Breeze

Richard Seltzer

ALL THINGS
THAT MATTER
PRESS

Gricks may rise and Troysirs fall (there being two sights for ever a picture) for in the byways of high improvidence that's what makes life-work leaving ...

Finnegan's Wake by James Joyce

... something about the metaphysical claustrophobia and bleak fate of being always one person ...
wasn't it also Crane who said that an artist is nothing but a powerful memory that can move itself at will through certain experiences sideways?"

Asymmetry by Lisa Halliday

To my wife Barbara (1950-2012)

Acknowledgments

I want to thank:
Rex Sexton and his widow Rochelle Cohen for their frequent helpful feedback and encouragement.
Nancy Felson, Homeric scholar
David Lupher, retired Classics professor
David Ratzan, Head, Library of the Institute for the Study of the Ancient World, NYU
Sophie Powell and Jennifer Barclay for their editorial help.
Fred Graf, Wendy Lehnert, Lynne Breslin, Diane Motowidlo, my son Tim and my sister Raven for their feedback.
Gabi Coatsworth for her monthly Writers' Rendezvous meetup sessions and her advice which led me to find my terrific publisher, All Things That Matter Press.
Phil and Deb Harris at All Things That Matter Press for their excellent editing.
And my son Bob for his continuing support

Brief passages quoted from *The Iliad* are from the translation by Robert Fagels, published by Penguin.

Part One ~ Slow Magic, Fast Magic

1 ~ The Goddess in Sunglasses

Breeze was lying naked, limp, and unconscious on Yannie's bed. Her pulse was strong; her breathing was normal, but her open eyes were glazed. Her long, curly black hair was wildly strewn across her breasts. One leg was straight and the other bent, with the knee leaning against the wall. Her body was alive, but it was as if no one was in that body.

The 911 operator had told Yannie not to move her. That could worsen her condition, whatever that condition was. The medics should arrive in a couple minutes. They had to. He knew the basics from TV shows. If her heart stopped—thank God, it was still beating—they would need to revive her within three minutes, or her brain would be damaged irreversibly.

The medics would ask him about her medical history and her family. Her life might depend on details that he could provide. But he knew nothing about her past, even though she had been living with him for over two months. What could he say? The medics might call the police, and the police would want to establish her identity and determine if there had been foul play.

She called herself *Breeze*. He didn't know her last name and didn't know where she came from. As far as he knew, she had no ID and no money. He knew nothing about her medical history. He didn't know if she had relatives or where those relatives might be. She had no friends that he knew of. He had never seen her do drugs, but that didn't mean that she didn't. Maybe she had over-dosed.

She could be a fugitive, and he might be guilty as an accessory to acts he knew nothing about. She could be seriously sick, not from drugs, but from some incurable disease. It could be contagious. He could come down with it himself.

He felt guilty for thinking such thoughts. How could he think about himself at a time like this?

Why was it taking so long for the medics to arrive?

He checked her pulse again. Still strong. She was still breathing. But she still wasn't there.

***

Yanni wasn't allowed in the emergency room because he wasn't a spouse or relative. He went back to his dorm room. He wanted to dig through her stuff, looking for anything with her full name or the names of relatives, any fact that might help in this crisis. Then the phone rang. By the clock, two hours had passed. He had no idea what, if anything, he had done in that time. He rubbed his face, scratched the back of his neck, scrunched his shoulders, stamped his feet—anything to regain his sense of himself as here in this place at this time. The phone rang again. Had it been ringing continuously, or had it stopped and started again?

An admin from Yale-New Haven Hospital was calling. He cringed. This wasn't a dream. They had moved Breeze from the emergency room to a regular hospital room. He could visit her now. The admin needed to see him today. She had questions about identity and insurance and payment and citizenship.

When he arrived at the hospital room, a nurse told him that Breeze was stable, but still unconscious. They didn't know what was wrong with her. Monitors kept beeping a maddening rhythm.

Breeze seemed to be sleeping comfortably, as if she could wake up at any moment, and life would go on as before. Yannie touched her hand, her cheek, her ear. He brushed back her long black hair so it no longer covered her eyes. He squeezed her hand. No response. He kissed her hand. He kissed her lips. He kissed her behind the ear and licked her there the way she liked him to. He wanted to talk to her but couldn't think of anything to say. He wanted to slap her, hoping to wake her up. But this was a hospital. You don't slap patients in hospitals. He was confused, paralyzed with indecision.

The next he knew, with no notion of how much time had passed, someone was talking to him. It was the same voice as on the phone—the admin person. Her tone was patient, but weary. She might have repeated herself several times already, trying to get his attention.

"What's your name?" she asked again.

"Yannie," he finally answered.

"Okay. That's what people call you, but what's your full legal name?"

"Yannie Johnson. Y A N N I E. Johnny in Greek, like Johnny Johnson with a foreign flavor. I spell it with an 'ie' at the end instead of an 's'. That makes it easier for people to know how to pronounce it."

"Your parents are Greek?"

"No. They're eccentric."

He spaced out for a moment, memories racing through his mind. Breeze had told him, "I like that you have a Greek first name. It's as if you have a Greek soul, and your parents recognized that the moment you were born."

"No way," he had answered Breeze. "I was named after an army buddy of my Dad's who was killed in Nam."

"War, yes. You're a warrior," she had said. "Greek warrior. Ancient Greek warrior."

He had always thought of himself as a nerd and had walked with a slouch. She made him feel proud of his looks. She took pleasure in dressing him up for public and undressing him in private. They would role play, and she would cast him as a character from the Trojan War. He stood tall for her and felt like a different person in her presence.

"And what's your occupation?" the hospital admin repeated.

Yannie remembered he was in a hospital. The Yale-New Haven Hospital. Breeze, who had been living with him in his dorm room for months, was comatose. He shook his head and scratched the back of his neck, trying to get his bearings. "What was that again?" he asked.

"Your occupation?" she repeated. Her patience was wearing thin.

"I'm a senior at Yale. Classics major. Literature. Latin and Greek. I live on campus, in Calhoun College."

"Where the girl was picked up?"

"Yes."

"And what's the girl's name?"

"Breeze. B R E E Z E," he spelled it out. "Like the wind."

"First name or last name?"

"Only name, as far as I know. She said her parents named her Briseis, after a character in the Trojan War. Did you see the movie *Troy* with Brad Pitt as Achilles? Briseis was his slave-girl lover."

"Strange name."

"Yes. It's hard to pronounce. So, her parents called her *Bris*. But that sounded too much like Jewish circumcision. So, they called her Breeze instead."

"That's a roundabout way of getting a name. And where are her parents?"

"I don't know."

"And what's your relationship to her?"

He hesitated. "Undefined."

"But she lived with you, right?"

"Yes, she lived with me in my dorm room for two months."

"So, it would be fair to say that you're *friends*."

"Yes, friends. Say we're friends."

"And you don't know of any other friends of hers who might know more about her?"

"No. Just guys at college who knew her through me. No one from before that."

"I realize that this happened just a few hours ago. You haven't had time to deal with the shock. But rules must be followed. Her vital signs are strong, but she's unconscious, and we don't know why. She needs to be hospitalized, but we don't know her name or if she has insurance or whether she or anyone else is in a position to pay for her care. We don't even know whether she's a US citizen, much less a citizen of Connecticut. You seem to be the only person around here who knows anything about her. So, we have a problem. You're a student, with no financial resources, and since you aren't married to her, no insurance of yours could help pay her bills. Not knowing anything about her, and her being in a coma, but in no immediate danger, we'll have to petition that she be made a ward of the court. Then she'll be transferred to a long-term-care facility, and this hospital won't be able to perform tests that might determine what's wrong with her and what should be done for her."

He buried his head in his hands. His mind was a blank. He felt numb. He had no sense of time. He had no idea what to do. When he looked up again, the admin was gone.

"Shit," he screamed in frustration, then buried his head in his hands again.

He needed to talk to someone, to Lauren. She wouldn't want to talk to him, but he needed to talk to her. They had been friends since childhood and lovers since freshman year, until Breeze appeared at his door a couple months ago. He hadn't spoken to Lauren since then. He had her number in his contacts. He hit it. Her phone rang. She answered.

"Yannie?"

"Yes, it's me."

"And to what do I owe this honor?"

"It's that girl."

"The girl who suddenly appeared at the door of your dorm room?"

"Right."

"The girl who put you into a trance at first sight?"

"It wasn't exactly first sight."

"Well, I don't want to go down that rat hole and find out you're an even bigger rat than I imagined. So, what about this love of your life? Have you popped the question? Are you so crass as to invite me to the wedding?"

"She's gone. That's what I called to tell you—she's gone."

"She dumped you? Big surprise. Congratulations. Get drunk. Wallow in self-pity, alone. Don't come crawling back to me. I'm doing fine, no thanks to you. The thanks goes to George from Dartmouth."

"You've found someone? I'm glad. Sincerely, I am. I'm sorry about the way I treated you. But you misunderstand. You see, Breeze—"

"Is that the bitch's name? Breeze? What kind of name is that?"

"I can explain. There's lots I need to explain. But none of that matters now. What I'm trying to say is that her body is here, but she's gone."

"She's dead?" Lauren changed her tone abruptly, now concerned and supportive. "What happened? Was she hit by a car?"

"No. She's in a coma, and the doctors don't know why and don't know if she'll ever come out of it. I'm at my wits end. I need to talk to someone. You were my best friend before Breeze came along, and I treated you like shit. And now Breeze is gone, and I can't think of anyone I'd rather talk to than you. Can you still be a friend to me at a time like this? Can you come down here to the Yale-New Haven Hospital and sit with me and let me talk it out and get a grip on myself?"

"So, you just found her unconscious? You stumbled over her?"

He hesitated, then mumbled.

"What?" she pursued.

"Not exactly," he admitted.

"God. It was a *Private Benjamin* moment, wasn't it? She conked out in the middle of screwing." She laughed nervously, loudly.

"It's not funny."

"Of course not. I'm sorry," she sounded sympathetic again, despite the pain he had caused her. "You must be ... I understand. I think I understand. You can count on me."

His memory must be playing tricks on him. His mind was switching off and on, in panic mode. The next he knew he was once again sitting in a plastic chair in a hospital room. Breeze was lying comatose in the bed beside him, and Lauren was staring at him from across the room.

He blinked and made a conscious effort to focus his eyes on Lauren and make eye contact with her. She was five foot four—about four inches shorter than Breeze. Short red hair. She wore a white blouse and a green plaid skirt, to the knees. She had dressed that way in high school. She felt comfortable and safe in that outfit. He guessed that she chose to wear it now, on this awkward mission, as a statement that she wasn't out to attract him again, and that she was comfortable being herself, for herself.

She had lost a few pounds since he last saw her. She was even more attractive than before. Elbows out, hands at hips, she looked determined and ready to take on the world.

Seeing her like this made him aware of how scruffy he must look. Rams jersey and sweatpants, both old and not recently laundered, the first items of clothing he had chanced upon. Hair over his ears, a couple inches beyond needing a haircut. Unshaven. There hadn't been time for grooming this morning. He slouched, self-effacing, unsure of himself. In contrast to Lauren, he looked tired and vulnerable.

He got up quickly and stumbled toward Lauren, arms outstretched, to hug her and be hugged.

"No," said Lauren, holding out a hand as a stop signal. "Don't touch me. Talk. Talk all you want. That's what I'm here for. Sit back down and tell me what happened."

"Well, the doctors—"

"Not the medical stuff. Not now. First tell me about you," she requested, gently, in the kind of voice she might use to calm a child who was hurt or angry. "However much I might try to be sympathetic, there's a part of me that's pissed at you, that needs an explanation. I came here for me as well as for you. After you, my best friend, the man I expected to marry, suddenly dumped me, I felt like shit. I feel better now, but I still need closure. So, start your story with how you met her. Help me understand how she made you forget me. You said on the phone that when she appeared at your door that wasn't the first time you met her. So, tell me, how did you meet her?"

He sat once again, with his elbows resting on his thighs, and rubbed the furrow between his eyebrows with the back of his clenched fists.

He breathed deeply, shut his eyes, and began, "I first saw her last summer in Athens."

"Saw her from a distance? Or saw her meaning you slept with her?" Lauren leaned forward; her eyes open wide.

"It's complicated. We met on the flat concrete roof of a house in Athens, where, for a euro a night, student tourists could stretch out with sleeping bags or ponchos, separated by just a foot or two of open space. I had heard about this place at a youth hostel. My money was running out, and I wanted to stay in Greece longer. I was doing everything I could to economize. That was my first night on the roof. I checked-in at 2 a.m. In the distance, I could see the Acropolis. The Parthenon was lit by flood lights. In the summer heat, the ground seemed to shimmer at the horizon. You could feel the presence of three thousand years of history."

2 ~ A Rooftop in Athens

Telling the tale to Lauren, Yannie relived the scene.

An hour after he lay down on the roof, when everyone else seemed to be asleep, a young woman walked up to an empty space near him and glanced in his direction. Maybe she noticed his half-open eyes, staring at her. With a teasing smile, she turned, as if to look at the Acropolis in the distance, then with one quick motion, pulled off her jeans, stripping down to her bikini underpants. Then she lay down beside him and pulled her poncho over her. It felt like a dream.

Maybe an hour later, he reached out to her. He didn't remember doing that, but he must have, because his hand was under her poncho, touching her naked thigh.

He wanted to pull his hand back, but if he moved too quickly, she'd wake up and catch him, and this could become a mess. He held his hand still for what felt like hours, suspended, barely touching her, not letting the weight of his hand rest on her. She shrugged and stretched in her sleep. And without moving his hand, he wound up caressing her thigh. Now his hand was resting firmly on her, and any attempt to remove his hand could wake her. She rolled this way and that, probably dreaming. Then her hand caressed his hand, as if his touch was becoming part of her dream. At that point, he wanted her to keep dreaming. He wished this moment would never end. He had never been this frightened or this aroused before. She rolled closer to him, so that, without moving his hand, his fingers touched the edge of her panties.

It felt like the beginning of a sex video. He didn't want this scene to end. But he was terrified that she might wake up and scream at the touch of a stranger's hand. He didn't want to stop, but he was afraid of accusations and consequences. At that time, police in Greece had no tolerance for public displays of affection, much less groping a stranger in her sleep. He could wind up in jail.

He breathed softly, for fear of waking her.

Then, whether by her movement or his, he found himself caressing her crotch through her panties, and caressing the crevices on either side.

Her eyes were shut. She was smiling. She was breathing fast. As the first rose-colored hints of dawn appeared over the Acropolis, she quivered with a small orgasm and opened her eyes.

He quickly withdrew my hand.

She looked around as if not sure if she had been dreaming.

Then she acted like she was falling asleep again, but stretched out even closer to him, perhaps inviting him to try again. He slipped a hand under her poncho and once again touched her thigh. She extended a lazy hand in his direction, mimicking the random movements of someone sleeping. Then she turned away from him, touching, through his trousers, his butt, his thigh; then rolled out of reach.

He knew that she knew what he had been up to. Did she want him to continue or not?

In any case, he wanted to say something to her, to open the possibility of getting to know her.

His back ached from lying on a concrete roof. And he couldn't think of what to say.

Then everyone started to get up and pack their gear.

If he could catch her eye, words would come to him. But she was wearing sunglasses. And his wallet was missing. He always kept it in his right back pocket, but it wasn't there. He checked his other pockets and felt around where he had been lying. Then he noticed that she was walking away. He stepped toward her; but before he could say anything, she turned toward him, moved her sunglasses down to look him in the eye, then slapped him on the butt, and maneuvered away through the crowd.

Then he realized that his wallet was back in his pocket. She had taken his wallet when they were lying close together, and she had returned it now and had deliberately let him know that she had. His credit cards, cash, and plane ticket were still in the wallet. Only his Yale ID was missing.

As she went down the stairs from the roof, she looked back at him over her shoulder, making eye contact, with a provocative smile, before she pushed her sunglasses back into place.

Is she a con artist? he wondered. Is this entrapment? Why didn't she keep the credit cards or the cash? Maybe she kept his college ID so she could track him down later. If she wanted to blackmail him, she'd have made a scene right there, with witnesses. But maybe she was a nutcase without a rational motive.

The incident felt unreal. He couldn't believe his own behavior, much less hers. Maybe he had dreamt it. But his ID was missing. That was real.

Having relived that scene in his mind, he found himself once again in the hospital room talking to Lauren, trying to explain his behavior when Breeze first arrived at the door of his room at Yale. "I didn't recognize her. I hadn't gotten a good look at her face on the rooftop in Athens. At my door, she was wearing sunglasses once again. When she took the glasses off, my mind flashed to the moment on the roof when she pushed the glasses down, looked me in the eye, and walked away. Then, standing at my door, she handed me my ID."

"And that was it," Lauren concluded. "She had you. Like magic."

"Pretty much. You were there. We had been in bed when we heard knocking. I had pulled on my pants and stumbled to the door. You saw me staring at this strange woman. After that, my mind is a blank."

"Post traumatic sex syndrome," she diagnosed.

"What happened next?" he asked her.

"Lots of shouting. Me shouting at her and at you. Her shouting at me. You didn't say much. You looked like you were in shock. You stared at her and were oblivious to me. That ticked me off."

"The next thing I knew, you pushed past me, backpack in hand."

"That was two hours later by the clock, years by what it felt like to me, years of hell."

"I didn't try to stop you."

"You certainly didn't."

"I treated you—"

"Like shit. Yes. Earlier that day, we had talked about what we could and should do after graduation and hovered around marriage—when, not if. Then this stranger knocked on the door, and I was nothing to you. Emotional whiplash, I'd call it."

"I'm sorry."

"At least now you admit that you had met her before, that you had felt her up when she was a stranger on a rooftop, that she let a stranger feel her up. A real winner that is. You deserve the likes of her."

"That rooftop thing was like a dream. I didn't tell you about it because I was embarrassed at how I had acted, and I didn't want to hurt you. Then, without warning, she showed up at my door."

"So, you dumped your steady girlfriend, your life-long friend, and invited this stranger into your room and shacked up with her?" Lauren felt sorry for herself and was willing to show it. She had been patient enough. Now she needed Yannie to show remorse, to show concern and sympathy for her.

"No, it wasn't that simple," he answered. "At first, we didn't sleep together. She kept her distance. We slept in the same small room, alternating who got the bed and who the floor. She only had the clothes she was wearing when she arrived. No suitcase. No backpack. She had no ID other than mine, which she gave back to me."

"And how do you know that?" Lauren asked.

"The first night, when she was asleep, I checked her pockets."

"True love."

"I didn't know what to think."

"When you checked her pockets, did she have cash?"

"Less than ten dollars. I paid for her meals at Calhoun. I bought her clothes. I thought she'd stay a day or two. I hoped she wouldn't tell anyone about Athens and make a stink."

"You hoped she'd screw with you," Lauren concluded.

"That too, but no such luck, not at first. Not until a month later, when I was totally obsessed with her."

"And she gave no explanation for who she was and where she came from?"

"She said she was a junior at Vassar. She had messed up—skipping classes, not turning in papers. After years of over-achieving, something snapped. She lay in bed and read romance novels. She ordered take-out pizza and burgers. She felt no obligations and no regrets. When it came time for mid-terms, she took a leave of absence. She hadn't told her parents yet. She didn't want to see anyone who knew her. She didn't want to have to explain, to have to sound rational. She didn't want to use credit cards because then her parents could trace her. She needed a floor to crash on for a few days."

"And Vassar? Of course, you checked with Vassar?" asked Lauren.

"They had never heard of anyone called Breeze, and no one fitting her description had taken a leave of absence. Nobody was missing. Later, when I asked her about Vassar, she just laughed. And when I introduced her to a friend's girlfriend who went to Vassar, Breeze asked the girl about details of daily life, like she had never been there herself."

"And it didn't bother you that she had lied to you?" Lauren prompted.

"She lied all the time, about everything, without guilt or apology. That was a skill she was proud of. She'd spin convincing tales about her past and then laugh at me for being so gullible as to believe her. That was part of her charm. Like the sunglasses."

"What about the sunglasses?" Lauren asked, still incredulous.

"Most of the time, even inside, she'd wear sunglasses. Those glasses were like an invitation to check her out, to enjoy looking at her without risking the intimacy of direct eye contact. I could be a voyeur, exempt from the interplay of eye catching eye. And she seemed to enjoy that same freedom, observing everyone around her from behind that shield."

"It sounds like she wore those sunglasses as a disguise. Didn't that make you distrust her?" Lauren prompted again.

"No way. She was so open with her tall tales; it didn't feel like lying. My friends and I would talk about her, guessing her back story. She was the mystery woman from some Humphrey Bogart movie. Suspicion and uncertainty added to her charm. And when she took the glasses off, like she did when she arrived at my door, eye contact was like an electric shock. Her eyes were so large, so dark, so deep that you couldn't look anywhere else. You had to believe her. You had to help her."

"So, what other lies did she tell you?" Lauren asked.

"She talked about reincarnation and the soul moving from one living body to another."

"Cleopatra reborn?" Lauren offered.

"Egyptian, yes, in one of the stories, but never historical people who you could check on."

"For instance?"

"Selima, the massage girl, who was working a cruise ship on the Nile. British and American tourists were headed from Cairo to Luxor. Breeze slipped into the role while she told the tale. She took off her sunglasses, twisted her long hair into a knot on top of her head, hiked her skirt halfway up her thighs. She set her lips thin and straight; her eyes wide open, sparkling with enthusiasm. Her cheeks seemed fuller, more childlike. She could have passed for fifteen or sixteen. She slid close to me on the sofa, until our thighs touched. She spoke in broken English with an Arabic accent. She offered to help me learn Arabic, Egyptian Arabic.

"She said, '*Eye-nah* means *where*. That's what the phrase books say. Say that in Morocco, yes. Say that in Iraq, yes. But in Egypt, true word for *where*, popular word, we say *fenn*.'

"She wrote the numbers from one to ten and made me repeat them till I knew them. She showed me how to write the numbers. Then she taught me the words for the numbers. Then the letters of the Arabic alphabet, holding my hand to guide it.

"Playing this role, everything about Breeze was different. She looked so young, so innocent, and yet so seductive. Her touch was shy, bashful, and yet insistent. She flattered me that I learned so fast. She asked if I had been to Egypt before, if I had travelled to other Arab countries, if I had an Arab girlfriend.

"I asked if she was a passenger on the boat, maybe traveling with her parents.

"No.

"I asked if she was the daughter of someone in the crew, maybe the captain or the pilot.

"No. She said she was a crew member.

"She asked me to guess her job, as she brushed her fingers lightly over the backs of my hands.

"I gave up.

"'Masseuse,' she said. 'Ten dollar,' she said. 'Just ten dollar, American. I will take you places you have never known. You will feel ways you never felt before. Make big memory. Ten dollar. Thirty minute. After, you dream this many times for free. I teach you Arabic too, Egyptian Arabic. Teach good.'"

Lauren asked, "Was it Arabic?"

"What?"

"The words she wrote."

"Yes. Later, I checked with a classmate from the Sudan. She was even right about the Egyptian dialect."

"So, what do you make of it?" Lauren asked.

"What?"

"The way you described her taking on the role of a massage girl, you knew she was conning you not just about that, but about everything. But you admired how well she lied, like admiring an actress for her performance."

3 ~ Melissa

Breeze lay unconscious in her hospital bed, motionless except for the steady rhythm of her breathing.

Lauren sat in a chair near the head of the bed, legs crossed, arms crossed, tired. She had arrived in an adrenaline rush, anxious to see Yannie, and half-hoping they might get back together. Now she had serious doubts about the likelihood of that and the wisdom of her having come here at all. She wondered when the next bus back to Mount Holyoke would be leaving. She could check on her cellphone but was in no hurry to do so. She needed time to collect herself. She felt emotionally drained. She looked away from her comatose rival, toward Yannie who was sitting on a chair near the foot of the bed. He was bent forward, pressing his fists to his brow.

"It was real," Yannie muttered again. "Not her stories, but my feelings for her and hers for me had to be real."

"What?" asked Lauren, her voice quivering as she emerged from the private world of her thoughts.

"It wasn't just her looks, standing there in her sunglasses. She charmed me with her words, too. We talked about everything."

"Except anything that would let you know who she is and where she comes from."

"One look at those big dark eyes, and I'd forget to ask questions. And then she'd start spinning tales like an improv artist, taking on one personality after another, and I'd want to believe whatever she said."

"She's a chameleon."

"What?"

"She has the ability to blend in wherever she finds herself."

"Yes. Definitely. Yes. No piercings. No tattoos. Long curly black hair. She could talk and act either street-smart or sophisticated. She could fit in anywhere. You'd have trouble guessing her nationality or social class or politics. One day she might show up for a gay rights rally, and the next a Young Republicans meeting. One day she'd protest for the rights of women in the Middle East. The next day she'd want to role-play as a harem girl."

"Like I said before, she's a con artist," Lauren concluded.

"No, there's no reason to believe that. She never asked me or my friends for money."

"Nor did she have to."

"What do you mean?"

"You gave her a place to live. You paid for her meals. You bought her clothes."

"She couldn't pay by credit card or her folks would be able to track her down."

"And she didn't want to explain her real problem to you because it was too embarrassing. And she needed time to sort out what to do next."

"Exactly."

"For two months."

"Yes."

"And you can't find her credit cards or ID."

"I looked everywhere. The only stuff of hers in my dorm room is the stuff I bought her."

"And her sunglasses."

"Right."

"Well, who the hell is she? What's she like?"

"She's most like herself when she's pretending to be someone else."

"The improvs?"

"Right."

Lauren took a deep breath, then re-engaged. "So, tell me about the improvs."

Yannie paused.

Lauren knew that this was why he had called her. He needed to talk it out to try to understand Breeze and her attraction. Lauren needed to endure this, difficult as it was. She had to let him know by her actions that she still cared enough about him to listen with compassion and understanding.

"Breeze was her nickname," he began. "Her real name was Briseis, like Achilles' slave in the Trojan War. She'd play her namesake, and I'd play Achilles. Or she'd be an Amazon queen and I her captive. Those improvs didn't require much dialogue. One way or another, we'd wind up in bed together. But we acted out other scenes like comedy improvs. Some we did over and over, so we knew the lines like in a play."

He shut his eyes and saw Breeze as she was a few weeks after she had appeared at his door, sitting on his sofa, leaning forward so she could look at him over her sunglasses. She was wearing a knee-length black skirt. Her legs were crossed. A sandal dangled, on the brink of falling, as she moved her foot up and down, rhythmically.

"Let's play a game," Breeze suggested. "You're a middle-aged businessman taking a bus from Boston to New York. Times are tough. That's why the bus. It's six in the morning. You have to make it to a meeting at eleven. You're tired. You expect to sleep on the way. Getting on the bus, there are a dozen empty seats, but no two empty seats together. You'll have to sit next to someone and be cramped. A fat guy is munching a sandwich, with an open bag of potato chips on the seat next to him. A woman is typing on a laptop, with paper notes on the seat next to her. A thin young woman, probably college age, with her seat back, is curled up, apparently trying to sleep, leaving the seat beside her empty. Her head is toward the window. A baseball cap is covering her face. You slide into that empty seat and recline."

"So, what's this game you're playing?" he asked her.

"You're the guy. I'm the girl. Improvise."

"What's there to improvise? On a bus like that, I'd shut my eyes and try to sleep."

"Honestly? You're sitting next to a cute girl. And you're going to be on that bus for four hours."

"You didn't say she was cute."

"I said she was me. That means that even if you're exhausted, you can't take your eyes off me. That means that even if you're married with kids, secure in your job, happy with your life, you're tempted to strike up a conversation to find out who I am and where I'm going, to flirt. You, as the middle-aged guy in this story, haven't flirted for a decade or two, for however long you've been married. But it would be like getting on a bicycle again. The temptation of it makes you feel younger, wakes you up. There's no way you could sleep."

"But I'm no good at starting conversations with strangers."

"It's me, remember. I'm curled up beside you. Every now and then I squirm to get more comfortable. My cap slides up a bit, so you see my face. I reach up to adjust the cap and my breasts snap to attention in my tight-fitting sweater. My eyes open a crack and I look straight at you and see that you're staring at my breasts. I smile. You have to say something to break the tension. I'm not going to let you off the hook. I'm going to hold your eyes with my eyes until you say something. So, what do you say? Say it."

"Would you like a cup of coffee?" he asked, sliding into the spirit of the scene she had created.

"What?"

"I bought two at the Starbucks in the bus station. But I only need one."

"But you don't have coffee cups in your hand.

"That's right. I don't. But I should have. Two of them, so I could offer one to you. How do you like your coffee?"

"Black."

"Perfect. This coffee that isn't here is black," he said, hoping to impress her with his ability to think fast.

"And yours?"

"Oh, I don't drink coffee. Take both of them. They're both black."

"But Momma said I should never take gifts from strangers."

"I'm Bill," he said, taking charge of the situation. "And you?"

"Melissa."

"So now we aren't strangers. Drink up. Enjoy."

"Thank you. That's the best non-existent coffee I've had today."

"So, you had some yesterday?"

"Yes, indeed. And the day before that. I often have non-existent drinks and non-existent food. You can't beat the price."

"Seriously?" he asked.

She laughed. "One minute you're a stranger, and now you're getting serious with me."

"Wow. You're quick. Do you play these games often?"

"Life's a game."

"Do you win?"

"Always," she replied.

"What's the prize?"

"A new life."

"Do you want a new life?"

"You do everything you can to stay on a steady course and be content with the one life you have. To you, immortality would be living that same life year after year. That's the kind of immortality the old Greek gods had—one life lived forever, one never-ending monotonous life. But it doesn't have to be that way. Just take my hand, check into a hotel with me, forget your appointments, forget your family and start a new life."

"God," was all he could say.

"Yes, if you can do that. You can forget the past and start a new life. That would be better than what the Greek gods had. That would be real immortality—living more than one life. That's the best that anyone can hope for."

"You mean drop everything?"

"Everything. Cut up your credit cards and ID. Go untraceable, like you were in witness protection. Start from scratch."

"I'd be lost," he replied, imagining what it would be like to actually do such a thing.

"Yes, wouldn't that be great? To have no idea where you'll be tomorrow and what you'll do—totally liberated."

Yannie woke up again in the hospital room, Breeze was unconscious in bed, and Lauren was sitting in a chair, facing him. He wasn't sure how much he had said to her and how much of that scene had just replayed in his mind.

Lauren stared him in the eye, held her knees, with both hands, and gathered her thoughts. Then she asked, "Okay. So, Breeze bragged about living serial lives. Didn't it occur to you that she could be a con artist, doing that kind of thing deliberately and repeatedly, latching onto strangers, living with them, having them pay for everything?"

"But why would someone as brilliant as she is want to do that?" said Yannie, with a far-away look as if he was asking himself as well as Lauren.

"I don't know. Maybe that's her shtik. Maybe she gets a charge flipping from one identity to another, living multiple lives instead of just one."

"Not a con," Yannie insisted. "She's not pretending. I think she has actually done that, moved from one body to another, like she said, living multiple lives, one after another. And she might be doing that again now."

"Bingo. No wonder you hit it off with her. She's nuts and you're gullible."

"It's like a goddess materialized in my dorm room. And when she vanished into this coma, maybe she went into another body. And maybe she'll come back here with a new improv to try out. Or maybe she'll stay in that other place and other time and live a new life."

"So, you think your girlfriend here is a free spirit … literally? She jumps from one body to another?"

"Okay, I admit, that sounds weird. But it could be true," he persisted.

"Reincarnation, soul migration, whatever you call it, I'd never want that for myself."

"Why not? You'd turn down eternal life?" Yannie asked, incredulous.

"Living is fine. But I don't like dying," Lauren explained "Dying once is bad enough, but to die again and again. That's not for me."

Yannie paused, and the muscles of his face tensed, like he was trying to pay attention to a faint voice he heard within. Then he relaxed again, and smiled, as if he now understood something he hadn't understood before. He explained, "We all live and die at least once. We don't have any choice about that. And if some people live and die again and again, I bet they don't have anything to say about that either. On the plus side, you can get used to anything. Dying the first time is probably awful. But the second not so much. And the third, the fourth, the fifth … maybe after a while it's not so bad. I'd like to think that Breeze is an old soul, and she's doing just fine right now, wherever she is."

"That's just magical thinking," Lauren countered.

"What?"

"When bad things happen and you're in denial," Lauren elaborated, "you get creative and believe outlandish things."

"But magic isn't all bad," he argued. "In myth, there are good witches as well as bad witches. And the way Grandma used to tell me, there's slow magic and fast magic. She's big on mythology, a Classics professor. Retired now. She's probably the reason why I picked Classics as a major, though I'd never want to teach it. I just love the intertwining stories and their variants. But I don't think Grandma found this idea in mythology. I've never read it anywhere, but it has a ring of truth to it. Maybe she heard it from her mother."

Lauren stared in disbelief. Yannie wasn't into the mystical and mysterious before. He was into literature, and he'd had great grades in Latin in high school. So, if he wanted to be impractical and pick a liberal art major, Classics wasn't any worse than English or History. He assumed that, regardless of his major, with good grades he could get a good job. That was how he had explained his choice to her and to his parents. That had nothing to do with the influence of a mystical grandmother. This was a side of him she hadn't seen before.

He continued, "You didn't choose your body, and I didn't choose mine. Over time, you come to accept the fact that you're not as tall or strong or attractive or intelligent as you wish. You forget how arbitrary and absurd it is that you are in this body. But your body ages, and the you inside it doesn't. Then one day you look in a mirror and see the face of a sixty-year-old. When you age forty years over the course of forty years, that stinks, but such is life. That's normal. There's nothing you can do about that. But if you age that much overnight ... "

"What the hell?"

"When I was six, Grandma explained to me about slow magic and fast magic. 'Everybody has slow magic,' she said. 'Twenty years from now, you'll have the body of a full-grown man, and you could have a son of your own. And sixty years in the future, your body will be old, like mine is now. That's slow magic. The changes happen so slowly that you hardly notice, until you bump into an old school friend and realize how much the two of you have aged. But if changes like that happened overnight, and you suddenly found yourself in a different body, that would be fast magic, real abracadabra magic. So, you could say that all magic is about time—making it go fast or slow, and forward or backward.'"

4 ~ Lauren

What the hell is he thinking?" Lauren wondered. Yanni's eyes were glazed over. Even when he looked at her, he didn't see her. He was lost in his delusions, where this other woman was still alive and might wake up at any moment.

"Magical thinking" Joan Didion called it, in her book about grief. He couldn't admit to himself that Breeze was gone. The process had to take its course. Nothing that Lauren could say could bring him back to reality. Difficult as this was, she needed to let it play out. He was focused on Breeze and on coming up with what seemed to him rational explanations for what had happened to her, and reasons to expect she'd come back, and that life would go on as it had before.

It was just as well he was out of it now. That was a safety mechanism. Shut off reality when it hurts too much. If he wasn't so out of it, he'd probably hate Lauren for being insensitive, nosy, impatient, self-centered. But there was no way she could empathize with him over his loss and pain.

The woman he had dumped her for was dead or dying. God. The only dead person Lauren had ever seen was her mother, and that was long ago, when she was a kid. Breeze and Lauren were about the same age and for no known reason—bam, she was gone. This was creepy, weird.

Lauren was the one who needed someone to talk to. Yannie had her as a sounding board, to prompt his memory and to help him vent his emotions and fears. Lauren was here to listen to whatever wild theories he might come up with. She'd let him talk endlessly about this woman he was obsessed with. But Lauren didn't have anyone to talk to. Yannie was so wrapped up in himself that he couldn't hear her, no matter what she said.

So, she played along, assuming the role he obviously wanted her to play: a loyal friend he could tell anything to as he tried to sort out what he remembered about Breeze.

Shit. He was still in love with this dead woman. He thought she was alive despite all the evidence to the contrary. When Lauren arrived at this hospital room, the doctor was telling Yannie that Breeze had almost no brain activity. But all Yannie could hear was, "There's brain activity." The doctor was trying to soften the blow, while telling him that it was over. Breeze's heart was still beating, and she was still breathing on her own. But nobody was home. That was a brain-dead zombie lying there. No one comes back from a coma like this. But Yannie grabbed onto the doctor's words like they were a beacon of hope.

Shit. What Yannie loved in Breeze, he could have loved in Lauren. She had it in her to be carefree, wild, acting out one fantasy after another. She could forget her responsibilities, forget the past and the future and live in the moment. That's a side of her that Yannie had never seen. To him, she was the girl-next-door, the childhood friend. She was a reminder of his parents' expectations of him and his expectations of himself. He had a fixed image of her as anchored, solid, predictable. There was no way she could compete with Breeze.

Yannie was a wimpy little kid when they became best friends in elementary school. He was vulnerable and sensitive when they held hands in seventh grade. Now he was this hunk, this brilliant guy who had no idea how handsome he was and who paid no attention to how he looked and how he dressed, but who with some regular exercise could have the body of a Greek demigod. If she met a complete stranger with a muscular body like this, Lauren would be drawn to him. But if Yannie were in a different far less attractive body, Lauren would still be drawn to him. They were in sync. They could talk openly to one another about anything. One word from him now, and she'd open up and connect with him again, even though she had every reason to hate him.

How heartless and insensitive could he be? How could he ask her to run to him like this so he could ramble on about her rival, the woman he dumped her for? Dumping her the way he did felt worse than when her mother died. Suddenly she was alone to a degree she had never imagined possible.

Sure, to save face, she could try to keep up the charade that there was a George from Dartmouth, that she had moved on and didn't care. But he wasn't likely to believe that for long. With other people, she was good at putting on a mask to hide her thoughts and emotions. But with Yannie, she had no mask. With him, she was naked no matter what she was wearing. The relief of dropping all pretense was part of the joy of their intimacy. But right now, he was emotionally numb. He hadn't a clue what she was thinking or feeling, and it didn't even occur to him to try to see things from her point of view. As far as Lauren was concerned, it might just as well be Yannie, not Breeze, who was in the coma.

Yes, Breeze was gone. She had disappeared as suddenly as she had appeared. But that didn't mean that Yannie and Lauren could pick up again where they had left off. That train had left the station. He didn't call her today because he wanted her again. He just needed someone to talk to. He was still obsessed with Breeze. But despite her resentment and her hurt, Lauren felt good that he had turned to her at such a moment and felt good being with him and hearing him ramble, even though he was talking about Breeze. A part of her still hoped that eventually they might reconnect. Maybe this was her version of Yannie's *magical thinking*. But she wanted to be with him when he came to himself again, and she wanted to be with him in the meantime when he just needed her as a sounding board. Then when he finally snapped out of this, she wanted to let loose with him in ways she never had before. Yes, they could be best friends and responsibly plan the rest of their lives together. But she also wanted to unleash the passion bottled up inside her. Shit, she wanted to fuck his brains out.

5 ~ Dreamland

Yannie woke up abruptly, nearly fell out of his chair, stood, shook his head, rubbed the back of his neck, rubbed his eyes, ran to the bathroom, splashed cold water on his face, then walked back to the hospital room, and sat back in his chair.

"Are you okay?" asked Lauren.

"A dream. It must have been a dream."

"A dream? We were just in the middle of a conversation, and you dropped off to sleep. Now, a minute later, you wake up and tell me you had a dream? You're really fucked up."

"I don't remember much. But it was a full-blown dream, like I'd been sleeping for hours."

Her disbelief turned to concern, then sympathy. "Right after my mom died," she confided, "I had hellish dreams. They felt so real. Then I started writing them down when I woke up and tried to sort out what they might mean. That made them less scary, so I could sleep. You can talk to me about that dream. I didn't come here to yell at you or lecture you. I don't mean to be a shit to you just because you were a shit to me. I want to help."

"I was lost in a city at night," he began. "I got there by bus. I was alone, but I knew that I had arrived with Breeze. We had checked into a Holiday Inn. No, I had checked in alone. Breeze would be arriving later. This was before the days of cell phones. We had no way to get in touch with one another. I headed toward a movie theater I saw ahead. Then I lost sight of it. I didn't know where I was. I had scraps of paper with scribbled words, and two plastic key cards from a Holiday Inn, in an envelope with the room number. I was afraid of losing the scraps of paper and the key cards. I had a backpack. It was late at night. It was a bad neighborhood. I sat down on the floor of an old-style phone booth, took out my wallet, and put the paper and the keys in my wallet. I wanted to get my bearings and decide what to do next. A cop found me there. I looked suspicious. I told him I was getting organized, checking my pockets for coins to use in the pay phone. He walked away. I got up. I was looking for someone, anyone to ask how to get to the Holiday Inn.

Then I saw the sign, ran toward it, and walked through the lobby to the elevator. That's when I realized I didn't have the key cards. They were in my wallet. My wallet wasn't in my pocket. I must have left it in the phone booth. I panicked.

"I raced back toward the phone booth. Then I stopped. My wallet wouldn't be there. There was no point in going back. Breeze must be in the hotel room. She'd have talked her way in. She had a credit card and cash. The front desk could call her for me. She'd let me in. Then I could call the bank and tell them I'd lost my credit card, so they'd cancel it and issue a new one.

"That's the whole dream. But retelling it now, I realize that I had lost my identity. Like that scene on the rooftop in Athens. That scene really happened. I'm sure it did. But it, too, meant that I had lost my identity. And I found my identity again, or a new identity, when Breeze gave back my ID card."

"I think I know what you're driving at," Lauren conceded. "Sometimes things that actually happen have meaning for you, like dreams do, only you don't recognize that meaning until later, and figuring it out is like opening a window to a part of yourself that you didn't know was there."

"Yeah," Yannie agreed. "That's intimacy."

"What?"

"Intimacy is what Breeze calls it. Getting close to your own self can be like getting close to someone you love ... close in mind, as well as physically. Telling each other things you've never told anyone else before. Remembering details and recognizing the importance of what you had forgotten. Bringing you back in touch with your true self at the same time as bonding with one another."

"You mean swapping tales of your sexual exploits?"

"Actually, the way I said that reminded me of you and me, the way we were before, that closeness. Breeze put into words what I had felt with you and then felt with her. With you, it happened slowly, over years. With her it was fast—fast magic. She explained that sex is the least of it. Life is short. If you see what you want, you have to do whatever you can to get it. True intimacy is difficult. You need to drop your defenses, share memories, plans, hopes. You need to read the same books, watch the same TV shows and movies. You need to do lots of stuff together—not just dates. She meant everyday being together. You need to build a common vocabulary of shared memories. She told me she wanted me and wanted me for keeps. Not just casual sex. I asked her how she could be certain. She said she didn't know how or why, but she was sure. Maybe it was an echo of a previous life. She felt a connection when she saw me on that rooftop in Athens. And now she had found me, she was going to keep me, was going to make me fall in love with her. She told me that the day she appeared at my door."

"Spooky."

"No, sexy, very sexy."

"So, you hopped into bed."

"No. Much to my surprise, no sex at all. We talked all night. She was upfront telling me what she was trying to do. She got me talking about myself, about you, about my childhood, about my mom who would love me no matter what I did, and my dad who is like an unscalable cliff."

"So, she must have told you about herself. You must know far more about her than you've been letting on."

"About herself, she said nothing directly. Rather, she told me tales that later we developed into improvs. She told them like she had lived them."

"So, it was a one-way street," Lauren concluded. "Jeez. She told you made-up stories, and you told her real memories. She gave you fiction, and you gave her autobiography. You wanted to get to know her, so you spilled out all your personal secrets, in hopes that she'd do the same. But she didn't reciprocate. She toyed with you, for God's sake."

"No, it was real sharing. Our styles are different—me direct and wordy, and she playful and elusive. But it was real sharing. That's what she insisted on. She said that sex is easy and uncomplicated. It's no big deal. But when you really know one another and connect to one another, that's when the ground starts to shake and the fireworks go off, and you forget who you are, and you become someone else, and you want to be that new person who you are when the two of you are together. She believed in that kind of experience and wanted to go for it."

"Searching for the Holy Grail. Fat chance," Lauren sneered.

"She said she knew it was possible because she had felt it before."

"Another boyfriend, of course. She was on the rebound from a bad breakup."

"No, not that. She had me do an improv where she was Briseis, soon after Achilles captured her. He refrained from touching her for weeks. He waited until she knew him and wanted him, and then it was the best sex she had ever had, and she connected with him as she never had with anyone else."

"What?" Lauren asked in disbelief. "She claimed she was the slave girl of Achilles in a previous life? You've got to be kidding."

"It was an improv. I don't know what she believed or didn't believe. What matters is that she wanted to feel close to me, and that story seemed to show her how she could turn physical attraction into love. We needed to share memories, experiences, and fantasies. And only when the time was right would we add the physical."

"Good God. You really didn't fuck her? You meant it when you said you lived with her for a month without doing it. How could you stand that?" asked Lauren. "That's not the way you were with me."

"She slept on my bed, and I slept on the floor beside the bed. Or we'd swap positions. We'd kiss goodnight. Sometimes we'd hold hands. Nothing more."

"That makes me feel just great. You'd rather hold hands with her than screw with me. Just what I wanted to hear."

"Actually, there was a sensual buzz to that whole routine—desire held back by self-restraint."

"B and D, without the handcuffs."

"I guess you could call it that. The restraint added to the passion."

"Fucking creative. As creative as jumping from body to body and living forever. Shit," exclaimed Lauren. "You're serious, aren't you? And all that intimacy stuff—keeping you restrained, tempting you but holding back—she really did that. That's a twisted imitation of Victorian courtship, and it worked for her. She made you fall in love with her."

"Not really," Yannie corrected her. "I fell for Breeze the moment she appeared at my door and took off her sunglasses. But I never told her that because it made her feel good to think she was in control. Sure, I did what she wanted. She wanted to make me fall in love with her. That was hot, that took away any doubt I might have had that I could attract her and keep her. With that kind of confidence, I enjoyed just being with her, just talking to her. When we finally got to it, the sex was great. But that wasn't a big deal. I was already committed to her and she to me."

"Okay, lover boy, you with all the answers. Sex isn't complicated. You can reinvent life and death. So, the money question should be easy for you, too," Lauren struck back.

Yannie heard these words but was slow to process their meaning. He was drowsy, sitting on a hard-plastic chair, with a crick in his neck. "What?" he asked.

"That's the big question right now, isn't it? Not love and commitment, but money. Who pays? She doesn't have insurance, right?"

"Not that I know of."

"And she doesn't have money. And you don't either. What does your dad say?"

"Dad?" he answered. "He doesn't know that Breeze exists, much less that she's sick, much less that I've been living with her."

"Talk to him, already."

"I can't talk to him. He'd explode. He'd call me an idiot, like you do. Only it will hurt worse when he says it. That's why I called you instead of him. I can take anything you say to me. We're on the same wavelength, or at least we were before, ever since elementary school. But Dad is different. I don't understand him. He doesn't understand me. He talks to me like I'm half my age, and then, I start acting the way he expects. I whine and make excuses, rather than standing up to him. Talking to him turns me into a different person. He's an unscalable cliff. I never live up to his expectations. I'm never good enough for him. I can't live that way anymore. I need to take care of this on my own."

"For God's sake, wake up. Your dad's a great guy. He's treated me like family ever since my mom died. He's given you everything you really wanted. And now you need a way to pay the hospital bills. Get your priorities straight. Maybe he has the money, or maybe he can think of another solution. If I were you, I'd get on the phone and talk to him now."

"But you're not me."

"By the grace of Chance Almighty."

Yannie bent over and covered his ears with his hands, not wanting to hear this.

"What about your mom?" Lauren insisted. "She thinks the world of you. To her, you can do no wrong. So, talk to her already. She can convince your dad for you."

"Sure, she thinks I'm the greatest. She has no idea who I am. And I have no idea who I am when I'm around her. I can't remember ever having a real conversation with her. When I'm around Dad, I'm the kid who can't get anything right and can't make a decision. When I'm around Mom, I'm the golden boy who can do no wrong and doesn't need to try. So, who the hell am I? I had to get away from them. But being at college wasn't enough. When Breeze appeared, that was like finding myself. I felt real. Weird as it sounds, with her, I felt like I was the right self in the right body."

"So that's your excuse now? I'm the girl next-door. I'm the one your parents expected you to marry. So, to break free of them, you needed to break free of me. Instead of me, you needed some mystery woman who appeared out of nowhere, with no past, or with thousands of years of past. You needed an exotic, unpredictable time-traveler."

"But it's not time travel. Her self or her soul moves from one body to another."

"Right," Lauren continued, caught up in the dialogue, forgetting there was no point in arguing with Yannie when he was in this state of mind. "So now you believe in something that isn't even a myth, something you just dreamed up. Miracle of miracles. The woman you love can materialize in another body in another place and time. And, yes, she can come back here again and live happily ever after with you."

"Well, she definitely has the power to reinvent herself, to start over fresh. I felt that in her improvs. And I felt it living with her. This was a new life she was starting with me, and that we'll start again when she comes back from this. I'd rather believe in soul migration, that that's how she could go suddenly and how she can come back suddenly. I'd rather believe that than that she's as good as dead."

"You mean, to hell with facts."

"No, I mean to hell with fate."

"Wishful thinking trumps all. Free the whales."

6 ~ Pregnant

Sitting on a plastic chair with no cushion and no arms, Yannie woke with a start and nearly fell over.

Beeping monitors.

Screaming woman.

The hospital room.

Across the hall, an old lady with a broken hip screamed in pain, "I don't want to die. Don't let me die."

Breeze was not alive, but not dead either.

She had an IV in her arm. She was unresponsive. Her eyes were closed. The medics had closed them. When she fell into this state, her eyes were open and glazed.

But shine a light in her eyes and the retina would react. Medical instruments confirmed that there was brain activity. Her pulse was strong. Her breathing, even without extra oxygen, was steady. The monitors were all in the safe range.

Yannie reached out and grasped her hand.

The clock on the wall showed five o'clock. It was still the afternoon of the day this all began. It was still Saturday. But it felt like he had been here for weeks or months, watching, waiting, hoping she'd come back. It seemed to make no difference whether he was here or not, whether he was asleep or not, whether he held her hand or not. She didn't even react to the screams of the old lady across the hall. At random intervals, her eyebrows would move, or her hand would twitch, or she'd smile. The doctors said those were reflex motions and meant nothing. Her body was here. But where was she now, really? What was she thinking? What was she doing? And would she ever return to this world?

Sitting, with his elbows on his legs, Yannie pressed his hands against his ears. He shut his eyes. He counted out loud, drowning out the beeping of the monitors, the screaming of the old lady, and even the sound of Breeze breathing steadily.

It might have been a minute or an hour later when someone took hold of his hands and forced them away from his ears.

"We got the test results," said the doctor who was standing next to him.

"And?"

"They were all negative."

"It's that bad?"

"Bad? No. The tests told us that there's no brain damage. Epilepsy was my first guess. But it's not that. No such luck."

"Having epilepsy would be 'luck'?"

"Better the devil you know. "

"So, there's nothing more you can do?"

"Not for her. But for the baby, yes."

"Baby?"

"I thought the nurse told you. There was one positive test result—she's pregnant. It's early. She probably didn't know. Did you use protection?"

"She said she was on the pill."

"And didn't that signal to you that she was sexually active, that you weren't her first partner? I'm surprised you weren't concerned about AIDS and other STDs?

"Is she ... "

"Like I said, all the tests were negative except for pregnancy."

"God. I'm not ready to be a father. I'm a senior in college, and I don't have a job lined up for after graduation. I don't know what I'll be doing a year from now. I haven't even finished Monday's homework."

"Okay. Take a deep breath. Maybe walk around. This is a lot to swallow at once. We learned about the pregnancy hours ago. I thought someone had told you, and you had had time to mull over the implications."

Yannie started pacing, in circles. "No one said anything, not even the lady with the paperwork and the questions about who can authorize care and who can pay bills."

"Yes, I'll have to speak to her," said the doctor. "I'll have to make sure she adds this to the record, because it changes everything."

"What do you mean?"

"Breeze is a puzzle. It would be a nightmare trying to give her the care she needs with no idea who she is and where she comes from and no one authorized to make medical decisions for her. But the child is another matter. From what you've said, you're the likely father. We could confirm that with DNA testing. From a legal standpoint, you can't be considered financially responsible for the child until it's born. But we could make a strong case that the father has an interest in the survival of his child. And in the absence of any other decision maker, the father of the unborn should be able to make health-related decisions for the comatose mother. Who pays for it is another question, though acknowledging paternity and assuming responsibility for making medical decisions might make you responsible for the bills. You need to keep that in mind before going ahead with this. But that would resolve the dilemma of decision-making, which would mean we'd have a much better chance of figuring this out and bringing her back."

Yannie stopped pacing and smiled. "Do the tests, the DNA tests. The sooner the better. Then I can talk to Dad, and Mom, too. I'll have to talk to them. Now this isn't a matter of some unknown woman I got involved with. It's their grandchild. They'll have to care. They'll have to help. I'll tell them we planned to get married."

"Did you?"

"Not exactly. We never talked about it. But now, yes. Definitely yes."

"So, despite the fact that you know nothing about her past, you want to marry her?"

"Yes, of course. It's like a Greek goddess materialized in my dorm room. Do you think I had a choice? Do you think I'd want a choice?"

Then he saw Lauren, dear reliable Lauren, who had been his best friend since childhood, whom he had presumed he would, one day, marry and whom he had dumped abruptly; and who, despite all that, had driven here as quickly as possible to help him in this crisis. Perky, opinionated Lauren was sitting just ten feet away and had heard all this and was silently staring at him.

His words had seemed so right and true when he was speaking just to the doctor. But he had been speaking to Lauren as well. He had to have known that she was there, right in front of him. She certainly presumed he was talking to her as well, his words like repeated slaps on the face. She took it without flinching, immobile, like a statue—a cute and sexy statue, like Venus de Milo with her head glued back on, finally, after centuries of blindness, seeing the world for what it was, and for the first time seeing Yannie.

7 ~ Lauren's New Role

Lauren grabbed hold of details, as if to prevent herself from drowning–details that she could see and details she remembered all too well. The Rams sweatshirt he was wearing, she had given him for his birthday, as a joke, after the Patriots beat the Rams in the Superbowl. He wore it so much the elbows had holes in them. Underneath that, in her mind's eye, she saw his smooth hairless chest, and the ragged scar, like the battle scar of an ancient demigod, which he had gotten in a car crash, back in the fifth grade. Back then she had helped it heal with the soft touch of her fingers, and had wanted to kiss it, but hadn't until they were in college.

While Yannie, still delusional, rambled on about Breeze to the doctor who had told him she was pregnant, and then kept talking, not noticing that the doctor had left, Lauren got up and walked past him, without him noticing, into the hall, then to the elevators, then to ground level, and outside. She needed to make a call. She had to tell his parents what was going on.

She was conflicted about what she should say and how she should say it. She could simply be a spectator in this drama, or she could, if she wanted, play a key role. If she understood the motivations of the others in this drama, she could take control of the situation, nudging the others in what she knew was the right direction.

Yannie's Mom had always wanted more kids. She had been an only child and didn't want her son to be one. She'd have been happier with four or five children, or even more. That's one reason why she took Lauren under her wing when Lauren's mom died. She'd have adopted Lauren if Lauren's dad had let her, but he wouldn't.

After Lauren's mother died, through junior high and high school, her father was often out of town on business and Lauren slept over at Yannie's house. Yannie and she were like brother and sister, close, but at a distance. No more handholding, like before. It wasn't until college, away from home, that they reconnected romantically. In high school they were friendly, but abrasively so. They were rivals in their schoolwork, and two years in a row they were opponents running for student council. She won both times. That felt good to remember. She often put him in his place, one-upping him and he tried to get back at her and put her down a notch, but he was nowhere near as good at that as she was.

The only parameter on which she couldn't beat him was height. What could she do about that? She hadn't chosen this body. He was five ten. She was five four, forced to always look up at him, which he didn't deserve. Breeze must be five eight or nine. Lauren couldn't help but estimate and compare. Long black hair. Lauren imagined that when Breeze was standing up and naked, that hair would hang just low enough to cover her nipples, so with an innocent flip of the head she could make the nipples play peek-a-boo with her hair.

Don't go there, she coached herself. She shouldn't compare herself to this rival she knew nothing about, whom Yannie really knew nothing about. It was the unknown and the forbidden that had entranced him. Lauren was sure of that. In contrast, Lauren was real, solid, predictable. She had short red hair and faded freckles that had once been prominent and cute. Her face and gestures were all too familiar to Yannie. She was the girl-next-door. She was his almost sister. Reliable, yes. Mysterious, no. He could count on her. He could turn to her in a moment of crisis, like this one. But her reliability was a strike against her. He'd jump over the fence to get to greener, less well-known grass. The cards were stacked against her. And the rival was stacked as well, as Yannie himself would crudely put it to his friends.

Unfortunately, the way Lauren had dressed today emphasized those girl-next-door associations. A white blouse and green plaid skirt she had worn in high school. Back then it was a statement of defiance, wearing what looked like a uniform in a school that had no uniform. She wouldn't compete in dress with the other girls. She wouldn't try to attract boys' attention with her choice of clothes. And her self-assured contrariness actually enhanced her popularity. Her three closest friends dressed as she did. It saved them time and hassle, not having to pick a different outfit every day.

She gave that up when she went to college. Lots changed when she entered that new world. But she still had a few of those blouses and skirts in her drawer. Getting ready to come here, she had chosen an outfit that made her feel confident. She needed confidence now, seeing her ex-best-friend and ex-lover and hearing him ramble on about how much he loved her rival and now learning that that rival was carrying his child and that he wanted to marry her. This outfit she was wearing was likely to make him think of her as sister-like, like he had in high school, and to forget that for the last three years, their relationship had been intimate, passionate, permanent. To Yannie, in comparison with his experience with Breeze, what he had had with Lauren must seem tame, distant, and temporary.

Lauren had lost a few pounds since Yannie last saw her. She had spent time in the gym, working out her anger and frustration on the treadmill and the elliptical. She had time for that now that she wasn't spending every weekend with Yannie. She had exercised for herself, with no thought of trying to win Yannie back after what he had done to her. But she looked better now. She was sure of that, though Yannie would never notice.

If what Yannie was going through was a dream, it was the kind of dream someone has when on the brink of launching into the *real world* and scared of the changes ahead. Describing his first encounter with Breeze on a rooftop in Athens, Yannie had concluded that it was dream-like, and about him losing his identity and then finding it again. He'd been sleepwalking. Breeze's style and the things she said and the things she did resonated with a need of his. In her presence, he felt the earth shake. But that didn't take much. Like the video in high school physics class where a bridge breaks to pieces because the wind hits at just the right frequency. That was physics, not magic. And his connection with Breeze wasn't love. Breeze happened to be at the right place at the right time, giving off the right vibes. That could have been Lauren, instead of Breeze. Lauren could have said those things. Lauren could have done those things. Lauren was clever enough. And Lauren could do Breeze one better. She wouldn't exploit his vulnerability and catch him by weakening him, like Breeze did. Rather, she'd rebuild his confidence, give him a plan, and reset his focus to the future, to their future together.

His infatuation with this strange woman and his wanting to drop out of his normal life were triggered by his anxiety about moving on to the next stage of his life, leaving the safe and familiar haven of college and going out into the *real* world. He had no bridge from here to there. He was scared. That was Lauren's entry point. That was what he needed her for. Not just a confidante. Not just a sympathetic shoulder. And not just a bedmate either. He needed a compass. And that's what Lauren could and would become for him.

His dad was key to finding a way forward. His dad was why he was a Classics major and being a Classics major was part of the problem. Such a major was unrealistic in the world of 2008. In his dad's day, the point of college was to find yourself, to grow up, to become a well-rounded and well-informed person. But, nowadays, no one could afford such a luxury. Good jobs were tough to get. Any job was tough to get. An impractical major labelled you as a loser. In his dad's day, liberal arts reigned, and one liberal arts major was as good as another. You followed your interests and your natural bent. That's what Yannie's dad did and his father before him, and that's what Yannie's Dad wanted for Yannie. In today's world, that was a rare gift that he gave to his son, sheltering him from economic realities. That was his dad's equivalent of his mom's babying. Indulgence. Privilege. So, his dad was filthy rich, and this was how he chose to express his love for his son, by giving him this anachronistic opportunity to find himself, to become a complete person, to prepare himself for success in a world that changes rapidly, to not let college, this once-in-a-lifetime opportunity, be degraded into short-sighted vocational training.

Sure, Yannie chose his major, and he felt obliged to defend it to his dad who listened in pride, delighted that his son had, on his own, chosen this path, and that his son thought this path was an expression of rebellion. More power to him. His dad had sense enough not to tip his hand. It was good for someone Yannie's age to rebel. And it was all a dad could ask for when his son rebelled by doing just what his dad hoped he would.

So, Yannie's dad was, in large part, responsible for Yannie being in this bind — having done nothing to prepare himself for what comes after college and suddenly sensing the chasm between this world and that. And it was his dad's wealth that let Yannie do that. So, he owed Yannie big time, and he had the resources and the know-how to help Yannie get through this mess, and then to help him launch despite his Classics major, despite Breeze, and even despite Breeze's baby.

This was the end of the first semester of senior year—a critical time. Fall recess at Yale would begin in a week and last for a week. Then a week of classes until exams. This was no time to screw up and miss classes and take short cuts. Yannie needed to buckle down. Breeze alive was bad enough as a distraction. Breeze as a zombie invalid could destroy his college career and irreparably mess up his future chances. He couldn't afford to mope, grieve, and act delusional. Breeze was not a close relative. He wasn't married to her. The college administration would not deem what had happened to her as an excuse for him not doing everything required of him. He needed to get back in gear, pronto.

He hadn't mentioned the existence of Breeze to his parents. Maybe he planned to stay on campus with Breeze over the break. That would have pissed off his parents, but he might have pleaded that he had work to do and needed access to the libraries, which would be open. Then, after exams, the dorms would close on December 21 and Breeze would have to move out. What then? He wasn't going to be able to keep Breeze a secret for much longer. How did he think his parents would react if and when he introduced her to them? And, even before Breeze's coma, he probably hadn't been working on term papers that would soon be due. He had been acting delusional. He hadn't planned ahead.

Yannie's dad needed to take on the financial responsibility for the hospital care and relieve Yannie of that worry. But he needed to do that with apparent reluctance. He needed to strike a bargain that Yannie would, in exchange, focus on his schoolwork and finish the semester with strong grades.

Then Lauren would need to get Yannie to focus on job possibilities, maybe in management consulting. His dad could use his contacts to set up interviews for the two of them, and then could coach them both to get ready for those trick-question mind games. But first things first.

What was first? The baby, of course, the baby.

That was first on Lauren's mind, but not on Yannie's. Thank God that wasn't on Yannie's mind, not yet. He wasn't thinking of himself as a father. To him, the baby was a way to get the best possible care for

Breeze and to bring her back to the world of the living. That focus would change over time. His bond with his child could be a barrier preventing him from ever bonding with Lauren, even after Breeze was long gone. So, Lauren needed to find a way to deal with the baby. Certainly not abortion. She didn't even know if he could legally make that choice in this tangled situation. But she knew he wouldn't choose that. And not putting the baby up for adoption. He felt responsible for Breeze, and certainly responsible for her being pregnant. He probably felt guilty that this happened to her and that he hadn't learned practical facts about her identity that could help in caring for her now. Lauren needed another alternative.

That's where Yannie's mother came in. With the right preparation, his mother might realize that she'd like to raise this child, as the second child she had always wanted. And she, in turn, could convince Yannie's dad to take responsibility for the medical bills, even though it could run to hundreds of thousands of dollars. Yes, the stock market was at a low point. Yes, news reports said that the wealthiest had lost as much as a quarter of their wealth. But he could afford it. And, properly motivated, he'd want to do it for Yannie, his only child. Of course, he'd never admit that he wanted to help, and he'd make as tough a bargain with Yannie as possible, to get the kid moving in the right direction and ready to become a business success, despite this mess.

It would make it easier for his dad to do all that, if his mom insisted that he do so, for the sake of their future grandchild. That way, his dad could act reluctant and thereby strike a better bargain.

This wasn't going to be easy. But now she saw a path to the future, a future in which she could have a life with Yannie, a full life in which they could share everything, and grow closer with every passing year.

8 ~ Friendship

"Okay, let's get real," Lauren growled at Yannie, then forced a smile.

In the fuzziness of his stressed-out mind, Yannie sensed that she wanted to play the role of a sympathetic friend, but that she was still pissed as hell at him. Asking her here, he had put her in an impossible position. Her bitter tone was well deserved.

She continued, "It's easy to imagine your live-in girlfriend moving from one man to another. But moving from one body to another is hard to believe."

"It could be like in that old TV series *Quantum Leap*," he replied. "She finds herself as a different person in a different place and time, and has to improvise, on the fly. It might be like swimming for the first time. You're pushed into the water, and you thrash around until you learn to control your fear and float."

"Or drown."

"Come on," he insisted. "You've heard of parents throwing their kids into the pool to teach them to swim. Have you ever heard of one of them drowning? Sure, it's scary at first, but you adjust by trial and error, and then it feels natural, and you start to take it for granted. That's what I imagine she's going through."

"Well, if you can believe that, more power to you. Go for it. Science be damned. Bring on the fantasy. Give it the works. Send her emails."

"What?"

"Talking to her while she lies there in a coma, like you've been doing, is depressing, for you and for me, too, having to listen to it. You know she doesn't hear you. And hearing yourself say that stuff has to hurt. So, email her. You need to talk to her, so do it quietly, by typing, and with the expected delay of email. With email, her not answering could be normal, like she's some place that doesn't have Internet access. Send her one email after another, not expecting replies, but knowing that when she wakes up, those messages will be waiting for her, and they'll let her know how much she means to you."

"She doesn't own a computer," he replied. "She doesn't own a cellphone. She has no email account. That's ridiculous."

"No more ridiculous than thinking she's in a different body somewhere. Pretend. Send the messages to yourself, with the idea that you'll show them to her when she comes out of whatever she is in. This is first aid for your mental health."

"I wouldn't know what to say."

"That's easy. Talk about her style, all the things about her that make her unique. Remember her in action. Replay videos of her in your head. Start with the sunglasses, the way she held them and put them on and took them off."

"With a flourish," he answered.

"What?"

"The glasses. She'd take them off with a flip and a twist. My eyes would follow the motion and lose track of what was moving. She was like a magician drawing your attention away from the trick. She did everything like that. She'd be talking and at the same time dangling a sandal from her toes, and I'd be watching the sandal expecting it to fall and watching the flex of the muscles of her calf, and I wouldn't pay attention to what she was saying. I'd hear the words. I'd know what they meant. But I wouldn't challenge them. I'd just accept what she said. And when she walked, she'd sway with a sideways motion, and I'd be so intent on watching her hips, her shoulders, her arms, that I wouldn't see where she was going or why, and I'd follow her, content to be in her wake."

"That's the idea. Just shut your eyes and remember her swaying hips."

He shut his eyes, and he must have fallen asleep. He felt a kiss. He must be dreaming. He didn't want to open his eyes. He didn't want to wake up. It was Breeze. Her tongue in his mouth–tasting, probing. No one but Breeze could kiss like that.

Then she pulled back suddenly, and he opened his eyes.

It was Lauren. "I didn't mean to do that," she mumbled, stumbling back to her chair. "Shit, I didn't."

"What?" said Yannie. Had he kissed her? Or had she kissed him? Either way, it shouldn't have happened. He'd ignore it, treat it like it was part of a dream. What you don't believe, doesn't exist. "I was asleep. What happened?" he asked.

"Nothing," she mumbled. "Nothing. I'm nothing."

"It must be this room. There's something strange about it and everything that happens here. Does it seem that way to you?"

Lauren seemed confused but welcomed this distraction. "What do you mean? A hospital room's just a hospital room," she shot back, regaining her edgy self-confidence.

"I mean that I'm never sick, and I don't visit people in hospitals. So, this is new to me. But this room feels like I've been here before."

"For God's sake, you watch too much television. Get a life."

Yannie chuckled. "Thanks, Lauren. Thanks for pushing back when I talk nonsense. I've been talking lots of nonsense. Thanks for slapping me with your words and waking me up. Thank you for coming here and knocking me into shape with your tough friendship. If you didn't exist, I'd have to invent you."

"Now that's a backward compliment."

"When I think about it, all the important people in my life are necessary pieces of me: you, my parents, Breeze. Without you I wouldn't know who I am. I'd feel incomplete. I'd have to dream you back into existence just to keep going. I'm glad you're here. Our friendship was and is important to me. I shouldn't have shut you out of my life when Breeze came into it. It was immature of me to think that caring is all or nothing. I do care for you. I always have. But it's different with Breeze."

"Yannie, for God's sake, please stop that. You think I want a consolation prize? Jeez. We've got something, all right. Leave it at that, okay? Don't put it in a pretty little box and label it. Leave some mystery, leave some buzz. Let me think you have to restrain yourself from taking me in your arms, that you hold yourself back not just because of her, but because of me, too, out of respect for me, not wanting to risk our friendship for a quick fling that we'd both regret. Make me think this is tough for you."

"It is."

"Wow. Thanks. I'm underwhelmed. That was convincing."

He laughed again.

She shot back, "Okay, daddy-to-be, laugh away. How the hell are you going to deal with this?"

"What?"

"So, you don't remember that, either? God. The doc told you, the DNA's a match. I called your parents for you and asked them to come here. Believe me, that wasn't easy. I must have been on the phone with them for hours. You were too out of it to do that yourself."

"Yes. Of course, I remember. You see how I need you."

"No. You don't need me. Your head's in a strange place. Suddenly you want kids. You want kids right now. When we were together, I thought maybe we'd have kids in five or ten years, and I thought we were both on the same page about that. And now you're ready to be a father before you're out of college. There's lots about you I don't understand. What if I were the one who was pregnant? I certainly could have been. Accidents happen. Even with pills and condoms. What then? Shit, we knew each other as toddlers. We were holding hands in the seventh grade. And for last three years, we were screwing like crazy until this stranger came along. And you knock her up right away? She probably blundered with her pills and as a prize for such brilliance, she wins you? That's dumb fuck, dumb luck."

"I wouldn't exactly call her present condition lucky."

"And my position is great now, isn't it? I'm visiting my ex in the hospital room of his pregnant girlfriend. Talk about awkward. I need to get out of here."

"No. Stay. Please stay. It's Saturday. You could stick around for another day."

"And where do you expect me to spend the night?"

"My room at Calhoun. I won't be using it. I'll stay here. Thanks for coming. Thanks for listening. And please listen more tomorrow. If you planned to see George, call and explain. This is a crisis. He'll understand."

"George?"

"George from Dartmouth."

"He's a myth. Breeze would call him an 'improv'. What would you expect me to say when you dump me after we'd been so close? You dumped me with no explanation. I didn't hear a word from you for months. Then you call me. Am I supposed to sound all happy and grateful to hear your voice again, like I've been moping over you? Well, I haven't been. But I haven't been going out with other guys, either. And

I didn't want to tell you that. I didn't want you to think I was a pathetic loser. So, I invented George from Dartmouth. It was spontaneous, an inspiration, an improv like the ones your Breeze came up with. I can be creative, too."

9 ~ Memories

A slap to the right cheek, then a slap to the left. Yannie shook his head, opened his eyes, and pulled back in shock.

"Dad?" Yannie said with a yawn. "How did I get home? No, this isn't home. Where am I?"

"Wake up, for God's sake," his father ordered. "It's time to get on with your life. You have schoolwork to do. You have exams coming up. You worked hard to get this far. Don't drop the ball now. You made a mistake. We all make mistakes. Now wake up and get in gear."

Yannie was still in the hospital room. Breeze was still unconscious in bed. What was Dad doing here? he thought.

"Ever since we arrived, you've been flipping in and out, drifting to sleep, then popping out of it. You're almost as bad as your grandmother."

"I haven't slept in ages, Dad. Give me a break."

"Okay. What do you want me to break?"

"That's not funny, Dad. This isn't a time for funny. But Grandma. What's wrong with Grandma?"

"Alzheimer's. Her consciousness is like a strobe light. It's on then off. Now it's more off than on. One moment she 's here and her old self. Then in the blink, she's gone, staring off into space, empty, absent. Or she'll flip between here and now, to talking as if she were in some other place and time. We can't take care of her at home now. She needs professional care, 24/7."

"Where is she?"

"On a chair in the corner, behind you. We had to bring her with us. She's on the waiting list for a nursing home. It could be months before she gets in. We do the best we can. It's hell for all of us." Then he smiled and shifted tone abruptly. "Well, congratulations."

"For what?"

"For changing the topic. But your victory is short-lived," he patted his son on the back, as if dismissing that thought and moving on to the next. "We can't stay here indefinitely. We need to sort this out and move on."

Yannie tried to get his bearings. Mom was beside Lauren, on the other side of the bed. Grandma was in the corner. He didn't remember his parents arriving in New Haven. He didn't call them. No, Lauren called them. Lauren had explained the situation and asked them to come. Since Breeze conked out, nothing had felt real. He had fragments of memories, as if he were outside himself, watching himself and hearing himself, as opposed to actually living through these events. He had vague recollections of interviews with the hospital administrator and the doctor. School work?

"What day is it?" he asked his dad.

"What day? Sunday. Of course, it's Sunday. Because it's Sunday, I could come here and not miss a day of work, and not have to reschedule appointments."

"Okay, Dad. Okay. It was yesterday morning that everything fell apart. Saturday. I haven't missed any classes yet. No problem. There's no need to freak out."

Yannie needed to get hold of himself and take charge. He couldn't space out and be the irresponsible kid his dad expected him to be. He needed to help Breeze. She was pregnant. The doctor said that he's the father, and because of that he could have some say in her treatment. There would be bills to pay, but this was a way to save Breeze, to get her care that might bring her back. Then everything would be the same. No, everything would be different. He'd be responsible for her and for the kid. He'd have to take seriously matters that he never thought about before. As if somebody had waved a magic wand, he'd have to become a different person. He'd be in the same body. He'd have the same name. He would be an adult, with responsibilities. No more drifting. Purpose. Plans. Job. Career. Shit. Not now. He couldn't think about all that now. He had to focus on Breeze. He had to talk his dad into paying for her care. He had to get his head in gear so he could convince his dad to help. He had never been able to convince him to do anything that mattered, now he had to. What would Breeze do in such a situation? She'd come up with an improv. If this were an improv, he'd understand his dad's perspective and come up with a way to play off that. What mattered to his dad? Where was the leverage point?

"You summon us here as an emergency," his father continued, "to see this young woman you think you knocked up and who has had a seizure or a stroke, and you want to talk us into paying her hospital bills."

"She's the mother of your grandchild. She's carrying your grandchild." Maybe that was the angle.

"Purported grandchild."

"Confirmed. They did the DNA tests. I'm the father."

"A one-night-stand."

"We lived together for two months."

"But you have no idea who she is or where she comes from?"

"We met in Greece last summer."

"Lauren," Dad turned and challenged her, "you didn't say that on the phone."

"I didn't feel that was necessary," she explained. "It wasn't easy saying all that I did on the phone."

"It wasn't easy hearing it either," his father replied.

"I should have told you about her long ago," Yannie admitted.

"You certainly should have."

"I didn't want to jinx it. I loved her. I love her. I realize now that I love her."

"Even though you have no idea who she is. You don't even know her name."

"She told me." Yannie improvised. "It's one of those long Greek names. *Papa* something. I know it. I just can't remember it. Traumatic stress or something. I even met her parents."

"What?"

"In Greece. Breeze and I met in Athens, on a rooftop, a make-shift hostel for tourists. We went to the Parthenon together, then took a bus together to Delphi." He made the story up on the fly. "We found a donkey trail behind the hostel that winds around the mountain to its flat top, with pastureland, that must once have been an island. Then we took a boat ride to the island of Skiathos, where we lived for a week in a tent on the beach. Finally, we went by boat to another island, the home of her parents, where the Greek army assembled before sailing for Troy."

He remembered the story about the army assembling, and unfavorable winds blocking the crossing, and the sacrifice of the king's daughter. Breeze and he had acted it out as an improv, with he as Achilles and she as the daughter of the Greek commander. In his current state of mind, he couldn't remember the name of the island or the name of the commander's daughter.

"Her father was a professor of philosophy and her mother a professor of ancient Greek," he invented more details. "They used to live in the US. When they retired, they returned to the place of their birth. Breeze was born in the US. She's a US citizen. She has dual citizenship. She was going to the University of Athens. She followed me here. I begged her to join me here. She was auditing courses and studying on her own, applying to colleges in Connecticut for next fall. We were going to get married"

That last line popped out spontaneously. He hadn't thought in those terms before. But saying it, he liked the sound of it. Maybe that was how to win his dad over. But no. Dad didn't flinch. Now Yannie had no more cards to play.

Lauren caught his eye, staring in disbelief. He waved her off with his right hand and broke eye contact with her, looking at the ceiling, hoping she'd get the signal, stay silent, leave well-enough alone.

"Do her parents know about this?" His father asked.

"That we were planning to get married?"

"No. This." He gestured toward the bed. "Her illness, her condition, whatever you call it."

"No. I don't have their address."

"They must have phone and Internet."

"I'm sure they do. But I don't know how to contact them."

"But you said you were there on that island with them."

"I have no address. And so many Greek family names begin like that—*Papa* something. I'm trying to remember so I can get through to them. With Google, I'm sure I'll find them eventually. But Breeze and our child need medical help now. And without proof of citizenship, she falls into the cracks of the healthcare system." He gave it one more push, "She and our child need help—now."

"You claim you were in her parents' house. You say you stayed with them for days. And you remember nothing that could help locate them now?"

Lauren buried her head in her hands. Mom reached over and hugged her, clearly sensing what she must feel, having to hear this. For years, his mom had treated Lauren like a daughter, since Lauren's mother died. For the last few years, she had presumed that Lauren and Yannie would marry. They had always been close. They looked so perfect together. And now this.

"I remember it all clearly." Yannie improvised again. Breeze would be proud of him if she could hear him. "At twilight each night, her father plays the trombone on the porch overlooking the sea. Neighbors up and down the coast listen. They look forward to his impromptu concerts and send requests. His solitary act, done for his own pleasure, has become an act of community."

His mother interrupted, "Your grandfather, my father, used to do that on the shores of Chesapeake Bay." She held Lauren tightly, stroking her hair, stroking the back of her neck to comfort her. "He met my mother, your Grandma, in Greece, while vacationing as a college student."

"Yes. I had forgotten that," Yannie quickly replied. "That's a remarkable coincidence." And now he did remember that story, though he hadn't thought of it when he began spinning this improv for his dad. He hoped that the similarity was close enough to make the story believable, without being so close to the original as to make his parents suspect he had made it up. To distract them from that tell-tale detail, he kept talking, "I'm sorry I don't know how to reach her parents. I never imagined I'd need to. But they know where she is, and sooner or later they'll try to contact her ... by cell phone. She talked to them by cell phone. Their number must be on her cell phone. But I don't know where her cell phone is. I've looked everywhere. When they try to call and don't get through, they'll find another way to reach her. They're parents. That's what parents do. Sooner or later. But Breeze needs help now. Please help."

"So where is this place, this island where her parents live?" his father insisted.

"All-something, I think."

"Not an island," Grandma suddenly interjected.

"What?" asked Yannie and his dad at once.

"Aulis is not an island. It's a port on the coast, north of Athens. Today they call it Avlida."

Yannie and his parents stared in disbelief.

"Don't look at me like that. Don't dare challenge my memory. I'm not a senile old lady. I have a PhD in Classics. I teach Greek. And I deserve tenure. I've earned it. My love of Homer is contagious. There isn't a student of mine who can't quote hundreds of lines of *The Iliad* in the original. Not because they have to. Because they want to. Articles in journals mean nothing. What matters is teaching, passing the torch of learning from one generation to the next. Love of the classics means intimate oral knowledge of what for centuries was an oral tradition. *Maynin ahayda thaya, Peliadio ... Peliadio ...* " Not finding the next word, she stopped short, and stared into space, silent.

Then the word *Akillayos* sounded loud and clear, from the bed where Breeze was lying.

Yannie jumped up, called for the nurse, and raced to the bed. He hugged Breeze and kissed her and pleaded with her to say more, to come back.

"*Akillayos*," Breeze shouted again.

"Yes, yes. Achilles," Grandma answered from her own world, oblivious of where she was or the commotion around her, just reacting to the familiar word. "*I sing the wrath of Achilles, son of Peleus.*" she added, quoting the first line of *The Iliad*. Then her face went rigid, and she sank into dark silence with a broad smile on her face.

The nurse rushed in and paged the doctor, who came soon after.

Yannie exuberantly explained that Breeze had spoken. It was just one word, but she had spoken. They had all heard her.

The doctor couldn't get any further response from her, though he did acknowledge that the monitors had recorded a brief spike in brain activity.

Mrs. Johnson led Lauren and her husband out of the room into the hallway, to give Yannie time and space to deal with what had just happened.

"You saw that. You felt that," she urged her husband.

"She said one random word," he mumbled in return. "It was a reflex. She hears this and says that. Just a reflex. No thinking required. Ask the doctor. I'm sure he'll say something like that. It means nothing."

"I didn't mean what she did. I meant what he did. Our Yannie. You saw how he reacted."

Lauren broke away from mom's grip, leaned against the wall and sobbed, "He loves her. You can see damn well, he loves her. For God's sake, do this for him, please."

Mrs. Johnson agreed, "He's in love with that woman. There is no doubt about that, the way he reacted to her voice. If we can afford to pay, we have to. We have to do whatever we can for her."

"We'd have to sell stock at a time when prices are at near-record lows. And there's no telling if or when her parents will turn up, and if or when they might share the financial burden."

"Just do it," Mrs. Johnson insisted. "Whatever you need to do, do it."

10 ~ Before the Beginning

The nurse waved a wand over Breeze's abdomen and a blip of light appeared, a rhythmic blip. "That's the heart beating," she explained. "That's all we can see at five weeks. We can't tell sex yet, or anything other than that it's a healthy heartbeat. And this is the earliest we can see anything."

"Can you record it?" Yannie asked.

"It's being recorded."

"Then can we have an electronic copy of the file?" asked Mrs. Johnson. "I'd like to send it to the baby's grandfather. This our first grandchild."

Mr. Johnson was back in Boston, at work. He had agreed to pay the hospital bills. Lauren was back at Mount Holyoke. Mrs. Johnson and Grandma were staying in New Haven, spending their days at Breeze's bedside, and their nights at a hotel. Yannie spent his nights here with Breeze and his days at school, going to classes, doing his schoolwork−−that was part of his deal with his dad. Except for now. This was the first ultrasound.

Breeze looked like a stranger, with close-cropped hair, like a cancer patient on chemo. After the first week, with no sign of progress, the nurses had hacked off her long curly black hair. Yannie couldn't blame them for that. The hair was soaked with sweat and knotted. It would've been too much work to wash and comb and maintained it. It would be a breeding ground for bacteria, a risk to her health. What surprised him was that as the hair grew back, the roots were red. She must have dyed her hair black. He hadn't known that. He knew so little about her.

But he did know that she loved the scent of sandalwood. So, despite the objections of the doctor, he burnt some of that incense each day, by her bedside.

As the nurse rolled the equipment away, his mom asked Yannie, "Did you and Breeze talk about the baby?"

Yannie scratched the back of his head, then scratched his ears. It felt like something was missing. A sound. Music. He'd feel more comfortable if there were a piano nearby and his mother were playing it. She didn't talk when she was playing the piano. He could feel close to her then, without feeling drawn into an emotional whirlpool of motherly love and concern. Red alert. Beware of the over-protective mother, soon to be a grandmother.

"No," he answered. "She didn't know she was pregnant."

"Did you want to have a baby together?"

"We didn't talk about that," he admitted. "We didn't talk about the future. We were too busy enjoying the present. I'm still trying to sort things out. Suddenly, I'm supposed to be a different person, a responsible adult. Or you could say I've experienced time travel. Before, all I thought about was the present. Now, all I can think about is the future."

"It's not easy growing up." His mother smiled sympathetically.

Yannie cringed, dreading a stream of reminiscences. Which of her oft-repeated speeches would Mom recite now? he thought. He rested his elbows on his thighs and his head on his hands and braced for the inevitable.

But what she said surprised and intrigued him. "Growing up is hard when it happens fast. For me it was fast, too, but not because of a medical emergency or accident. It was like there was a switch in my head, and suddenly it was flipped, and the world looked different, and I knew who I was, and I was a new and different person. One day your dad and I were having fun together, as we had for months. Then something clicked, and I knew, and he knew that what we had together was real and important and would have consequences. One day what mattered was where to go to dinner that night or what movie to see next. The next day we were talking about our future together and talking about you. Not that I was pregnant. But, rather, we realized that it wouldn't be a bad thing if I were and that sooner or later, we wanted to have children together, that we wanted to have a life together, to be responsible for one another, that we needed to plan together."

Yannie looked up, puzzled. This didn't sound like his mom. The voice was the same, but she had never talked this way to him before.

She continued, "I can't help but wonder when you began. Not when you first screamed, and we were relieved that you were alive and breathing. Not making love with your father. Yes, bizarre as it sounds, your parents had sex, enjoyed sex, enjoyed one another. I mean *began* in the meaning-of-life sense. That's just as much a mystery as death. Is there a beginning and is there an end?

"Okay, I'm making you uncomfortable talking about such things. But those are the kinds of thoughts I've been having since you've been away at college. Empty-nest philosophy, I guess you could call it. The older I get, the more I think about the *big questions* that I hadn't paid attention to since I was in college, back when the meaning of everything was all that mattered.

"Your dad and I wanted you so much. As soon as we married, we tried hard to have you, but it didn't happen. Sure, we enjoyed the trying. Making a baby was a good excuse for doing what we wanted to do. But then we crossed a line, and expectations changed. It wasn't a sure thing anymore. We were afraid that you would never be. And wanting you, we were conscious of you. You were very much in our thoughts long before you were physically conceived.

"But your little Yannie, if he's a boy, you should call him Yannie Jr., until the doctor told you Breeze was pregnant, no one thought of him. I wonder, as awkward as it sounds, can someone be conscious if no one is conscious of him?"

Yannie did a double take, intrigued by the idea, and amazed that it was his mother who was saying this. "The quantum theory of childbirth," he shot back, as he might have said when joking about the meaning of life in the dining hall at college.

"The watched kettle," Mom offered back.

"What's childbirth got to do with kettles?"

"That's old kitchen talk for the observer being part of the experiment. A watched kettle never boils."

"Or the tree in the forest."

"And what if the guy who hears the tree fall forgets about it?" asked his mom. "What if he's confused and doesn't understand what he's hearing? What if he has Alzheimer's?"

"Maybe we are all thoughts in the mind of God."

"And maybe God has Alzheimer's," she suggested with a smile.

"So, you mean," Yannie guessed, "if nobody knows there's a baby, is the baby real?"

"I'd phrase it differently. Is the baby really conscious?"

"And you're wondering, what does *conscious* mean?"

"Yes, that's the kind of question." She was delighted that her son could talk to her like this, now that he was about to become a father.

"I've been wondering like that, too," he added. "For the last few days, I've been trying to make sense of Breeze being with me one moment and gone the next. What was there one moment and then not there the next? It's like automatic thinking, thinking I can't stop. Like hearing voices in my head. But I don't think *consciousness* is the right word. And the word *soul* carries too much religious baggage. Maybe the *self*. What is it? When does it start? When does it end?"

"Yes," she answered quickly, interrupting. "That's what I meant about Yannie Jr."

"Well, Breeze, too. Where is she? Can she ever come back? Like you, I wonder where does the self reside? In the head? In the body? When does it begin? When does it end? Does it ever begin or ever end?"

She smiled, pleased to have such a conversation with her son, "I don't understand what religion or philosophy has to say about such matters," she admitted. "But I know in my gut that you aren't just in your own body. There's a model of you in the minds of everyone who knows you and loves you. And that's part of who you are, part of this *self* you're talking about. You're a part of me, even though nowadays we only see one another a few times a year. When someone you love dies, heaven forbid, the folks left behind keep an image and a voice in their minds. Not just a memory. A real presence. Sometimes when I'm troubled and confused, as I drift off to sleep, I hear my dad, your grandpa. He talks to me like a conscience might, but it's his voice, nudging me back to the right track, helping me find my true north, as he'd say."

"I get that," Yannie admitted. "There's this voice in my head now, only I don't know whose voice it is. And what about Breeze? The doctor says her brain is still working, that she isn't brain dead. She must be having experiences of some kind. When she comes back, how will she have changed? Who will she be? I also wonder about me, about all of us."

"In what way?"

"What happened to Breeze, whatever the hell it was, was none of her doing. But what about the rest of us, who live ordinary lives, who don't suddenly go to the brink of death? Is it possible to transform yourself, in good ways and by an act of will? I wonder if you can become a new person through little changes, by changing one habit, then another and another. Can little changes trigger big changes? Can you truly become a new person, not just the same self in different circumstances? To put it another way, you probably can't control what will happen in the world around you, but you can change the who you are who reacts and decides. Forget about fighting fate. Focus instead on habits and gestures, small stuff. How you do what you do. How you think what you think. This is like the old idea Grandma had about slow magic and fast magic. She was talking about aging, which, slow or fast, is out of our control. But what if there's another flavor of magic that relates to growth as a person, little changes that we can consciously direct and that can slowly transform us."

11 ~ Decision Point

Well after midnight, Yannie was still immersed in writing a paper on "Paradise Lost and Mythical Visions of Heaven and Hell" when he was interrupted by a knock.

Annoyed by the interruption, he shuffled to the dorm-room door and, his weary eyes unfocused, he was greeted by hungry lips and arms that hugged tight. The lights went out. His body responded automatically before he could think. He was hugging back. His tongue was touching her tongue. He was exploring her mouth as she explored his. For a moment, he thought he was dreaming, and that in the dream this was Breeze. The kiss, the style, those were classic Breeze. He shut his eyes and enjoyed, not wanting to wake up.

When she finally broke the kiss and nuzzled his neck, and licked his ear lobe, he muttered, "Déja vu."

"Let's déja screw."

She switched the lights back on. It was Lauren.

When she took his hand and led him to the bedroom, he felt the tingling sensation of mutual stimulation that he used to feel with her and that he had felt with Breeze, as well.

Wide-eyed he asked, "This is a dream, isn't it?"

She slapped him in the face. "You didn't dream that. You might have dreamt a kiss, but not a slap, no way. You're awake," she insisted. She grabbed him in the groin. "You're very much awake."

They fell onto the bed, she on top.

He shut his eyes, wondering out loud, "Is this therapy or seduction, or both?"

"Shut up and fuck me," she replied.

After the passion and pleasure peaked and subsided, Lauren sat up and prompted him, "Well, are you going to congratulate me?"

He smiled broadly. "Certainly. That was a ten. No, I'd give that a 20."

"Not the fuck, stupid. The job. I got the job. Didn't you read my email? I'll start at Mathers and Jones in September. Management consulting. The job your father pointed me to. And you got the job at

B.F.D. Your dad told me. We'll both be in New York. Both with dream jobs. Wake up and smell the coffee."

"Sorry. I haven't checked my email. I've been trying to make sense of heaven and hell, the ways of God, and the fate of man. But even if I got the job, I'm not sure I want it."

"There's no doubt that you got it, and no doubt that you should take it."

"But Breeze and the kid. I can't give up on Breeze. And I should raise the kid myself. Little Yannie should be mine. It'll be tough, but I can swing it with online jobs. Maybe I should marry Breeze. Can you marry someone who's in a coma? I'll have to check the Web. Maybe it's the right thing to do. And maybe if she and I were married I could get insurance that would cover her."

Lauren slapped him again. "You screw me, and then you think of marrying her? That's a hell of a way to say, 'thank you ma'am'. As for insurance, forget that, buddy. You know damned well that would get you nowhere. Pre-existing condition. We've been over that before. Are you delusional again? Repeat after me," she took his head in her hands and brought their faces close, so their noses touched. "I'm going to take that job."

He stared wide-eyed.

"Say it, for God's sake." She slapped him again.

"I'm going to take that job," he muttered.

"Louder."

"I'm going to take that job."

"Good. You can take orders. You've healed. You've come a long way. I love the way you've changed. Don't act like a deer paralyzed in headlights like you did when Breeze collapsed. That's not you anymore. You can think ahead. You can plan. You'll do what I want you to do, because that's what we both want. And I won't need to use handcuffs."

"Handcuffs?"

"I've changed, too, kid. Give me credit. I know what I want, and I take it."

Her hair was different. She had let it grow longer. It now hung down to her shoulders. And the color was darker. She must have been dying it, and he hadn't noticed before. When changes happen slowly, it's hard to notice them. She had changed a lot over the last few months. He hadn't realized how much. He liked the new revised edition of his best friend and lover. Her decisiveness was refreshing. He was sure she had his best interests at heart. She seemed to know him better than he knew himself. The management consulting had been her idea. She had cleared a path for him from the world of college to the *real* world.

He felt a surge of relief. A burden of responsibility and guilt had been removed from his shoulders. He shrugged. "I'll take the job," he repeated and smiled.

"We'll rent an apartment in Brooklyn. We'll live together. Maybe one day we'll get married. So, get back to work. Figure out the meaning of life and ace that paper. We're a team now, kid. I want to see A's, and nothing but A's."

She hopped out of bed and dressed quickly.

"What are you doing?"

"Getting the hell back to Holyoke. I've got work to do, too."

12 ~ When is a Triangle Not a Triangle

It was graduation day. It would be a month before the doctor would induce labor and the baby would be harvested. Yannie and Lauren were all packed and ready to move to Brooklyn. Everything was settled. The rest of his life was about to begin.

Then a call came from the hospital. It sounded like the same administrator who had called months before. Breeze might be going into labor. Weak contractions had started then stopped, then started again and stopped again. They hadn't expected that would happen naturally. That's why they had planned to induce. It probably didn't mean anything. It would probably go away. But the doctor wanted him to know. The doctor had said that if she was ever going to come out of the coma, the pains of childbirth might trigger it.

Yannie was shocked by his first reaction to that. Instead of racing to the hospital, ecstatic at any hint that Breeze might recover, he hesitated. He was afraid to tell Lauren. He was afraid how this news might hurt her. A part of him didn't want to give up the idea of a future together that he and Lauren had built over the last few months. Now the road of his life had suddenly diverged: there were two paths forward and he didn't know which way to go. He flashed back to the moment when Breeze first appeared at his door, when he said and did practically nothing while Lauren and Breeze shouted at one another, until Lauren, enraged at his indecision, stomped out, hoping that her leaving would shock him out of his funk, and he'd run after her, but he didn't.

***

Now Yannie and Lauren were in the hospital room. He told Lauren. She insisted on coming with him. He dreaded to think what she must be feeling now. He had this blank in his memory.

As hope of recovery had faded to nothing, Yannie's visits to Breeze had become shorter. He had kept up the routine of daily visits, but he rarely stayed more than a few minutes. He would squeeze Breeze's unresponsive hand, ruffle her close-cropped red hair, and kiss her on the cheek. Then he'd put his ear to her distended belly and listen to the baby, maybe feel a kick.

Now Breeze looked the same as she had yesterday, the same as she had every day for months. No sign of labor.

Lauren said, "Something's wrong, very wrong."

"Of course," Yannie replied. "She's still in a coma. What they thought was labor was probably a muscle reflex. False alarm. Same as usual."

"I mean it's been seven months, and she hasn't changed."

"Like you don't notice the hair and the pregnant belly?"

"Sure. Sure. But her face, her muscle tone. She looks the same as she did when I saw her here in November."

"Yeah. Big surprise. That's what being in a coma is about."

"For God's sake, listen to me, Yannie. She should have lost weight and muscle-tone. She should look wasted. Haven't the doctors or nurses said that it's weird that she looks so good?"

"You expect them to complain that she's doing well?"

"This doesn't feel right. This doesn't happen in nature. This is like somebody's idea of somebody in a coma, and the person with the idea doesn't know a damn thing about medicine. Besides, this is the same hospital room, in the same hospital. I thought they moved her to a long-term-care facility long ago. And her sheet is wet, soaking wet. That's not piss. That's water. What's going on?"

Breeze screamed and convulsed in the contractions of labor.

Yannie doubled up in pain, excruciating pain. He slipped and fell and lost consciousness.

***

When he woke up, Breeze was standing beside him.

She took his hand. She kissed him on the lips. She hugged him.

She was fully recovered. He smiled. He'd have felt ecstatic if he weren't so groggy.

She said, "Thank God you're okay."

"What?"

"Your life: it's a gift. I was afraid you were gone."

Then he realized that he was in a hospital bed. He was the one who had just woken up in a hospital bed. He was the one who had nearly died. He was surrounded by a crowd of well-wishers. It took a while for him to sort out who was who. His grandma and mom and dad were there. Lauren was there, too, with George from Dartmouth. Breeze was a student at Yale, a senior.

He had been in a coma, and on news that he was finally coming out of it, they had assembled to help him recover from his amnesia, to help him make connections to his past.

He heard a baby crying.

"The baby? Where's the baby?" he asked.

***

He must have drifted off to sleep again because he woke up again.

He first saw a woman's legs, crossed, the calf of the upper leg pumping nervously, a sandal dangling from the big toe of her bare foot. He couldn't focus.

"Breeze," he thought. "Breeze," he muttered out loud.

The sandal fell. "For God's sake," the woman exclaimed.

"Lauren?" he thought at the sound of her voice.

She kissed him and inserted her tongue in his mouth, and his tongue responded. And he knew that it was her—Breeze, no, Lauren. He knew that whoever it was, she was the woman he loved and who loved him. He held her tight and pleaded, "Don't ever leave me again. Keep this body. Stay in this one. Please let me love you like this forever."

Then he realized that the woman he was hugging and kissing was an old lady he had never seen before, nearly as old as his grandma, with short gray hair.

"This is a trick," he screamed. "Somebody's playing a nasty trick. Or my mind is gone. Who are you? Who am I? This isn't the world I live in."

"You're my best friend," said the old lady.

"I am?"

"Yes. You always have been since we were toddlers."

"Toddlers," he repeated automatically, trying to get his bearings.

"And my lover," she smiled.

"Lover?" he muttered, unconvinced.

She laughed. "What else would you expect? We've been married for forty-four years."

"What? We're still in college."

She laughed again. "Yes, it does feel like that was yesterday."

Then he noticed his hands, and they were the hands of an old man.

"How old am I?" he asked.

"Same as me. Sixty-seven, of course.

He sat up, grasped at his sheets, pressed his fists to his brow, then lay back down again in pain.

"It's all right," she tried to calm him. "Relax. Everything will be clear soon. You'll get back to your old self. You're still coming out of the anesthesia. I shouldn't be in here. I talked a nurse into bending the rules. This is the recovery room. You've been out for over six hours. The doctor said that waking up might be confusing. It could be like an out-of-body experience."

"What's your name?" he asked tentatively.

"What?" she laughed.

"Your name. Please indulge me. Don't presume I know anything."

"Lauren, of course," she laughed again. "You'd think that after forty-four years of marriage you'd remember my name."

"Lauren?"

"Yes. Now you're coming around. And when we role play, which we both love to do, often I'm Briseis, Achilles' Briseis."

"Yes, yes."

"And then your pet name for me is Breeze, which is so much easier to say than Briseis."

"And the baby?"

"What?"

"I heard a baby. I hear a baby now, out in the hall. I thought you were having a baby. Then I thought I was having a baby."

She laughed and Yannie joined in.

"That's our granddaughter, our first grandchild, Dela. All four of our kids are here and your daughter-in-law and your parents. They're waiting to see you, waiting for you to be rolled out of here to a regular hospital room, so they can see you."

"And why am I here? What happened?"

"You needed an emergency operation. You nearly died, but you're okay now. That's why everyone is here for you. You had sharp pains in your gut. You thought it was gas or indigestion, but I insisted on taking you to the emergency room to make sure it wasn't serious. We were lucky that a doctor on duty guessed that your intestines might be twisted, cutting off circulation. An MRI confirmed that that was the case. They rushed you into surgery. That was six hours ago. The operation took more than four hours. The doctor says the operation was a complete success. They caught it in time. You'll be fine."

"The doctor, what's her name?"

"We had a good laugh about that before they rolled you away. She's Greek by ancestry. Her name is Thetis, like the mother of Achilles who took him to the land of the dead, as a baby, and dipped him in the River Styx to make him immortal. I told her she should do it right this time."

"What?"

"That she should heal you totally, dip your heel all the way in the water so you'll live forever. And she did."

"She what?"

"While you were under, I drifted off to sleep in a chair in the waiting room. And I dreamed we were both college age, and she was a goddess disguised as a holy-roller preacher, and we were standing in a river, and she took hold of both of us, and dunked us, and held us under. It felt like I was drowning. Then she pulled us both up and told us we were saved, that our immortal souls were saved."

Yannie said, "And I dreamed that we were college kids, and you nearly died, and you were in a coma for months. Or was that real and this is a dream? I can't believe that this is you. Where are your sunglasses. Where's your long curly black hair?"

"And where are my firm breasts and shapely legs? Where are the snows of yesteryear?" she laughed.

"Who are you, really? Why should I believe you?"

She smiled indulgently and explained, "We grew up together. We lived on the same block in Boston, in West Roxbury. Back in elementary school, at St. Theresa's, we were best friends. We held hands in the fifth grade. We kissed in the seventh grade, sitting in the back of a movie theater. Then I moved away. We lost touch. Eight years later when we were both in college, the summer after our junior year, we met on a rooftop in Athens. You didn't recognize me at first. In eight years, I had grown from a little girl to a woman, four inches taller, and with a body that you said was *to die for*. My hair which had been short and red, was long and black. And sunglasses, too. Back then, I wore sunglasses all the time. Thinking I was a stranger, you came on to me. I suspected that I knew you but couldn't place you. Then your fingers brushed mine, and I felt something electric. Then you kissed me, and I kissed back, and I knew it was you, against all probability. That was a night to remember. I can see it now like it happened yesterday. We'll talk about that when you're well enough to go home, when we can share that moment and act it out again in bed. That will bring back your memory. All of it. The magic of Athens, of Greece. The next day we took the bus to Delphi and hiked up the donkey trail to the top of Mount Parnassus. And there we picnicked near an old olive tree and ate pomegranates and golden apples and bread and cheese and tomatoes. And we talked about our future together. And lying there under the stars that night, the ancient gods granted us our happily ever after."

He stared at her, trying to grasp what had happened, and where he was and when he was and who he was. And he wondered if he'd wake up once again, and where and when that would be.

She watched him patiently, waiting for a reaction.

Finally, he said, "A minute ago we were college kids. Now I'm sixty ... "

"Sixty-seven."

Epilogue ~ 1~ 20 Years Later

Yannie woke up again. He was in a hospital bed. A young woman with short red hair sat in a chair by the foot of his bed, and the little girl on her lap, seeing him open his eyes, jumped up and ran to him and shouted with joy, "Tell me another story, great-grandpa."

After the shock of hearing that name had sunk in, and he realized how old he must be, memories strobed through his mind. Once before, long ago, he had awakened in a hospital room like this, and learned that the love triangle that had been the story of his life had been no triangle at all, but rather long intimacy with the same multi-faceted woman. Breeze and Lauren were one. And now, he remembered with a jolt, that she was dead.

In this state of mind, with his whole life in his mind at once, he wanted to tell this little girl what Grandma had told him when he was her age—to explain to her about slow magic and fast magic. But, from what he had just experienced, he now understood that real magic is for the old, not the young.

The younger you are, the slower time goes, the older the faster. He was now in the realm of fast magic, where ten years could go by in a blink. To her, magic would be nothing but fantasy. To him, it was a fact of life.

So instead, he showed her the deep scar on his shoulder and told her the story of his life, beginning with his mother holding him by the heel as she dipped him in the River Styx, and the death of Patroclus, and his epic battle with Hector, and his love for Briseis, and his fated death before the walls of Troy, and then his second life with Briseis among the Amazons. And he wished he had a lyre so he could sing the tale, as it should be sung.

Part Two ~ Cheating the Gods

13 ~ You Cannot Cheat the Gods

Breeze was falling up, slowly. No one falls up. No one falls slowly. But Breeze did. She drifted up toward light, bright and rippling, like the surface of water.

She broke the surface, took a deep breath, then sunk, and pulled up again.

Another breath. She took in and spit out water, salt water.

She was at sea.

How did she get here? Plane crash? she wondered aloud.

Her calf muscles cramped.

"Breathe slowly. Relax," she warned herself. "You're alive."

She floated on her back, shut her eyes, and conjured up calming images.

She was at a resort on an island in the Caribbean, in the South Pacific, in the Aegean. She was relaxed and confident. The sea was mirror calm. The tide was coming in. She knew, without knowing why she knew, that she didn't have to swim to save herself. If she just stayed afloat, she would drift ashore. She shut her eyes. By the time she reached the beach, she would probably remember where she was and who she was and why she was here. Temporary amnesia. Drugs? Alcohol? Maybe, like in a movie, she would have a humorous time trying to fit in by reading clues and improvising until she figured out what was going on.

Maybe she wasn't in water at all. She was asleep in a college dorm room and having a dream. When she woke, she would find she was naked in bed with a boyfriend. As she fantasized about this boyfriend, snapshots of one guy after another raced through her mind like matches on Tinder swiping by so fast the images blurred together. Then she saw pictures of herself, slide-show style, on the smartphone of her mind, at different ages, in different places, in different bodies, in different lives. All the photos were of her. She knew it was her she saw.

Now she saw a young girl, dressed in white, with garlands of daisies streaming from her hair and ribbons fluttering in the wind. This was someone else, not her. Breeze viewed this scene from above, hovering in air, not water. Standing tall and proud, this girl in white strode down a long path defined by spears crossed above her, thousands of spears forming a corridor hundreds of yards long. An army was lined up on either side of her. The sun reflected off the polished helmets and breastplates.

The girl in white advanced at a ceremonial pace. She looked confident. She knew what she had to do and how to do it properly. She smiled, pleased at the extent of the preparations, beaming in anticipation.

The size of the assembled army and the girl's gold necklaces and bracelets suggested this was a royal wedding, an historic event. Breeze free associated, as she would in a trivia contest: army, ancient Greece, Troy, Trojan condoms, the movie *Troy*. Brad Pitt as Achilles, his slave-girl lover Briseis. Who played that part? Julie Christie as Thetis his goddess mother. Peter O'Toole as Priam, king of Troy. Brian Cox as Agamemnon, commander of the Greeks.

Breeze made the connection. The bride must be Iphigenia, daughter of Agamemnon. For reasons she never understood, Breeze knew the story of the Trojan War as if it were hard-wired in her head. Reading the story for the first time, as a child, had been like refreshing her memory about events she had lived through.

Here and now, wherever here and now was, whatever flavor of reality this might be, Iphigenia was thinking she was about to be married and didn't have a clue what was really going on. Breeze needed to warn her and save her but couldn't make a sound.

Iphigenia probably thought that she had lucked out in the arranged marriage game. Her father had ordered her to marry Achilles, the greatest Greek. Preparing for war against Troy, the Greek army had come in a thousand ships from dozens of small independent states, nominally under the leadership of Agamemnon. Through this marriage, Achilles would acknowledge Agamemnon as his superior, and Agamemnon would welcome Achilles as his closest ally, strengthening Agamemnon's authority.

Just a few days before, Agamemnon's heralds had abruptly fetched Iphigenia from home in Mycenae. Her mother was offended that there was no time for traditional preparations, but the name *Achilles* had silenced her objections. By renown, he was the finest match in all of Greece.

As if this were a movie, the sound of that scene, the soldiers cheering, continued as the scene changed.

Breeze reclined in a huge metal tub. Young girls, dressed in white togas, washed her hair, and scrubbed her back and arms. She heard the name, *Iphigenia*. She realized that now she was Iphigenia. She was seeing through Iphigenia's eyes, against a backdrop of Iphigenia's memories. Breeze knew what Iphigenia was thinking, and also had her own knowledge of what was about to happen, but she had no way to communicate what she knew to the person whose body she was now sharing.

She knew that Iphigenia had arrived earlier that day, the day before the wedding, without her mother, without friends, without her personal slaves. Iphigenia wondered why she hadn't seen anyone she knew, not even her father. She had been isolated and closely guarded in a temple of Artemis.

She had seen Achilles only once before, at Argos. That was two months ago, soon after he was recruited for war against Troy. Back then, she was considered a little girl, too young to be married, and Achilles was the most important man in the world. Then, just a few weeks ago, she had her first period, making her a *woman*. Now, by royal decree, she was Achilles' bride-to-be.

To Iphigenia, the name Achilles meant heroism, glory, esteem, power. She was delighted that her father had made this match for her. But to Breeze, the event to come evoked horror.

There were two separate people in this one body, with very different ideas of what was going on and what they must do.

Breeze grabbed her new head with both hands to relieve the pain. She wished she were at sea and drowning, anything but in this body, about to suffer the fate of Iphigenia.

Breeze saw a moving light. Whatever was happening would soon be over. She would die or wake up. And if she died, she might wake up in her real world, wherever that was.

The light was a torch coming toward her.

She was sitting on a pile of rugs on a stone floor. Aside from the torch—now hot, close to her face—the room was dark.

Breeze guessed this was the temple, on the night before the wedding.

The man holding the torch was Achilles.

Breeze realized that Iphigenia didn't believe what she saw. She thought she must be dreaming. Achilles wouldn't enter her sleeping quarters before they were married. He wouldn't want to dishonor her father and incur his wrath. Besides, the guards wouldn't let him. This couldn't be happening.

She stood and reached up with both hands, touching his cheeks, his chin, his neck.

He didn't move, didn't speak.

His torso was in shadow. She felt the outlines of a jagged scar on his shoulder. She caressed his chest—muscular, hairless, and smooth. Curious and aroused, she reached lower, then lower still. He was naked. He was hard and ready, bigger than what she imagined a man could be. She'd never have a dream like this. This wasn't a dream.

The bride-to-be fell back in shock.

Achilles caught her. "Have no fear, my little princess. I won't hurt you, and I won't let anyone else hurt you. You've heard the rumors. They are lies. You will be mine."

"Yes, yes," she mumbled uncertainly. "What rumors?"

"They say your marriage to me is a ploy to lure you here. They say that Calchas, the priest, asked for you."

"And am I to marry him instead of you?"

"No, my sweet. They say that the gods are making the winds blow foul, preventing us from sailing to Troy. They say that Artemis demands a human sacrifice. And Calchas says the victim must be a virgin daughter of Agamemnon."

"That's horrid. Father would never ... "

Achilles shook his head.

She protested, "Stop. You're frightening me."

"Then I'm a blundering fool. I came here to calm your fears and to take away all reason for them."

"How?"

"Artemis wants a virgin sacrifice. So, I'm going to make sure you aren't a virgin."

She slapped, then hugged him. "You trickster. You joker. I never dreamt you were so devious. Do you think you can seduce me with a tale like that? Do you expect me to feel flattered that the great Achilles wants to dally with me, to risk offending my father, just hours before I will be given to him in marriage?"

Achilles didn't answer. She had expected more flirtatious lies. The silence was unsettling. She blustered on, acting self-confident to feel self-confident. "There's a hint of fear in your eyes. The great Achilles can fear. I could love you for that, all that divine strength, with a dash of human vulnerability."

She kneeled and caressed his legendary heel, then, suddenly, grabbed it and pulled hard. He fell over backwards.

She kissed his heel, his foot, his leg. She kissed his hardness, and she mounted him, as she heard in stories and saw in paintings. She thrusted down, regardless of the pain, until she opened. Then, slowly and softly, she continued, as he hugged her and caressed her.

Breeze zoned out. This was too weird. Having sex while in someone else's body was beyond her limits. She wondered, "He's hot. And for that time and place, he's a rock star. He doesn't need a trick to get in a girl's pants. He knows that, and she knows that he knows that. So, she's flattered that he bothers to make an excuse and that he takes risks to seduce her, when he doesn't even know her and when she will be his property after the wedding.

"Okay, she wants him, and doesn't have any qualms about letting him know that. In this time and place, there are no blushing brides; and if a bride isn't a virgin, that's no big deal. For a girl to have sex for the first time isn't to lose something of value. It's a step in becoming a woman."

Breeze drifted to sleep in a maze of myth and woke up again in Iphigenia's body and with Iphigenia's consciousness, alone now, with dried blood on her thighs. "I actually did it. It wasn't a dream." Iphigenia had never guessed that she had it in her to be such a person. She savored her memories of that night. Then she cleaned up the evidence, before slaves arrived to help her dress for the ceremony.

Then once again, Breeze was separate—a spectator hovering above the wedding procession. She saw Iphigenia up ahead, walking slowly, deliberately, on the open ground a hundred feet in front of the altar where her father stood with Calchas the priest.

Breeze heard the girl's thoughts, "Where is Achilles? This is no time for joking. The entire Greek host is assembled and watching. He can't be late. He wouldn't oversleep on our wedding day. If need be, the heralds would wake him and drag him here. Father would make sure of that. Once father decides on something, no one and nothing can stop him."

Her head swung left, right, behind, unceremoniously. Still no Achilles.

When she reached the altar, she whispered anxiously to her father, "Where is he?"

"Who?"

"Achilles."

"Drugged, asleep in his tent."

"But that's impossible."

"There's no need for him."

She took a deep breath. "Then the rumors are true?"

Agamemnon's face was cold and calm. "I had hoped that you'd hear those rumors. That makes this easier."

"Easier?"

"The gods demand a virgin sacrifice."

"But I'm not a virgin. Achilles made sure of that."

"A minor technicality," he replied, grabbing her by the hair.

She reached up, struggling, unsuccessfully, to free herself.

She took a deep breath, preparing to scream. But Calchas the priest forced the altar cloth into her open mouth, with a graceful flair, as if that were part of the ceremony.

"You cannot cheat the gods," Agamemnon whispered, raising high his blade.

14 ~ Beware of Gods Bearing Gifts

There was a splash. Falling into water again. Then up again. Naked. In a new body. Heavy breasts. Standing, Breeze pulled back her shoulders and tried to find her new balance, to stand straight. Her waist had too much flesh, but she wasn't obese. Chubby. This was a body built for another time and place. Renaissance Italy. Ancient Greece. For such a time, this would be a voluptuous body, built for self-indulgence and luxury.

***

Breeze took a deep breath and tried to get her bearings. This wasn't the sea. The water was just two feet deep. A pool. Fresh water. An offshoot of a river, near its mouth, near the sea. She's wearing a white woolen tunic, the bottom of which is pulled up and tucked in at the waist to keep it out of the water.

Dozens of young women dressed like Breeze were dancing in the pool around her. They were shouting, laughing, splashing, playing, and working. Yes, working. That was cloth not sand under their feet. They were stomping on clothes, washing them by dancing on them. What in the future would be a chore, these women have turned into a party. Breeze joined in, dancing with enthusiasm.

She recognized that this was ancient Greece, where goddesses spin and weave, and princesses do laundry, where shared labor is shared joy.

Two dozen guards, in bronze armor, their helmets and spears on the ground, drank and laughed, enjoying the spectacle.

Off to the side stood the wagons used to haul the laundry. And in the field beyond, the mules were free to graze.

Beside the pool, other young women spread their freshly washed clothes on the grass to dry, then smoothed their skin with oil. Others played ball or lay on the grass and ate, savoring their food with no concern about gaining weight, hoping to put on more flesh to be more attractive to their men.

Breeze scanned the horizon. The sun was low in the sky. Probably soon after dawn. Off to the left, near the shore, a wooden stockade extended for a mile or more. Inland, in the distance, casting a long dark shadow, loomed a walled city: Troy. She was sure it must be Troy.

"Briseis," called a man's voice.

Her head turned automatically in the direction of the voice. Her left foot was stomping on laundry, without her having willed that. Her thinking and her moving were disconnected. She tried to turn her right foot to find out if she can control her new body. It moved, not as much as she wanted, but it moved. She smiled at that minor success. Then she staggered to keep her balance, while out-of-control muscles twisted the other way. The scene around her faded out of focus. She stumbled. A woman beside her caught her before she fell.

She tried to say, "thank you," but couldn't make a sound.

"Too much wine," the woman laughed. The meaning was clear to Breeze, though she didn't know how. She didn't know what language the woman was speaking, but she heard it as English.

"Out. Out. Out," another voice shouted inside her head.

The voice protested, "What are you? And what are you doing here? Are you a goddess who took over my body to play at being human? I've heard the tales, but I thought they were fantasy. Why would a goddess need to sneak and hide? Or why would you need to use me to deliver a message? You could write it in the sky or have a mule speak it. You don't need my body to do your work. Get out. Let me get on with my life."

A wind of will blew against the self that was Breeze. Her vision dimmed. She no longer had control over her limbs. Her eyes closed without her willing them to close. She felt cold water again. She's on her back in the pool. She must have fallen. She heard laughter.

She willed her eyes to open, and they opened. The women around her laughed, splashing her playfully. Some gripped her under her arm pits and helped her to her feet.

An old man with a long white beard, ran toward her. Breeze recognized him as the priest from the wedding sacrifice.

"Calchas," she said aloud. She was surprised that she could speak now.

"Briseis," he exclaimed, giving her a warm hug. "You are sick. Such good fortune. Thank the gods."

"What?"

"My child, you must have had another fit of the falling sickness. You must have heard the voices again. I sought you out in hopes of this, and my prayers were answered. The crisis is upon us. We need guidance from the gods, and once again they have chosen you as their messenger. Tell me quickly, what have you heard?"

"Falling sickness?"

"You don't remember, do you, my child? That, too, is common when the gods possess you. You lose consciousness. Your mouth clamps shut. Your muscles twitch, as if you no longer control them, as if your body were emptied of your soul. That's when the gods speak to you and through you. And you are not alone in this. Cassandra of Troy, daughter of King Priam, has such fits. All will be well. Believe me, my child. Relax. In calm, your memory will return, and you will be able to tell me what the gods have told you."

He led her out of the pool and onto the grass. Then he massaged her forehead, focusing on the spot between her eyebrows, as if to coax her memory back.

"Shut your eyes, my child. Breathe deeply. Think of our current crisis. A plague is spreading through the Greek camp. Another dozen soldiers died of it last night. Two days ago, Apollo, speaking through you, told me he is angry. Chryseis, Agamemnon's favorite slave, is the daughter of a priest of Apollo. The priest tried to ransom her. Agamemnon refused. Then the priest prayed to Apollo for revenge, and now Apollo has brought this plague upon us and will only end it if Chryseis is released to her father. I begged Agamemnon, but he won't budge. He wants to save face to maintain his authority. We must find another way to appease Apollo. Otherwise, many brave warriors will die of disease, without glory, without honor. Those who survive will abandon the war and straggle home. Have the gods told you what we should do? What do they say? Speak the first words that come to you."

Breeze struggled to regain control of her tongue, then blurted out, not knowing where the words come from, "You have no need for worry.

Agamemnon will release Chryseis, as you wish, and the plague will end."

"At no cost? This miracle will happen with no payment due? The gods are greedy and devious. Beware of gods bearing gifts."

"Yes, there will be costs. One problem will lead to another. Such is life. You know that better than I," her automatic speech continued.

"Then tell me what you know so I can prepare to face these problems."

"Agamemnon will take Achilles' slave girl, Briseis, as compensation for his loss and to reassert his authority."

As Breeze spoke, she recognized the story from the beginning of Homer's *Iliad*. She didn't mean to say what she said. The words just came out of her mouth.

"You, to Agamemnon?" asked Calchas. Then he beamed. realizing the implications of her words. "Yes, my child, yes, A problem for you, but salvation for the Greek army. That has a ring of truth to it. You'd never suggest that of your own free will. To be taken from Achilles who is devoted to you. To put yourself at the mercy of Agamemnon. You would not wish that on yourself. Thank you, my child, thank you for being an honest spokesperson for the gods."

Calchas continued, "I will go again to Agamemnon, and point out to him that you are a worthier prize than Chryseis. He will welcome the opportunity to put the arrogant Achilles in his place. Agamemnon will save face. Apollo will be appeased. This is a brilliant ploy. The gods be praised."

In the original story, Briseis never made such a suggestion. But the outcome, triggered by the rivalry of Agamemnon and Achilles, could be the same. This was an alternate path to the same story line.

Calchas spoke again, "But how will this end, my child? Did the gods tell you that? When Apollo stops the plague, and I have faith that he will, is that the end or the beginning of our troubles? Need we fear the wrath of Achilles? Will we have a war among ourselves, another war over a woman, and this time you the woman?"

"War?" she asked, wide-eyed.

Breeze was able to say that. She could speak what she thought. Breeze was in control. The voice in her head was gone. The push-pull tension in her legs and arms subsided. She wiggled her arms and kicked her legs. She was on her own in an alien world. She could understand what was said, and she could make herself understood. But she didn't have a clue as to what she should say or do.

Calchas looked at her in sympathy, seeing her antics as the aftermath of her having been possessed by a god. "Have no fear, my child," he reassured her. "And have no shame for this."

"Shame? What shame?"

"You have soiled yourself."

She felt, then danced away from the yellow puddle at her feet.

"That, too, is a sign. You speak the truth, the truth of the gods."

15 ~ Achilles

When Breeze again opened her eyes, her back was sore, and the room dark. Hard bed. No, she was on the floor. Stiff scratchy material under her. A rug? Her hair was wet and strewn across her face. She pushed it aside. What's that smell? Sweat? Oil? Then she remembered the women washing clothes in the river. Oil for the skin. Maybe for the hair as well. Sticky, smelly. She needed a long, hot shower.

She was in that same fleshy, overweight body she was in at the beach, with the laundry and the priest Calchas.

She heard sounds of horses and wagons in the background. She guessed she was inside a lodge in the Greek camp. She wondered about how much time had passed since she talked to Calchas? Where had she been and what had she done in the meantime? What happened to this body when she wasn't in it?

She needed to gather clues and improvise. Her life depended on it. People here were superstitious. If she stumbled in this new role, they'd think she's a witch.

And who was the naked man lying beside her here in the dark?

She needed clues. She reminded herself that Homer's *Iliad* is a story, not history. How could she expect that events would unfold the way Homer said? And could her words and actions change that story? Did she have any control over what she said and did? And if so, what were the limits of her free will?

She might, at any moment, awaken from this here-and-now to another. But while she was here, she was probably subject to all the dangers of this place. She couldn't risk presuming otherwise. She needed a plan. She knew that some voice speaking through her told Calchas what would happen in the immediate future. She presumed that Calchas, acting on what she said, suggested that Agamemnon give up his captive slave girl to that girl's father, a priest of Apollo, and that Agamemnon take Briseis away from Achilles. That's the way Homer's story went. That way, the gods were appeased, and Agamemnon saved face, but Achilles was enraged. In the twist on that story that Breeze found herself in now, Briseis was to blame for the rift between Achilles and Agamemnon. In any case, she would be turned over to Agamemnon.

She was on a rug on a rough wooden floor. Not what one would expect in the residence of the commander-in-chief. And the large muscular man asleep beside her feels like he could be the Achilles she saw *rescue* Iphigenia.

As her eyes adjusted to the dark and her mind adjusted to her circumstances, she began to distinguish outlines, where one thing or person ended, and another began. One of the man's legs was draped across hers, pinning her down. She made out what seemed to be deep scars on his left arm, his left shoulder, and his chest. She felt an electric tingle as her fingers lightly caressed him, touching the tips of the light body hair on his shoulder and neck.

Her nipples were erect. Her labia were swollen and moist. But she didn't remember having had sex.

She knew the story of the Trojan War well but could hardly imagine what it would feel like to be a slave, to be owned and used by a man renowned for his cruelty and for his skill in slaughtering people.

She didn't know how to dress, how to walk, even where to go to urinate and defecate in this time. There were no bathrooms. Maybe there was something like an outhouse or a trench.

For reasons unknown, Calchas understood her words, as she understood his. But what about body language? She wouldn't be able to interpret the intentions of others, any more than they'd be able to interpret hers. And Achilles was a total stranger to her. She knew what he said and did in the story but had no idea what to expect outside the story, between the scenes that Homer wrote.

When Achilles woke up, she thought, would he strike out at her, enraged to discover that he was in bed with a creature from another time?

She wanted to take charge of the situation and make the best of it. She knew that she was from a world 3,000 years in the future, a world of computers and cars, of hygiene and medicine; a world with bathrooms and cellphones, with tampons and contraceptive pills. While she knew the story of the Trojan War, she knew nothing about everyday life at this time. But she did know men and how to please them and how to please herself with them.

Her body responded spontaneously to the nearness of this naked man. His leg lying across hers heavy but titillating. Her fingers, acting on their own, caressed him.

She leaned forward and felt his shoulder against her cheek. With just a few points of contact, her flesh carried on a dialogue with his flesh, independent of her will.

According to the story, Achilles loved Briseis, but he may have only known her as a body, this body that's now Breeze's body. If he was shallow and horny, she might be safe. The less he knew and understood Briseis as a person, the better. The vainer and more self-centered he was, the more likely he wouldn't notice the difference between her and the *real* Briseis.

He shrugged and turned and nuzzled her neck with his face. Probably dreaming.

She thought to kindle his passion while he slept so when he awoke, it would be with desire.

She reached out and stroked his nearly hairless chest and kissed a scar on his arm as she might kiss a child's scratch.

The feel of him and his responses triggered memories from Briseis' past.

She saw the ruins and ashes of what once was Lyrnessus, the town where Briseis grew up. Briseis was sprawled on the ground in the dirt path in front of what had been her home. Her bare feet sore and bloody. The ends of her hair were singed. Her tunic was torn. Towering over her, stood Achilles, bare-chested, but still wearing his helmet. His entire body was smeared with blood.

The more Breeze watched, the closer she identified with Briseis, the victim on the ground. She cringed in pain as someone cauterized a wound on her arm with a red-hot sword. Achilles had killed her father and her three brothers. That blood on him is theirs. She was his captive. She hated and feared him. She didn't know whether he was going to rape her or kill her or both. She trembled, then struggled to control herself.

The remembered scene changed to the Greek camp, months later, among the lodges of the Myrmidons, Achilles' troops. Achilles was riding a chariot, returning from battle. Breeze guessed that the man standing next to him was Automedon, his charioteer. In the next chariot was Patroclus, Achilles' best friend, who resembled Achilles, but with red hair. In a chariot on the other side of Achilles, stood a regal-looking, white-bearded man, Achilles' other close friend, his old tutor, Phoenix.

The chariots stopped. Achilles stepped down and Briseis ran up to him. From the look of surprise on his face, Briseis was greeting him like this for the first time. Her smile said that she was delighted he had returned from battle alive and unwounded. She reached up and helped him take off his breastplate, then gently stroked his chest. Then, just as suddenly, she ran away, like a child playing hide-and-seek.

Breeze was puzzled by this memory. Now that she had seen the destruction of Lyrnessus, now that she had vicariously felt wave after wave of grief for her father and brothers, Breeze couldn't understand how Briseis could forgive Achilles, how Briseis could flirt with him and care for him.

As Breeze now remembered, Briseis waited, submissively, expecting that sooner or later, Achilles would take her and use her roughly, as was his right. But night after night, he passed her by and chose other slaves to share his bed. Sometimes she caught him looking at her. Then he'd shrug and look away as if his look were an accident and meant nothing. He ignored her so consistently that it had to be deliberate. He must be aware of her as she was of him. And his overt indifference might be a sign of consideration, giving her time to grieve and to adjust to her new role as a slave. Perhaps this legendary brute could be sensitive. Briseis believed that such hopes were unrealistic, but nevertheless, they enlivened her daily routines of cleaning clothes, polishing armor, and straightening up after meals.

Then one night when, by chance, they were alone together in his lodge, Briseis dared to reach out and touch his leg as he walked by. In response, he laughed and grabbed her, and threw her over his shoulder, and carried her to a corner where rugs were piled. There he took her roughly, then explored her body with his hands. She had wanted him. He hadn't forced her.

That first lovemaking took place just a few months earlier.

Now, with him nuzzling her neck, Breeze realized that she, as Briseis, adored Achilles, and believed he was worthy of her worship. She believed the rumors that he was the son of a goddess, and that Zeus, king of the gods, insisted that his mother marry a mortal because the Fates had foretold that if she mated with a god, the offspring would be greater than Zeus himself, and would overthrow him.

As these memories subsided, Breeze was once again aware of Achilles' naked body pressed close to hers. Then without warning, Achilles rolled over, grabbed her, flipped her, and took her from behind. She surrendered. Despite herself, her body enjoyed his body. This man had the brash force of a professional wrestler, but he had gentle self-control as well.

When he was done with her, she squeezed free from his limp body, then stroked and kissed his cheek, his lips. When he didn't respond, she kissed him again and inserted her tongue into his mouth. He drew back as if surprised. Maybe she blundered. Maybe in this time and place people didn't kiss that way.

Then a sliver of dawn light from a crack in the wall reflected off the sweat on his face. He was smiling broadly, perhaps responding to the pleasure of such an unexpected sensation. Or perhaps he expected his slave girls to be submissive and patient, nothing less and nothing more. Perhaps he didn't expect a gesture of tenderness and willful desire. Maybe he didn't think the pleasure of sex could be reciprocal.

He leaned down. She opened her mouth. Her tongue caressed his.

Then another distant memory forced itself on Breeze, signaling that something was wrong. She remembered that she, as Briseis, kissed Achilles that way hundreds of times. He had reacted with surprise the first time she did it, but by now it was part of their regular repertoire of mutual pleasure-giving. Yet to this man, such a kiss was out of the ordinary.

She realized that the man on top of her, the man inside her had bright red hair.

This wasn't Achilles. This was his look-alike friend, Patroclus.

She heard grunting in the corner of the lodge and turned her head to see the silhouettes of what she now guessed were Achilles and another slave girl, probably Patroclus' slave, Iphis.

Breeze guessed this was the night after Achilles' argument with Agamemnon when Agamemnon threatened to take Briseis away. The story said nothing about that night. It jumped ahead to when Agamemnon's heralds came to get her. But it could have been like this. Achilles, angry and spiteful, could have given her to his friend for a night of pleasure and might have taken his own pleasure with Patroclus' slave. If he couldn't own Briseis, he wouldn't want her—not now, not ever. His pride would not allow him to admit his feelings. Agamemnon insulted him, and Agamemnon and the entire Greek army would pay a price.

Without Achilles and his Myrmidons, the Greeks were no match for the Trojans. The Greeks would beg him to forgive Agamemnon. Agamemnon would offer to return Achilles' trophy slave girl to him, and to give him rich gifts as well, anything to get him to rejoin the war. Achilles would laugh in Agamemnon's face. He would pack up and leave for home, taking his army with him, throwing away his fated glorious death. He would lead a long and quiet life, savoring the knowledge that the Trojans crushed the Greeks because he, Achilles, withdrew, because Agamemnon was so foolish as to insult him over a slave girl. It was a matter of pride and self-respect, not love. If it had been love, he'd have killed Agamemnon on the spot. Briseis, as a person, didn't matter to him. That's what he must be proving to himself by taking Iphis instead of her. That's how he must be explaining to himself his moment of cowardice in Agamemnon's presence.

The way Breeze interpreted the story, although Patroclus loved Achilles as a best friend and repeatedly risked his life for Achilles in battle, he envied and resented Achilles. He wanted to be Achilles himself. Yes, in the story, Patroclus would have his one shining moment when he would ride forth in Achilles' armor, pretending to be Achilles, leading Achilles' men. And in the guise of the greatest of the great, he would rout the Trojan army, even kill Sarpedon, reputed to be a son of Zeus himself. And the death of Patroclus would wake Achilles from his funk, would wipe away Achilles' argument with Agamemnon, would reduce his feelings for Briseis to nothing. Achilles would come raging forth, a killing machine intent on revenge, determined to hunt down Hector who had killed Patroclus, and slaughter him like a beast. Women were nothing to a man with rage like that. Revenge and pride were all.

Breeze now knew that she could feel pleasure in this new body of hers. That meant that she could feel pain as well. And she was about to become the property of Agamemnon, a man who sacrificed his own daughter in hopes that the wind would change to help his fleet sail to Troy. She would be at the mercy of such a monster.

She shivered with the realization that if she wasn't executed as a witch or slaughtered by an enraged warrior, she could get pregnant by Achilles or Patroclus or Agamemnon or anyone Agamemnon might lend her to. And childbirth here, with the primitive medicine of this time, was often fatal.

She felt something foreign and itchy inside her vagina. She reached in with her fingers and pulled out a sponge-like thing. Not a rubbery sponge-like in the twenty-first century. A sea sponge. Filthy. It smelled of fish and vinegar.

It was probably meant for birth control. Could anything so primitive work? She hoped so.

16 ~ Iphis

A week later, when Agamemnon's heralds were about to fetch Briseis, Iphis helped Briseis choose her wardrobe, and Diomede, another slave girl, fixed her hair. Everyone expected the exchange to happen immediately. Instead, Agamemnon delayed a week, heightening Achilles' humiliation. The wait also made matters worse for Breeze, giving her time to appreciate what she was about to lose.

Both Diomede and Iphis accepted Breeze as Briseis, without question. When she stumbled in her speech and actions, they presumed she was distracted and depressed by the prospect of having to leave Achilles for Agamemnon. Breeze wished that she could confide in them, wished she could explain to them that she was a different person from a different time, to let them know her fears, and ask for their help in dealing with the unexpected challenges of everyday life. But she held back, uncertain what the consequences would be if she revealed too much of what she knew or does anything else to break the pattern of the story.

***

Diomede was short, blond, and light-skinned, with delicate features. She was a slave by capture, but a princess by birth, a cousin of Andromache, wife of Prince Hector, the greatest of the Trojan warriors. Diomede was keenly aware of her former status, and repeatedly reminded others of it. With men, regardless of their rank, she was perky and sassy. She walked with her head held high and boldly look\ed every man in the eye. She flirted and bossed and talked constantly. But with other slave women, she was quiet and relaxed, treating them like she did her sisters at home before the war.

Iphis was tall, thin, muscular, and athletic. She was born a slave, as was her mother before her. By training and habit, with men, she was quiet and obedient. She walked with her head slanted downward and her eyes half-closed, avoiding direct contact. But with her fellow slave girls, she was talkative and assertive, speaking confidently on every subject and delivering good advice.

Breeze herself was forward and open with Achilles. He seemed to like her that way, and that's how she felt most comfortable with him. She tried to avoid other men, except when she was carrying out orders from Achilles. She stood tall and stared straight into Achilles' eyes. But with other men, by facial expression and posture, she made herself look less attractive, bending respectfully and avoiding eye contact. She even shied away from Patroclus, with whom she slept only once, that night, when Achilles, seething with anger at Agamemnon, shunned her. The following nights, Achilles' anger cooled, and he sought her out and made love to her. It was selfish, violent sex, modulated with moments of tenderness when he realized how selfishly he was acting. She sensed that his passion was driven not so much by the knowledge that he was about to lose her, as by the shame that he had let this happen. By taking her roughly, he proved his manhood to himself. She obeyed and submitted. She let him do whatever he wished. She acted as she imagined the real Briseis would. She sympathized with him and wanted to ease his pain, while at the same time realizing what a self-centered ass this amazing hunk of a man was. He paid no attention to her feelings or desires. After he finished his business, he rolled over and went to sleep. She finished herself.

Despite his egotism, she found him attractive. If she was stuck in this world, she would much rather be his slave than anyone else's. During the day, when she had the chance, she flirted with him, using teasing gestures to capture his attention. She did peek-a-boo motions using a veil, like she used to use her sunglasses in her other world, covering, then revealing her eyes. Sometimes she dangled a sandal from her big toe, precariously, until it looked like it was on the brink of falling. Then she adjusted it with a quick motion of foot and leg, displaying lots of leg.

Whenever Achilles was near, she glowed. Both Diomede and Iphis told her that she seemed even more taken with Achilles than she had been before, her emotions probably heightened by the prospect of losing him.

With the other slave women, Breeze wasn't quiet, but she didn't speak first. She listened for clues about what's appropriate, then improvised, cautious not to be conspicuous.

The attention and praise of Calchas made it difficult to be inconspicuous, as did Achilles' overt preference for her. So, she went out of her way to defer to the other women, to ask for their advice, to compliment them on how well they dressed and how well they did whatever they did. And she was the first to volunteer to help the others with their laundry and other chores.

Now, just as Breeze was beginning to feel comfortable in this new time and world, everything was about to change.

"You must move on," Iphis advised her. "Your fate has taken a new turn. Don't brood over what you can't change. Start your new life as well as you can. Agamemnon knows you only by reputation. Dazzle him at first sight. Go before him submissively, but not as an ordinary slave, rather as a captive princess, like Diomede. But don't be as forward as she is; that wouldn't work with a man as vain as Agamemnon. Act confident, but obedient. You know your importance, but you know your place as well. You have the self-respect you were born with. You have pride in the status that Achilles' favor conferred on you. But you accept the path that the Fates have prepared for you. You're a slave, and now you're the slave of another man, a very different man, who will treat you differently. Whatever he demands of you, you should strive to please him. You should make the most of your new circumstances. He must sense a balance of self-respect and obedience in your every gesture, your every word. For today, you should wear a robe that's simple and white, but with a belt of gold. Diomede will comb your hair, so it looks natural and wild. Wear a veil that lets you see and yet not be seen, that invites him to savor the sight of you without the awkwardness of direct eye contact."

Breeze thought, "Like sunglasses." But she said, "Yes, I can imagine how I might use a veil. Please remind me of that later, after I've settled in. There will be so much that's new for me to deal with, I'll rely on your help."

"I wish I could continue to help you. But we will probably never see one another again. Agamemnon will prize you for what you mean in his contest of will and power against Achilles, as a symbol of his authority. He will keep you closely guarded. That's all the more reason for you to try to attract him, but without the intimacy of eye contact. Let him know who you are. Teach him to prize you for your beauty and for the pleasure you can give him. But keep your proper distance as a slave. You are inexperienced in these matters. Achilles has been your only master, and he has spoiled you. Accept that there will be no emotion between you and Agamemnon. If Agamemnon wishes to enjoy you, do what you can to heighten his pleasure. But keep it impersonal. That's what he will want. That's what most men want from a slave girl."

"All I know of Agamemnon is what I've heard, and that frightens me," Breeze admitted. "He killed his own daughter as a sacrifice. Were you there at Aulis when that happened?"

"Yes. That was ten years ago when the war began. Already then, I was Patroclus' slave. I watched from a distance. I've never seen anything so horrible. His own daughter. I am reminded of it every time I hear my name."

"Why is that?"

"Because my name, too, was Iphigenia. Achilles never wanted to hear that name again. So, he renamed me 'Iphis', and that's what everyone calls me now."

"So, Achilles loves her still?"

"Love? No, not love. Iphigenia was important as a token of power in his struggle with Agamemnon, as you are now. Your closeness with Achilles is uncommon. Don't let your brief time with Achilles spoil the rest of your life. You need to adjust your expectations. Some day you may again find pleasure with another man, a new owner, or a fellow slave. But that's not yours to choose. That's a matter for the Fates and the whim of your master, whoever your master may be."

"But unlike you," Breeze protested, "I wasn't born a slave. I was a free woman. I wasn't a princess like Diomede, but I was the daughter of a wealthy man. I can't get used to the idea of being someone's property."

"Don't be ridiculous. That's the way it's always been. And that's the way it will always be."

"For you, perhaps."

"For you as well. For all women. First, you were the property of your father, and if there had been no war, you'd have become the property of whatever husband your father chose for you. Now you are the property of Achilles. Soon you will be the property of Agamemnon. A woman's life is defined by the man who owns her. Never forget how fortunate you are to be owned by a king."

"King or no king, I want to choose the man I'm with," Breeze dared to say, needing to vent to a friend, and hoping this degree of familiarity would not have repercussions.

Iphis answered soberly, "Say whatever you want to me. But within hours you will be with Agamemnon, and he won't put up with such insolence from a slave. You need to catch his eye and catch his seed as well as soon as you can."

"That would be horrible."

"That would be the best thing that could happen to you, to bear the son of a king, to have a son who has a chance for wealth and power, who might someday become king himself."

"But when you don't want to get pregnant, what do you do to prevent it?"

"I do what we all do. Sometimes you scare me, with these blank spots in your memory. Things that we all take for granted, to you seem strange. How far has stress thrown you off?"

"And what do we all do?"

"If you are so foolish as to not want to bear a king's child, you can always be friendly."

"What do you mean by *friendly*?"

"Friendly with your hand, with your mouth, with your tongue. Do whatever you can so the seed is spilled where it can't take root."

"But that's too risky. He could force me."

"Then pack your sea sponges. I know you have them. We gathered them together at the shore. If he's drunk enough, as he's likely to be, he won't notice. And take your vinegar, too–that's what you've used in the past to soak sponges in. I prefer to soak them in the juice of oranges when I can get it, in case the man is in the mood to taste."

"I use a slice of lemon instead of a sponge," Diomede added. "That's just as good. There are other choices, too—lots of them. I've heard that in Egypt they use honey, soda, and crocodile shit, but I don't know whether they insert that or eat it."

"Use a sponge," Iphis insisted, confidently.

"Sponge, yes. I'll go with the sponge," Breeze agreed. "Thank you. But if that doesn't work, what's the alternative to giving birth?"

"Herbs can deal with that," said Iphis. "Any slave girl could provide details if you still don't remember."

"Thank you. It's important for me to know that I have a choice, that my fate isn't at the whim of a man who thinks of me as his property."

"Where do you get such ideas? Yes, we can prevent pregnancy, most of the time. But we have no choice about the life we live, and it's a good thing we don't. If you could go from this man to that one on a whim, you'd never feel committed to the life you find yourself in, you would never feel the extremes of fear and joy. Everything would just be make-believe to you because you could leave at will."

"My mother used to tell me that," said Breeze, improvising to draw attention away from how far her ideas were out of line with the accepted truth of this time.

"I don't think you've ever told me about your mother."

"How long have we known each other?" Breeze tried to calibrate how well Iphis knew Briseis before Breeze became Briseis. Reminders of the change still made her feel like she was plunging into water, nearly drowning, struggling to surface again.

"Over two months."

"Yes, thank you. That's when Lyrnessus fell, and my family was killed, and I was captured. My memory sometimes plays tricks on me. Have you noticed that I'm sometimes distracted?"

"I'm amazed that you cope so well. First you lost your family and were forced into slavery. And no sooner do you adapt to your new life than you become the property of someone else. That's one life after another after another."

"It's that, yes, and maybe trauma, too. My mind is sometimes in more than one place at once. It's difficult to explain. Have you wondered why Calchas the prophet sometimes seeks me out?"

"He claims he's a friend of a relative of yours who is concerned about your welfare but can't afford to pay ransom for you. I thought, despite his age, your looks charmed him, and he sought excuses to be near you. No fault of your own."

"It's because I'm different in ways that are difficult to explain. I have spells. The *falling sickness* Calchas calls it. When I'm in that state, I see not just what's here and now, but what might be and what must be. And sometimes I'm not sure which is which."

"Like living more than one life?"

"Yes. Sometimes it feels like that."

"It must be wonderful to know the future, even if dimly."

"Sometimes I see it clearly, and it isn't wonderful at all. Imagine what it would be like to be a mother holding her newborn son and seeing the moment, thirty years in the future, when he will die. Imagine what it would be like to feel his death agony as a warrior when you hold him and kiss him as a baby, singing and rocking him to sleep."

"Like Thetis, the goddess mother of Achilles."

"Yes. Like that."

"Then you're telling us that you're a goddess?"

"No. I'm telling you that I know too much and that such knowledge colors what I see and turns times of joy into times of sorrow, unless I can keep my balance, and learn to savor the now, even though I know what happens next."

"But sometimes it might be a blessing, knowing the details of a tragedy to come, even if we can't prevent it. Life is brutal and short, but if we knew for sure what was going to happen, that could make us more aware of the present. Like you just said about yourself, we should savor what we can, while we can, and live this one fated life of ours to the fullest."

"Then if you had the choice, you'd want to know?"

"Of course."

"You think that now, but what if you knew what was going to happen and you couldn't undo the fact that you knew it, and hence you couldn't go on as before?"

"What do you know that you hesitate to tell me? What do you know of me or Patroclus? Yes, Patroclus. I can see it in your eyes. Fates be merciful. Patroclus will die. He will die soon. Why do you tell me this horror? Why do you do this to me?"

"That's what I was afraid of. That's why I didn't tell you."

"Then it's true?"

"No. You guessed wrong. I have no such power. I was making up stories to distract myself from my dread of Agamemnon. Forgive me, please, and forget I ever said any of this."

"But you already told me. Once heard, there is no forgetting. You have the power. That's why Calchas comes to you. That's why you sometimes walk and talk in a haze. That's why you'll look sad when you should be happy, and happy when you should be sad. That's why you sometimes stumble in your speech. It's because you know so much and hesitate to let others know, to give them knowledge the gods never intended them to have. Well, you've done it now. I'll never be able to look at Patroclus the same. We all know that Achilles must die here at Troy, gloriously. That's the price of being the great warrior that he is, son of a goddess. He proudly wears that fate. He's fierce and unstoppable because he doesn't fear death. That's part of who he is and how everyone sees him. But Patroclus is an ordinary man, with no knowledge of his fate. Each day for him has its risks and hopes. I had hoped that I'd be his for years to come, sharing all with him. But he will die soon. I believe you. Tell me more."

"More?"

"You cannot unsay what you have said already. You cannot undo the pain that brings. So, tell me when and how he will die. Give me all the details you can. Free me from the anxiety of the unknown. Free me to live to the fullest the time we have left together. Is it an honorable death? A glorious death? Ares, grant that it be a death in battle and not death from illness or accident. Let his death be worthy of his life. But no, that cannot be. You must be wrong. Achilles says that for us the war is over. Because of you, Achilles won't go to war anymore, nor will any of his men. Once you go to Agamemnon today, we'll pack up and go home. Later, for reasons no one knows, Achilles will come back here and die here. The Fates have said he will die here, and the Fates will never be cheated. But Patroclus and the Myrmidons aren't part of that fate. We're going home, and we can stay home. Patroclus and I can have a new life back in Thessaly. That's what he told me just yesterday. And now you tell me that Patroclus will die soon. But how will he die? Please tell me it will be in battle, however that could be. Any other death would be shameful for a man such as he, a man with all the courage and skill of Achilles, but without the fame and the noble divine birth. Tell me true. Tell me how it can be. Make me believe. Free me from the anxiety you have brought me. You owe me that. Tell me quickly, before the heralds come for you."

Breeze answered, "Achilles will sulk, but he won't leave. He'll linger, wanting to witness the defeat and humiliation of Agamemnon and his army. And Agamemnon will beg and grovel, offering to return me and to give Achilles rich gifts as well, but nothing will move him. The Trojans, sensing that the Greeks have lost the will to fight, will strike in full force. They'll push the Greeks back and break into our encampment and threaten to set fire to our ships.

"But Patroclus will not sit idly by. He loves Achilles and has repeatedly risked his life for Achilles in battle. And yet he has always envied Achilles and wished that he were Achilles himself. So, for the good of the Greek army and for his own glory, Patroclus will put on the armor of Achilles and pretend to be Achilles and lead Achilles' Myrmidons in battle."

"I can see him now."

"And you will see him soon in a scene that will be remembered for thousands of years, standing tall in Achilles' chariot beside Automedon, raising his spear to the cheers of the Myrmidons who race to arm themselves and follow him in his shining moment, as he rides into the breach in the wall where the Trojans are pouring into the encampment. He will face single-handed the foremost of the Trojans. Then the Myrmidons will join him and the whole Greek army—a hundred thousand strong—yelling loud enough to shake the ground and charging reckless and frenzied. He will fight like a demi-god and inspire them all. They will believe that he's their champion, the unbeatable Achilles, not Patroclus, a mere mortal with dreams of glory. Patroclus will concentrate all his strength, all his life into one brief moment, to change the tide of the war, to change the course of history, and to be remembered for all time."

"And he will do it," Iphis echoed, in awe.

"In battle, he'll do all that the world's greatest warrior could do. In hand-to-hand combat, he'll kill Prince Sarpedon, reputed to be a son of Zeus himself. He'll lead the Greek army to the walls of Troy. And there he'll die at the hand of Hector, greatest of the Trojans."

"Zeus be praised."

"You're all right with that?"

"Of course."

"That when Patroclus is given the choice of living with you or dying in glory, he'll choose glory?"

"As he should and must; for so it is fated. So, you have seen it. So, it will be. Thank you for telling me the whole story, for letting me know now, so I can tell Patroclus and share the story with him in anticipation of his glorious moment."

"But knowing the future could change it."

"What will happen is fated. But knowing what will happen can change how we experience it. Thanks to your gift of prophecy, we can control what we make of it, what it means to us."

17 ~ Agamemnon

When Agamemnon's heralds came for Briseis, Patroclus, not Achilles, handed her over to them. After that, Breeze's memory blanked out. When she regained consciousness, she was lying on the ground. Her eyes were shut tight. She was afraid to open them but didn't remember why.

She stood and reached out, like a blind person getting her bearings. Her hands touched metal. A rough hand pushed hers away, and a gruff voice grumbled, "No more games."

She opened her eyes. She still had trouble seeing. The veil. She was wearing a veil, as Iphis suggested. She didn't dare remove it and look the angry man in the face. She was far too close for direct eye contact with a stranger, much less with a *king of kings*.

"Keep the veil on," Iphis advised her. "Never let an angry dog sense your fear. Never let an angry king take offense at the expression on your face. Don't let him read your thoughts."

Keeping her head still, standing rigidly straight, and getting used to the veil, Breeze scanned the room in front of her. A structure like Achilles' lodge, only larger. Details gradually come into focus. Unpainted wood. Gold ornaments hung here and there, as if someone with no taste tried to add a touch of opulence to a log cabin.

She was now Agamemnon's slave. She was completely at his mercy. If she pleased him, he might want her as his plaything, maybe even as mother of his children. If not, she could become his drudge, or he might, to spite Achilles, humiliate her, torture her, even kill her.

Then she remembered the passage in *The Iliad* where Agamemnon relented and offered to return her to Achilles and begged Achilles to go back to battle. He has his heralds relay his words:
"... and I will swear a solemn, binding oath in the bargain:
I never mounted her in bed, never once made love to her —
the natural thing for mankind, men and women joined."

In the story, Agamemnon didn't touch her. For all his bluster in his competition with Achilles, he didn't want to make the breach irreparable. He was a politician. He wanted to assert his authority and make Achilles acknowledge that authority in public. But if that failed, he would need to make amends. Her well-being was important to his backup plan, though he'd never acknowledge that to her.

Everything, so far, had gone according to the story. In the story, she was safe. Patroclus would disguise himself in Achilles' armor and be killed by Hector. Agamemnon would return her to Achilles, untouched. Achilles would, once again, lead his troops into battle. He would kill Hector in revenge. And a few months later, Paris would kill Achilles with a poisoned arrow in the heel, at the gates of Troy.

But she shouldn't be here. No one living through these events should know what's going to happen before it happens. Even if no one figured out that she doesn't belong here, sooner or later she would mess things up, acting on what she knew and telling others what she knew. She already told Iphis what would happen to Patroclus, and Iphis telling that to Patroclus would probably change what Patroclus does. That could throw the story wildly off-kilter. And here and now, if she said the wrong words to Agamemnon, or if her tone or gestures aggravated him, this *king of kings* could break her neck or slit her throat. End of story.

***

Agamemnon stood in front of her, his face an inch from her veiled face. He was tall compared to other men in this time. He was beardless, with a narrow Captain-Hook mustache. He squinted. She guessed he was near-sighted and that that was why he brought his face so close to hers. She imagined that a physical defect like that could lead to body language that intimidated people in his presence. Breeze held back a smile. The veil covered her full face, but Agamemnon still might be able to discern her facial expressions. She reminded herself that she had to control every muscle of her face, like a movie actress in a closeup.

He had a pointy nose and chin. In the flickering candlelight, his skin had a sickly pallor. He probably thought he looked haughty and regal, but she saw him as blustery and insecure. She hoped he had no idea what she was thinking.

He glared at her and what he said in a whisper shattered her confidence. "No more games."

Breeze wondered what he's referring to. Maybe he had hit her, and she had lost consciousness. But she felt no pain. It was more likely that the in-and-out craziness that had plagued her since she took over this body had struck again. What did she miss? She could play many roles, but she needed clues to choose rightly. How did she anger him? she wondered.

She guessed this was her first day with Agamemnon, that she had caught his eye. She had been lying down, probably with him beside her. He was probably sampling the new merchandise—her.

Maybe she hadn't been submissive enough. She was used to the flirtatious foreplay of the twenty-first century. He was used to the obedience of frightened slave girls. If he wanted a submissive, that's how she should play it.

But maybe he wanted her to be more sexually aggressive, to pretend that she was attracted to him because he's so powerful and manly. But not too much, not too fast. She should stroke his ego however she could, make him believe that she wanted him, but that she was restraining herself out of respect and decorum. If he wished, she could be both active and submissive in the dance of their lovemaking. She could show him that his pleasure could be far greater if she participated in it, if he treated her as more than an insentient plaything.

She couldn't decipher the meaning of his silence now.

She dared to move the corners of her mouth, even attempted an obedient, but friendly smile. Would he notice such a smile behind her veil?

"Stop," he bellowed. "Don't think you can seduce me as you did Achilles."

He grabbed her and pushed her down, shouting, "On your knees, slave."

She remembered that phrase and that tone of voice. She had been on her knees in front of him before.

She remembered that she had used the veil as she'd have used sunglasses, pushing it up and letting it fall to make and break eye contact. She had misinterpreted his body language. She had seen what she thought was the bulge of an erection. When he had put his hands on her shoulders and pushed her down the first time saying, "On your knees, slave," with her face at his crotch, she had, reluctantly, but for survival, done what she thought he wanted. She had reached out and grabbed him, only to discover that what she held was the scabbard of a dagger. She had reached again and had taken hold of something limp and small, embarrassingly small and unresponsive. He had pushed her away and she had fallen on the floor. That's why she was lying down when she regained consciousness.

Holy shit, she thought. "I will not tell, master."

"You what?"

"Your thing, your highness," she said. She almost made the blunder of saying, "Your little thing."

"That? You think I'm ashamed of that? You fool. That's the source of my strength, though fools like you would laugh and whisper. And you dare not whisper, do you?"

"No."

"No what?"

"No, your highness, your merciful, all-powerful highness of highnesses."

"Stop sniveling. And don't ever try your feminine tricks on me. I'm above such nonsense. Women have no effect on me. You are my trophy. I have no other use for you."

He ripped off her veil. "My slaves don't wear veils."

He grabbed her hair, pushed her head back, and brought his face close to hers. "Look at me. Look up. Look into my eyes. Let me read the truth in your eyes. Calchas says you see the future. Then you must know what I'm going to do if you lie to me now."

"I didn't know, your highness. I didn't know your—"

"My little secret. Yes, little. Yes, secret. But not shame. This is my strength, my God-given strength. This is how the gods protect me from lust, protect me from the likes of you. So, tell me, you, who see all, with those magic eyes of yours. You, who know all. Surely, you knew this before you saw me, before you dared to touch me. Surely, you told Achilles. That was why he dared to challenge me. And when I demanded you, he backed down far too quickly. That was your plot.

Admit it. You'd be my slave. Then you could bear witness to what you think is my deformity, you could bear witness not as a prophet, but as a whore slave. Admit it."

He let go of her hair, and she dropped to the ground.

He muttered in disgust, "No. There's nothing but fear in your eyes. The fear of an ignorant fool. You didn't know this before."

"I'd never have thought, no one would ever think. You are the father of a son and daughters."

"So I wish people to believe. So they believe."

"Orestes? Isn't he your son?"

"If he were my son, he would be here by my side, learning command and kingship."

"Then Iphigenia ... that wasn't your daughter you sacrificed?"

"She was no blood of mine."

"And your wife, Clytemnestra?"

"That's enough prying. Don't test the limits of my patience. Would that my brother Menelaus had been as blessed as I was, with no lust and no jealousy. Then we might have been spared this endless war. Yes, Menelaus should deal with you." He called, "Talthybius! Eurybates!"

The heralds appeared in the doorway.

"Take this wretch to my brother, Menelaus. She doesn't please me. Perhaps he will choose to make use of her. Or perhaps he will give her to his men."

"But that isn't in the story," Breeze protested.

"What story? The only story here is the one I tell."

With a chill, Breeze remembered the wording—Agamemnon would never mount her. But that didn't mean he wouldn't give her to others.

18 ~ Menelaus

Once again Breeze found herself inside a rough-hewn wooden lodge. This time she knew it was the dwelling of Menelaus, king of Sparta, brother of Agamemnon, and husband of Helen of Troy.

Here rugs were piled on rugs, many layers deep, giving the springy feel of mats in a gymnasium. Heads of boar and bear hung on the walls.

In a corner, a slave girl with long blond hair kept her head down, focused on her weaving. The girl was barefoot and her thighs, all the way up to her bare butt, were visible through the many slits of her short tunic. Breeze had heard that Spartans made their women dress provocatively. She dreaded that she might soon have to wear garb like that.

After her experience with Agamemnon, Breeze didn't dare speak to anyone without first being spoken to. She stood off to the side, careful not to block the doorway and awaited the arrival of Menelaus or anyone else who might tell her what to do.

Calchas the priest walked in, leaning on a walking stick that was carved to look like a swirling mass of snakes. He was followed by a short, stocky, bearded man who was athletic, in his thirties, and who gestured and spoke with an air of authority. "I had him," he insisted. "One more pounding stroke and his shield would have shattered. Then that damned fog came out of nowhere."

"The will of the gods," replied Calchas.

"Damn the gods," he bellowed. "The outcome of the war was in my hands. Single combat with Paris. A fight to the death. Winner takes all. And winner gets all the glory." He swung his arms wide and accidentally hit Breeze in the face with the back of his hand.

"You," he exclaimed, surprised, not angry, but offering no apology for hitting her. "It's my good fortune that Agamemnon had no use for you. Calchas here tells me you could be helpful."

Catching her balance and taking her cue, she responded "As you wish, my lord." This must be Menelaus.

"Calchas and I often talk about the future," he continued. "But instead of getting to practical matters, we argue over fate and free will."

Calchas replied, "We are drops of water in the ocean. The ocean is nothing but drops. And we are nothing without one another."

"Yes, talk like that has a poetic ring. But I need facts I can act on and win with. Calchas tells me you know things no one else could guess."

"Indeed, your highness," Calchas confirmed. "She speaks of the future as if it had already happened, and she had seen it happen."

"Well, do that for me now, Briseis. The Trojans are pressing hard. My single combat with Paris came to nothing. Now they know that Achilles refuses to fight, so they come at us with new-found confidence. Our prophet here says we will win the war. But how in Hades' name are we supposed to do that?"

"It doesn't take a prophet to know that," Breeze answered quickly and confidently. "The answer to your question is easy. You need Achilles," she insisted.

"You aren't his slave anymore," Menelaus reminded her. "You're mine. So, drop your loyalty to Achilles, and talk straight to me. I'm the one you need to please. Besides, that answer of yours leads us nowhere. Achilles refuses to help."

"Patroclus is the key."

"No one, not even his best friend Patroclus, can make Achilles budge."

"Patroclus has the same build as Achilles and is an outstanding warrior in his own right. He will act the part of Achilles. Dressed in Achilles' armor, even Achilles' own men will believe that he is Achilles."

"What?"

"Patroclus, pretending to be Achilles, will lead the Myrmidons in battle. He will fight as well as Achilles would have. He will push the Trojans back."

"You think we can win this war with a trick? Wars are won with muscle and skill, not treachery. Such a ruse might fool people for a while, but when the lie is uncovered, what with the disappointment on our side and the relief on the side of the Trojans, the Trojans would crush us."

"That's just the beginning. Patroclus will die, killed by Hector. Then Achilles himself will rush into battle, with new-found fury, determined to revenge the death of his friend."

"Good. That trick might work. Calchas, you heard her. Go to Patroclus and tell him about his glorious fate. Convince him to sacrifice himself this way. That's not an easy matter. But it must be done. I see no other way out for us. Get him primed to do it and do it soon, before we lose more men."

Breeze interrupted, "But what I said is fated. It will happen without your telling Patroclus. It will happen no matter what you do."

"So, you believe, and so it may be. But I don't believe in taking unnecessary chances."

"But you bet the entire war on your single combat with Paris."

"That was a sure thing if it weren't for the fog. I'm the better fighter. Calchas, go and tell Patroclus the story. Throw in some of your mystical language. Make it sound like your voice is the voice of Athena. Make a believer of him."

"Yes, your majesty." Calchas hurried away.

"So now, Briseis," Menelaus continued, "tell me more. Tell me everything."

"You win the war. What more do you want?"

"What matters to me is that I, personally, get the credit and the glory. I want to be the winner. I want the win to be by my strength, and by my orders and strategy. I don't just want victory. I want it to be my victory. I need to know what will happen, in detail, so I can be in the right place at the right time to take credit."

"And you want Helen, too, of course."

"Of course."

"I can't help but be curious. In these visions of mine, I know what happens, but not why it happens. Do you want her because you love her or because you want to punish her for being unfaithful?"

"Love? It was a political marriage. I'm king because she chose me as husband. She ran off more than ten years ago. Why should I blame her? She gave me an excuse to rally this army, to unite the cities of Greece as they have never been united before. She gave me an excuse to conquer this city and open the eastern Aegean and the Black Sea to Greek trade. She played an important and necessary role. If the gods had granted me foreknowledge of this, I wouldn't have tried to stop her, though I'd have made everyone think I did. I'd have put her up to it. I'd have begged her to do it. And if I do come out of this with all the honor and glory, I'll welcome her back with thanks and joy, and we'll reign together proudly for the rest of our days. What matters to me is how to get the honor and glory in my lifetime."

"But that may not matter."

"Not matter? This is my life, my only life."

"Maybe. Maybe not. You remember Iphigenia?"

"My niece, yes, sacrificed for the good of the cause, poor child."

"She had a second fate, a second life. In that alternate story, the gods relented at the last moment. They substituted a deer to serve as a sacrifice in her place and moved her, magically, hundreds of miles away to Tauris, where she serves as a priestess of Artemis."

"And how does that fairy tale relate to me?"

"There's a second version of the story of your life, as well. In that one, there are two Helens. The one here is an illusion, created by the gods. The real one never went to Troy. All these years she's been in Egypt, waiting for you."

"You mean all of this has been a sham, for nothing?"

"Nothing? You get everything you wanted, but you're fighting for a symbol of your wife, not a real person. And in that second version of your life, you have a faithful, loving wife, as well."

"But I, personally, get no honor, no glory? I'm not known as the conqueror of Troy?"

"After Troy falls, when you learn the trick the gods played on you, you set out on a quest to find the real Helen. After eight years you land on an island off the coast of Egypt. There you wrestle Proteus, a shape-shifting sea god, and you win. You and Heracles are the only mortals ever to defeat a god in hand-to-hand combat."

He smiled proudly. "Now that's glory. If I could believe that I wouldn't mind that I, like everyone else, must die."

"But you don't die, not in that version of the story of your life. Proteus tells you where to find Helen. And he tells you that Helen is really a daughter of Zeus. Zeus, in the form of a swan, raped her mother, Leda. She wasn't born as mortals are born. Rather she hatched from an egg. And she won't die. Zeus has a special interest in her and in you, as well, because of your marriage to her. After your long and happy reign as King of Sparta, Zeus will transport you and Helen to the Islands of the Blest, at the far end of the ocean to the west, where you will live forever."

"With that you overstep the limits of belief," Menelaus objected.

"I can't explain why, but I know the story we are living here at Troy. And I know that other story of how you fight Proteus and find Helen in Egypt. How can they both be true? How can the same person do different things in different places at the same time? Much is beyond my understanding."

19 ~ Return to Achilles

Breeze heard the wind rush through the trees, then felt it on her thighs. She was wearing the Spartan garb known as *thigh showers*. This outfit was as short as a mini skirt, with many slits. She didn't know how to stand, walk, or sit without feeling like she was making a spectacle of herself. Little more than a torn rag covered her butt and crotch. What she was wearing was more like a grass skirt than a tunic. But she had to maintain a dignified pose, like the Emperor marching through his capital city in non-existent clothes. Once she got used to this garb, she wouldn't think about it. Strippers got used to less. Anybody could get used to anything. She had to get over the adolescent notion that everyone was staring at her and talking about her.

She stood still. She didn't dare walk or sit. She wanted to reach down and hold the shreds in place as the wind whipped by. But that would call attention to her problem.

Someone sneezed. It was Iphis, the slave of Patroclus, comfortably wrapped in her ankle-length woolen toga.

"Iphis? Is that you? Am I back in Achilles' camp?"

"Yes, of course you are. Are you all right? You've been speaking in tongues. I didn't know what to make of you. Rumor has it that Agamemnon kept you in solitary for fear that harm might come to you, and that Achilles might hold him responsible. That must have been horrible. No wonder you're disoriented."

"Disoriented? Yes. I've blanked out, I don't know how many times."

"What did Agamemnon do, aside from dressing you like a Spartan whore-slave?"

"It was Menelaus, not Agamemnon, who dressed me like this. Please help me find something else to wear, quickly."

"Don't you remember? Just a few minutes ago, Phoenix asked for your help."

"Phoenix?"

"By Zeus, don't you remember anything?"

"Phoenix. The name is familiar. Yes, friend and teacher of Achilles. But I don't remember him saying anything to me. Not today. I don't remember anything from today."

"Maybe what happened to Patroclus knocked you into this state, as it did me and Achilles."

"Then that's happened? Is Patroclus dead already?"

"Yes."

"And you told him beforehand?"

"No, I mean yes. Yes, I told him, but that had nothing to do with him doing what he did. He had heard already."

"From Calchas?"

"No, from Achilles himself. It was Achilles' idea, so the Greeks could be saved from destruction without his having to give in to Agamemnon and lose face. Now Achilles is mad with grief and guilt. Day and night, he mutters about Hector and revenge."

A white-bearded warrior, Phoenix stepped out of the shadows and joined their talk. "Patroclus and Achilles were two parts of the same man. And now Achilles without Patroclus is someone else. It's as if his soul has already crossed over to the land of the dead, as if Patroclus were his soul, and the physical body of Achilles remains here for one purpose—to kill the killer of Patroclus."

"Yes, that's what happens," Breeze affirmed. "I remember now, that's what's supposed to happen."

"That's a strange way to talk about what's happened already. You need to get hold of yourself," Phoenix insisted. "We need you to distract Achilles. We need for you to get him drunk, to do anything to break him from his suicidal grief. That's why I asked you to wear that Spartan garb, however uncomfortable it might be for you. The sight of you like that might catch his eye."

"Please be careful, Briseis," Iphis warned. "When Achilles is like this, he may forget his strength, and he can crush a man's skull with the grip of one hand."

"Please pardon me, Phoenix" Breeze answered. "My memory keeps switching off and on. Now I remember a story about you and your mother and father."

"What?" asked Phoenix in disbelief.

"Your father left your mother for a young slave girl."

"Yes."

"Then your mother pleaded with you to seduce that slave girl and to please her so much that she'd lose her taste for your father."

"Yes, I did that," he admitted. "And it worked as mother wanted it to. Except that father was enraged when he found out. He tried to kill me. I fled. That's how I ended up at the court of Peleus and became tutor to his son Achilles. But how could you know that? The only person I told was Peleus. You mean you know the past as well as the future? That could be a dangerous gift."

"Past and future are the same to me," Breeze tried to explain. "I don't know why or how. And sometimes I get lost in time. I need to orient myself, to check what's real and what's not, what's happened already, and what's yet to come. I remember that Achilles loved me, that he threatened to leave the war and undermine the Greek cause for love of me. But now that I've returned, you say that I have to dress like this to catch his eye? What am I missing?"

"You seem to remember only one side of Achilles," Phoenix noted. "Sometimes a darkness comes over him, an anger that blots out all human concerns, like a werewolf when the moon is full. That's what he is now. We need to do whatever we can to bring him back."

"So, you want to throw me to this werewolf?"

"We have no choice."

"And if he doesn't recognize me?"

"Then he might tear you to shreds, as he might do to me or Iphis or anybody who approaches him. But you see the future. You know that doesn't happen. Hence you can act with confidence, and you'll need confidence to deal with the wild beast that he is now. The smell of fear could provoke him to violence."

"I wish I knew."

"What?"

"We're in the cracks of the story."

"You're speaking in riddles."

"I know that the Amazon queen will come with a dozen warriors to help Troy, and that King Memnon, too, will come with a black army from Ethiopia. Achilles will kill them both. Then Achilles will die. Then the Greeks will win the war. But I have no idea what happens to me today. I don't know if I live beyond today. I don't appear in the story again."

"What does that mean?" asked Phoenix.

"Anything could happen to me."

"And us?" asked Iphis.

"I don't know about you or Phoenix, either. None of us show up in the story beyond this point."

"So, you don't know what will happen, and that scares you?" asks Phoenix.

"Yes."

"But that's the way the rest of us live every day," he continued, "not knowing when or where or how we'll die. We use the courage the gods gave us when we were born. You sniveling child. How could Achilles ever have loved such a coward? Take off that rag and give it to Iphis."

"Yes, Briseis, give it to me. I'll do it."

"That's the spirit, girl," Phoenix encouraged Iphis. Then turning to Briseis, he explains, "While you were gone, Achilles slept sometimes with Diomede and sometimes with Iphis. He has lusted for Iphis before, and he might again now."

"But it's me he loves," Breeze insisted.

"I don't know who you are. Yes, you have the face and body and voice of Briseis. But you don't speak or act like her. All this talk of the future and the past, and *love*. I'd never have expected that from Briseis. And your not knowing how to deal with Achilles when the dark anger is on him, that isn't Briseis. She wouldn't need these Spartan rags, nor would she need prompting. She'd have gone to him at once, regardless of his madness, regardless of whether he'd greet her with hugs or tear her apart."

"Shit," yelled Breeze. She tears off the Spartan rag and tosses it at Iphis, then strides naked into Achilles' lodge.

"Now that's Briseis," said Phoenix.

20 ~ The Middle Voice

As Breeze entered Achilles' lodge, a cold wind hit her from behind as if to hurry her along. A polished bronze shield hung from the wall on the other side of the lodge near the hearth. She approached it and wondered at her reflection while warming her naked body. She still felt uncomfortable in this body, with large breasts and big belly, muscular legs and arms, and calluses on her hands.

Then she realized that Achilles was standing behind her, staring at her as she stared at the reflection of herself.

She turned to face him.

Achilles had dark, penetrating eyes, accented with thick eyebrows that met in the middle. He was beardless and his chest was nearly hairless. He was over-weight by the norms of the twenty-first century, but he was muscular by any standard. She reached out and touched his arm where a scab had broken loose from a recent wound. A drop of blood appeared. Without thinking, she brought her fingers back to her mouth and licked the blood, then her lips kissed the wound.

He smiled. "Thank you." His eyes showed that she had done that before. Despite her ignorance of what she should and shouldn't do in this time and place, she often acted as Achilles expected Briseis to act.

Achilles lifted her, cradled her in his arms, and carried her to a stool near the hearth fire.

She noticed long streaks of dried blood on his chest and remembered that in the story he just slaughtered a dozen noble Trojan warriors on Patroclus' grave as a sacrifice.

But this wasn't a brutal fighter standing before her. This wasn't the young athlete of legend who could throw a spear farther than anyone and could run fast enough to catch it before it struck the ground. This man was approaching middle age at a time when, even without war, few men lived beyond middle age. He had a full-grown son. And now, disillusioned and weary, he looked his age.

His best friend was dead. He had killed Hector in revenge. His rage had cooled. He had no further objective, no reason to do anything. He was a shell of his former self and had had enough of war, enough of life.

He wrapped her in a blanket, then sat with her on his lap, picked up his lyre, and played and sang melancholy songs. Where was the beast that Phoenix spoke of?

He talked to her about the deaths of Patroclus and Hector. Then he admitted that he missed her and that he needed her now more than ever. He said he wanted to impregnate her before he died and that he would die soon.

Then her ability to understand his language faltered. Her mind had been like a radio tuned to his language channel. She knew what he meant without thinking about it. She simply understood what was said, and others understood her when she spoke. The flow of meaning between her and others was as natural and easy as breathing. But now she heard a word that sounded like English but didn't make sense as English.

"No, no, no," he said, but she knew he didn't mean the English word *no*. He wasn't protesting his fate, like Dylan Thomas not wanting to go into *that dark night.* In childhood, his goddess mother told him his fate, and he accepted it, proudly. To rebel against fate was foreign to him.

"What do you mean?" she dared to ask.

"Not I, not we, just 'no'. The number two. The two of us. Two people who by nature always belong together, like twins–not singular, not plural, but dual. It means the closest two people can be. It means the two of us love one another, inseparably and by nature. To use that word with you is to caress you. Surely, you must know that."

She stared at him in disbelief, then jumped as high as she could and threw her arms around his neck and pulled herself up to kiss him on the lips. He lowered her gently to the ground and they made love, slowly and tenderly.

But still, she felt a dissonance in the way he spoke to her, something more than the use of the *dual,* something about the automatic translation that she had come to take for granted, without understanding how it worked, wasn't working now. Something about the verbs was off when he talked about the two of them and also when he talked about revenge.

When next he spoke, she asked, "Why do you use that form of the verb?"

"What's a verb?" he asked in return.

"Where I come from, a verb is a word that tells of action."

"And you come from Lyrnessus, a Phoenician colony."

"Yes, Phoenician. In Phoenician, we speak in terms of what you do yourself or what someone else does to you. But the way you speak feels different. I believe I understand the drift of it, but what exactly do you mean?"

"I learned that way of speaking from my mother, Thetis. Like her and the other gods, I feel connected, permanently connected, to everyone with whom I have serious dealings. The connection never ends. The act of love leads to a child, who will one day have children, and they will have children, and so on. Spoken that way, the word *love* means all of that—not just the moment, but all the generations that come from it. I am connected forever to those I love and to those I kill, as well. Revenge ties man to man, family to family, across generations. When you kill a man, you create a bond with everyone connected to him, a blood obligation that leads to the shedding of more blood."

"I don't understand. That pattern of thought is foreign to me."

"Mother could explain this better than I."

"I wish that I could meet her."

"You will in the fullness of time."

"I understand the tie of love and how that can connect you to future generations. But I don't see how you could be closely tied to people you hate and kill."

"You don't always hate the ones you kill. Sometimes you must kill to pay a blood debt, even though you respect or even care for the person."

"Death and killing are foreign to me."

"Nonsense. You, too, have a blood debt, but you choose to ignore it. By blood debt, I am your enemy and will always be your enemy."

"You mean I have an obligation to kill you?"

"Yes. I killed your father and your three brothers. If ever there was blood debt, that's one."

"And you'd expect me to kill you in revenge?"

"Strange, but true. I know that I must die, and soon. But I'd rather that it be by your hand, for what I did to those who were dear to you, than that it be by the hand of some random Trojan. Since by my death I will be connected to my killer forever, I'd rather that it be you who does the deed."

"That's sick. I could never kill you."

"That's the one flaw in our love for one another. You don't feel the compulsion of the blood debt. Or perhaps you don't have the courage to do it. But that means nothing. You couldn't kill me even if you wanted to. My mother told me my fate long ago. I will die near the gates of Troy, shot in the heel with a poisoned arrow."

"I, too, know that. Perhaps that's why I don't feel the responsibility of blood debt."

"Do you know that with confidence, from your prophetic powers? Or faintly, from general rumor?"

"By special powers. I've seen it happen. I wish I could stop it from happening, or at least stop seeing it happen over and over again. But that's beyond my control."

She got up from his lap and fetched a pot of water, then kneeled in front of him, and tenderly washed his right foot, paying special attention to the heel and kissing the prominent vein that stood out on the ankle. Once again, she saw the scene of his death. She cringed and kissed the heel that would be the death of him.

Once again, he played the lyre, and memories surged through her mind. She saw the father of Briseis teaching her brothers how to throw the javelin. Then she saw them all impaled by javelins thrown by Achilles.

Once again, she saw the sack of Lyrnessus. This time she saw the scene through the eyes of Briseis and felt what Briseis felt. She was curled up with her legs crossed tightly, cowering on the ground at Achilles' feet, struggling not to urinate. Her bladder was full to the point of agony, and she didn't dare say anything. More than rape, more than death, she dreaded losing control and befouling herself in front of this arrogant conqueror, shaming herself like a helpless child. Holding it back was her last shred of pride and dignity.

Later, she heard the screams, the laughter, the grunting, as the rest of the Myrmidons took their pleasure with their captives, night after night. She remembered her surprise that Achilles let her sleep alone the night he captured her, and many nights after that, though he could have forced her any time he wanted.

She heard that Achilles chose her, and only her, for himself. She heard, too, that he wouldn't allow anyone else to touch her. She felt his eyes rest on her from a distance. But he never called for her. He never spoke to her. He never even gave orders for her to do chores. She was free to sit and mope or to walk around the Myrmidon camp or to spin and weave and wash clothes at the river or to help Patroclus with the cooking.

The time came when she warmed to Achilles and wanted him despite what he had done to her family, and, at her instigation, he took her, and it was good. She felt both desire and hate for him. She both expected and feared that after that first time, he would take her again and again, that she would become his favorite plaything slave. Instead, he kept his distance.

Then one day, back at the Myrmidon camp by the shore in front of Troy, over a month after Lyrnessus was reduced to ash and rubble, she picked up a lyre and played old tunes her mother played for her when she was a child. That must have been long ago because her mother died when Briseis was just four.

Then she heard other notes, not the same notes, but in harmony with hers. She turned and saw Achilles playing and gazing at the waves as they crash on the rocks. For hours, they played music together and yet not together. Sometimes he responded to her notes, improvising on the melody she started, and sometimes she took her cue from him. For five nights in a row, without exchanging a word, they settled in the same positions and played. On the sixth night it rained, and, on impulse, she entered his lodge. He was alone, playing the lyre by the hearth fire. She curled up on his lap, with her head on his shoulder. He welcomed the feel of her body against his, but still, he said nothing, continuing to play the lyre, until she got up and went back to the lodge that she shared with other slave women.

The following night it rained again, and again she went to his lodge. Only this time when she got up, she lay down on the stack of rugs that served as his bed and waited for him to join her.

Only after they made love tenderly, as they did that time, did they seek out one another's company, and it became common knowledge that the bond between this master and this slave was uncommonly strong.

Her memories stopped, and she found herself once again on Achilles' lap. The time for playing music was about to segue to the time for making love, when they heard a wagon stop in front of Achilles' lodge. Puzzled, since no one should be moving around the camp at this hour of the night, Achilles, followed closely by Breeze, went to the door.

An old man and his subservient companion climbed down from the wagon.

"Priam," Breeze whispered.

"Surely you joke," Achilles whispered back. "The king of Troy wouldn't come unattended and unarmed to the lodge of Achilles."

"Believe me," she repeated. "This is in the story. That's Priam, in disguise, under the protection of the gods. Hermes helped him pass the guards. He's come to beg you for the body of his son Hector, so he can give him a proper funeral."

"Stay," Achilles ordered her, and stepped outside to confront the old man.

Breeze was out of earshot, but she could imagine the dialogue, straight out of the last book of *The Iliad.* This was her favorite scene, where Achilles showed his sensitive, sympathetic side. His drive for revenge and glory was over. All that remained was to kill Trojans, mechanically and efficiently, and then he himself would be killed. At this point in the story, Achilles understood the plight of Hector's father, as he understood what his own father would soon feel at his death. He felt a bond of revenge blood-debt with Priam, and he also sensed their common mortality.

That's the story's human perspective. But, as Breeze also knew, *The Iliad* included, as well, the gods' perspective. Humans knew that they would die, and knowledge of their mortality gave meaning to their lives, made every moment precious. For the gods, all action was trivial. Regardless of what happened to them, they couldn't die. Like cartoon characters, you could bash them, blast them, do anything to them, and they'd pop up again and continue to do rash and silly things. The gods provided comic contrast, heightening the tragedy of the mortals who strove and died, who played the game of life for keeps.

Achilles ordered his slaves to prepare Hector's body for the journey back to Troy. For the interim, just as in *The Iliad*, elderly Priam and his sole companion napped on the porch of Achilles' lodge.

Breeze once again joined Achilles near the hearth. She knew that he was trapped in a fate that couldn't be changed. He would grant Priam an eleven-day truce. The Trojans would mourn Hector for nine days. On the tenth day, they would bury him. On the eleventh, they would build a high barrow over his body. And on the twelfth day, the war would begin again. Then, after a few more weeks of fighting, Paris would kill Achilles, shooting him in the heel with a poisoned arrow.

With her head resting on Achilles' shoulder, Breeze wondered what meaning life could have if all that happened was predetermined. Achilles would nobly accept his fate. He had the courage to continue doing what he felt he must do, even in the face of death. But such fatalism was foreign to her.

Gently, he lowered her to the floor and mounted her, missionary style, then stopped abruptly.

"Take it out," he shouted at her. "The sponge. With me, you don't use a sponge. What are you thinking? I want our love to have consequences. I want our love to live beyond us."

Caught off guard, she reached in and removed the sponge, then welcomed him again.

Then she interrupted him with a question that had never occurred to her before, "But what will happen next?"

"You mean after I die?"

"Yes, what will happen to me and to our child, if we have one?"

"You don't know? You, who know so much, don't know this?"

"The main story ends here, with this scene. There are other fragments that tell of your death and of the fall of Troy and some of what happens after that. But nothing more about me and no mention of a child of ours."

"You're a beautiful woman. You'll be prized for yourself. And you'll be prized too for the fact that you were my woman. Any man would welcome you to his bed. I wouldn't be surprised if the greatest warriors here were to fight for the right to possess you, as they might fight over my armor."

"If it were just a matter of me, alone, I could imagine that, even though there's no such scene in the story as I know it. But me pregnant with a child of Achilles? No. My fate would be decided when your son Pyrrhus arrives at Troy to take your place at the head of the Myrmidons."

"Yes, Pyrrhus. He was only seven when last I saw him. He must be a man by now."

"He's enough of a man now to understand that if I should bear a son by you, that son would be your heir and his rival. Knowing what I know of his brutal character, I'm sure he'd eliminate me, quickly, to avoid any such complication."

"I can't control what happens after I die. I can't even control when and where and how I die. Such is life. All I know is that I want you, and I want you now. And I want to make a child with you so our love can live beyond us."

"Well, if I'm going to have our child, what do you expect me to do? What can I do to survive and to protect our child? "

"Join the Amazons," he laughed, entering her again.

"What?"

"If there were such a thing as an Amazon, I could imagine you becoming one. You have the build for it, and the brash independence."

"You mean Amazons aren't real?"

"Amazons are no more real than centaurs."

"But I heard that a centaur taught you as a child."

"No way. Everything I know about fighting I learned from Phoenix, who is still my friend and companion. Don't believe everything you hear or see in that story of yours."

"But your mother is a goddess, right?"

"Yes, of course, And the earth is flat. And the moon is half empty."

"And the sun also rises?"

"Yes, of course."

Then she remembered the last mention of Briseis in *The Iliad,* in the final book:

"And deep in his well-built lodge Achilles slept with Briseis in all her beauty sleeping by his side."

So, she did appear one more time in the story, at this very moment. She needn't have feared the dark anger of his grief. She was safe up to this point in the story. But beyond this point, anything could happen.

21 ~ Polymusa The Amazon

Breeze cringed with pain. She was lying face down in a moving wagon. The wagon hit a rock and bounced up. On the down stroke, she banged her temple. She held her head up and stayed alert for more such bumps.

It was night, and she was under a pile of hay with a man lying beside her. She had to be careful not to wake him because he probably didn't know she was there.

Where was she in the story? Where were they going and why? she wondered.

The man smelled of perfume. He was dressed like he's coming from a wedding feast. You didn't dress up for a trip like this. Maybe he was involved in a drunken fight and was hurt and was unconscious. But he didn't smell of alcohol. In any case, he must have been a fugitive, trying to sneak out of the Greek camp in darkness.

Another rock. She had to move fast to avoid touching the man as he rolled in her direction. Now she was pressed up against the side of the wagon—no more room for retreat. She must have been mad to have gotten herself into this.

She remembered going to sleep in Achilles' arms. Outside, King Priam, disguised as a farmer, was resting on the porch with his herald. Slaves of Achilles were washing the corpse of Hector and preparing it for the journey back to Troy.

Priam had arrived in a wagon with a load of hay and would be returning in that same wagon, drawn by two mules and two horses.

She bit her tongue to stop from screaming. This wagon was that wagon, Priam's wagon. Her quiet companion was the corpse. No wonder he was so large. That was Hector himself. She had stowed away on Priam's return trip to Troy.

She felt nauseous. She shut her eyes and counted to a hundred, pacing her breathing, slowly, one breath for every number. It worked to her advantage that she was traveling with a corpse rather than a living man. He wasn't going to wake up. And no one would expect a stowaway to be cuddled with a corpse.

According to the story, even though Hector had been dead already for twelve days, the gods had preserved his body. There was no decay. Out of respect for Priam, Achilles had had his slaves wash the body and anoint it with preservatives and perfumes. But it was still a corpse. And Breeze had never seen a corpse before, much less shared the back of a wagon with one.

This was no time to be squeamish—not if she wanted to survive. She crawled over and pressed up close against the body so that any observer noticing the uneven distribution of the hay would guess there was only one body, not two. Taking a deep breath, she rested her head on his shoulder as a cushion against further bumps.

The wagon stopped and she heard footsteps. An exchange of words with guards. Breeze lay as still as she could—coma-like, clutching the corpse. They started up again. They were leaving the Greek camp. That meant they had to cover another four or five trackless miles, bumpy ground strewn with the gruesome residue of battle.

According to the story, the gods would protect Priam's return to Troy, but there was no reason to presume that the gods would protect hers as well.

A few exceptional fighters, like Odysseus and Diomedes, sometimes crossed from the camp to the city on night raids without getting caught. If caught, someone of their stature would be held for ransom. Ordinary soldiers and slaves, like her, would be executed on the spot as spies.

Why was she there? Achilles would never have risked her life like this. She must have done this on her own account. She must have wanted to slip into Troy unnoticed. She must have had a good reason for doing so, but what was it?

The name *Andromache* flashed through her consciousness. She wanted to meet face-to-face with Andromache, Hector's widow.

Andromache came from the town of Thebe, an ally of Troy and a neighbor of Lyrnessus. While Andromache was safe inside Troy, Achilles destroyed Thebe, killing Andromache's father the king, and Achilles' Myrmidons killed all her brothers and sisters as well. Achilles claimed Andromache's mother as his captive slave and raped her, then ransomed her. That was the dark, beast-like side of Achilles.

Breeze also knew that Andromache was raised with her brothers, as their equal, trained in the use of javelin and bow. Seeing Hector in danger, Andromache was tempted to rush into battle herself.

Trying to sort out how she got there, Breeze remembered that after Priam arrived and slaves started preparing Hector's body for return, she fell asleep in Achilles' arms, only to be awakened by a commotion outside the lodge. That's when guards brought in a young woman, tall and muscular, with dark curly hair and intense eyes that showed determination, not fear. She resembled Breeze and could have passed for an older sister of hers. But this intruder had the breastplate and shin guards of a warrior. She had been hiding under the hay, in the back of Priam's wagon.

Priam claimed to have no knowledge of her. His confusion and embarrassment were convincing.

The guards disarmed the woman and bound her hands. They presumed she was a spy or assassin.

"I am Polymusa," she announced proudly. "I report to Penthesilea, Queen of the Amazons. Andromache ordered me to protect King Priam."

Achilles laughed and gestured to the guards to do away with her.

Acting on impulse, Breeze intervened. "She lies."

"What, Briseis? Of course, she lies. She's no Amazon. There are no Amazons. Why should I care about this woman? Guards, get rid of her. I have more important matters to deal with."

"No," Breeze blurted out, following her instinct to save someone who looked so much like herself and curious to learn what, if anything, she could about Amazons. She sensed that Amazons were important to her in this world. "I mean she lies about the reason she stowed away on Priam's wagon. She's my cousin from Lyrnessus. She came for me."

Polymusa grabbed this cue and improvised, "Yes, I lived in Lyrnessus, but ran off to join the Amazons rather than marry a rich old man my parents had sold me to. I heard that Lyrnessus had been sacked, and that Achilles had made Briseis his slave, had taken a fancy for her, and wouldn't accept ransom for her. I rode to Troy with my queen, Penthesilea, and a dozen other Amazons, hoping we'd find a way to rescue her. I heard that King Priam was going to Achilles' camp in disguise. Never would there be a better opportunity. I hid under the hay, telling no one. King Priam knew nothing."

"And what did you intend to do after you rescued her?" asked Achilles.

"We'd return to the land of the Amazons, many hundreds of miles to the east, in Hyrcania, beyond the Caucasus."

"An Amazon?" he asked. "An Amazon in the flesh? And with two breasts?"

"Of course. Don't believe every legend you hear. You don't need to cut off a breast to handle a bow."

Achilles smiled. "Then as a cousin of Briseis, you're welcome here and now. A month or two from now, you could prove useful. Then Briseis may need saving. For now, let's make merry with food and drink. And you can entertain us with tales of the Amazons."

Polymusa regaled them with stories.

At first Breeze listened with interest, curious about the lifestyle of these women warriors. But Polymusa, encouraged by Achilles, spoke of her queen, Penthesilea. And, remembering the next episode of the story, Breeze felt uncomfortable.

"With a bow, no one can match Queen Penthesilea, daughter of Ares, the god of war."

"Do you really believe she's the daughter of a god?" asked Breeze.

"When you see her, you, too, will believe," Polymusa insisted. "You think I'm tall and strong. She's a head taller than me and once, in a wrestling match, she lifted me over her head and threw me three body lengths."

"Does she look like a man?" Breeze prompted her.

"Imagine the strength of Heracles combined with the beauty of Helen. For her, physical beauty is a weapon of war. Once, when a battle seemed lost and she was surrounded by enemy soldiers, she took off her red helmet and shook loose her long blond hair, and her enemies bowed down to her in awe and surrendered."

"Has she ever met a man who was her equal?" asked Achilles.

"Not yet, but she hopes to find one here, on the field of battle."

"Is that why she came to Troy?" he pursued.

"In part. But she has other reasons as well. Last year, while hunting deer, by accident, she killed her sister Hippolyte. She was conflicted, owing a blood-debt to herself, obliged to kill herself in revenge for the death of her sister. Wild dreams haunted her sleep. A priestess of Ares told her that only in service to Troy could she cleanse the pollution from her soul and appease the Furies. That was when a messenger arrived from Andromache, pleading for help."

"What did the messenger say?"

"He said that Achilles had killed Hector and desecrated his body. He painted a picture in words of Achilles as a demon who must be destroyed. The Queen dismissed that plea—why blame a warrior for being a good warrior? But she asked the messenger to tell her more about Achilles. And the messenger said Achilles could throw a javelin farther than anyone and could run so fast that he could catch that javelin before it reached the ground. He said that the Greeks and the Trojans both believe that no one can match his skill in battle. Those words aroused the Queen's interest. She wondered if Achilles could be her equal."

Breeze interrupted, "Enough. All of this will lead to nothing."

"And how is that?" asked Polymusa.

"I have a power," Breeze continued. "Gift or curse, I don't yet know. I have the ability to see the future. And, in that future, Penthesilea and all twelve of the warriors she brought to Troy, including you, will die at the hand of Achilles."

"Some fates are fixed," insisted Achilles, "like the death of Hector by my hand, and my death here soon. But the gods don't worry themselves with the doings and deaths of every common person. Fate is only for the great."

"Queen Penthesilea is no common person," insisted Polymusa.

"Far be it from me to insult your queen," said Achilles. "But also, far be it from me to kill her, or you, or your companions."

Though tempted to tell all she knew about the story, Breeze restrained herself. She was uncomfortable remembering what would happen next. Achilles would strike down the Queen in hand-to-hand combat. Then he'd take off her helmet and discover that this was a woman who had fought so well. Struck by her beauty, he'd fall in love with her as she died in his arms.

As Breeze escorted Polymusa from Achilles' lodge to a lodge for slave girls, Priam started his wagon journey back to Troy. Seeing her chance, Polymusa dashed through the bushes toward the wagon. The driver saw her and halted the wagon. Priam reached down and helped her climb onto the seat beside him, wrapping her protectively in a blanket.

She hadn't come to save Briseis. Of course not. That was spontaneous make-believe. She was a spy or assassin who had failed in her assignment and now wanted to return to Troy.

On impulse, Breeze ran after the wagon and jumped onto the back of it, banging her head. When the wagon struck a rock, she awoke, face down, under the hay, beside the corpse.

22 ~ Andromache

Not far from the Greek encampment, riders on horseback met the wagon, received news and orders from Priam, and then rode away. The wagon halted again, abruptly. Breeze rolled away from the corpse and squeezed herself tightly against the other side of the wagon, shutting her eyes and holding her breath.

Soldiers removed the body.

Breeze heard shouted orders and footsteps. An honor guard formed to escort the body to the gates of Troy.

Still covered with hay, Breeze went unnoticed.

The wagon started up again, then stopped. "Alert," shouted the driver. "There's something in the back of the wagon that shouldn't be there. The load is off balance."

Within seconds, a pair of soldiers grabbed Breeze roughly by the ankles, then her thighs, making free with their hands as they caught glimpses of her exposed flesh in the torchlight. If she didn't come up with a good story fast, she'd be tied up as a spy and left at the mercy of men like these.

She needed someone to whom she could plead her case, someone in authority and yet young enough and vain enough to be susceptible to flirtation and flattery.

She heard the name *Deiphobus* and remembered that he was a son of Priam, next in line after Hector. He was standing beside a chariot, preparing to leave.

Swinging an elbow at the face of one of her captors, and a foot to the groin of another, Breeze sprinted five steps and slid feet first, with her back to the ground, stopping inches away from Deiphobus. With her legs spread carelessly wide, she leaned back on her elbows so her breasts pointed up. This was no time to act lady-like. She needed to catch his attention or she was doomed.

He dropped his torch. She caught it.

Then, after a moment of confusion, he reached down and helped her to her feet, at the same time signaling to the guards to back off.

Breeze guessed that he was new to command, having always been in the background behind his older brother Hector. This incident could be an opportunity for him to show off his new authority.

"Young lady, what do you think you're doing?" he boomed at her in a deliberately deep voice. He was nowhere near as tall and strong as Hector was, and he was well aware of that.

Priam, Priam's driver, and Polymusa probably didn't know that Briseis had stowed away. They had already left the scene. No one here knew who she was, so Breeze could pose as anyone she wanted.

"Your highness, thank you for deigning to listen to me," she answered quickly, sitting up, then dropping her head back submissively and by so doing making her bust more prominent. "I am Diomede, daughter of Phorbas, from the island of Lesbos. I was visiting my cousins, the daughters of King Eetion of Thebe, when Achilles conquered that city and took me captive. I have been his concubine for a year now."

"And Achilles stoops to use his concubine as a spy?"

"No, your highness. I'm not a spy. Let me explain—"

"So, you decided on your own to stow away and go on a pleasure ride with a corpse? And Achilles—"

"He has no idea I'm here."

"So, you're his castoff? He tired of you? For a woman with your looks, that's not a likely story."

"I used to be Achilles' favorite. Then he captured Briseis. Have you heard tell of her? Achilles nearly pulled out of the war with all his men for her sake."

"We heard something like that but gave it little credence. Achilles revels in bloodshed. Achilles without war would be like an eagle without flight. He'd never willingly withdraw from the greatest war the world has ever seen, not for a mere woman."

"If you were to see Briseis, you'd know what I mean. Next to her, even Helen is nothing."

He laughs, "Surely, you jest."

"I wish that were so. Once he had Briseis, he cast me aside and passed me off to his lieutenants. Then when Agamemnon took Briseis away, my fortunes rose again. Sometimes Achilles chose me to share his bed, and sometimes he chose Iphis from Scyros, who had been the favorite slave of Patroclus.

"Now, just this morning, Briseis returned. Learning that Iphis and I had gained favor with Achilles in her absence, she flew into a jealous rage. She bribed soldiers to bear false witness against us, accusing us of spying for Troy. Iphis was carried off and has probably been executed. I managed to escape in this wagon. I was hoping to find Andromache, daughter of Eetion, Hector's widow. She is my cousin."

"Diomede?"

Breeze spun around toward the new voice and saw, silhouetted against the rising sun, Mount Ida, the walls of Troy, Hector's funeral procession, and, in the foreground, a tall regal woman carrying an infant.

"Diomede," the woman repeated, with authority. "My mother told me about you. She said that you were captured with her and that Achilles favored you so much that he wouldn't accept ransom for you."

"Andromache? And how is your mother now?"

"She died."

"Oh."

"In childbirth, from a stillborn son of Achilles."

"Then you have many reasons to hate Achilles."

"Far too many. Come with me. I'd talk with you further."

Breeze guessed that the infant in Andromache's arms must be Astyanax. At the fall of Troy, Pyrrhus, son of Achilles, would pick Andromache as his trophy slave and would bash her baby's skull against the walls of Troy.

Cuddling and nurturing her baby now, Andromache knew that he was doomed. She knew that when Troy fell, the Greeks would not allow a son of Hector to live and seek revenge in the next generation.

Revenge was the connection, Breeze realized. Andromache was tied to Achilles by revenge debt.

Walking toward Troy, keeping pace with Hector's body in the procession, Andromache whispered, "My cousin Diomede is short and blond. She was like a sister to me before I wed Hector."

Breeze stumbled but kept walking, silent, at a loss for how to follow-up after such a blunder.

"No need to fear. I'm not about to denounce you as a spy," Andromache insisted. "If you're a spy, you're too inept to pose a threat. My instinct tells me to trust you."

The procession approached the Scaean Gate, the main gate of Troy. Thousands thronged along the ramparts. Thousands more lined the streets leading to the gate, all shouting as if this were a victory march. They had grieved and despaired when Achilles slew Hector, tied his feet to the back of his chariot and brazenly dragged the corpse around the walls of Troy. But that was two weeks ago. They had presumed that Achilles would desecrate the body, feeding it to his dogs. Hector would never get a decent burial. The Trojan cause was cursed and doomed.

But now, miraculously, Priam had brought his son's body back, in honor. And rumor had it that the gods had shown their favor to Troy by preserving the corpse from the brutal acts of Achilles as well as from the natural process of decay. Troy had reason to celebrate.

"You claim to know Achilles," Andromache stated.

"Yes.

"He must die," she said with assurance.

"Prophets say that he will die soon, here at Troy."

"But his death must be by my hand or by my orders. His death must belong to me," insisted Andromache.

"They say that he's the son of a goddess, that he's invulnerable, that no man can kill him, except at the fated moment and in a fated way."

"Yes, *no man* can kill him. I've heard that, too, but I interpret that differently than you. *No man*, but woman makes for a different story."

"An Amazon?" asks Breeze.

"Yes. You think like I do. That's why I summoned Amazons to Troy. Penthesilea and a dozen of her finest warriors are here now. Polymusa you met. She rode with Priam to the Greek encampment. She was to kill Achilles if the opportunity appeared. That didn't work, but she escaped unharmed, to try again another day."

"You want to break the chain of fate?" asked Breeze.

"I want to do everything I can for revenge. You cringe. Your face tells more than you want to say. You care for Achilles, the butcher. You love him and hate him at once, like he's two different people. You wish you could kill the one, and not the other. I know what it's like to be of two minds. From the look on your face, you fear for him. That's good. That means my plan rings true to you. You think that fate can be undone but wish it won't be. Thanks for the vote of confidence. I believe you are sincere. At some point you could prove helpful to me. If the Amazons fail, I'll kill him myself."

"You'd go yourself to the Greek encampment?" asked Breeze.

"Priam, an eighty-year-old man, got past the guards, met with Achilles, and returned home safely. I won't need to come back. All I'll need is a chance to strike down Achilles. Polymusa just told me that you're Briseis, trophy slave of Achilles. You could help me get close to him. But tell me truly, explain why you're here. Why did you, the favorite of the great Achilles, risk your life to come to Troy?"

"I heard that Priam had safe passage. If I was going to leave, it had to be then or never. I acted on impulse."

"So, you'd rather be a Trojan slave than a Greek one?"

"I'd rather be an Amazon," her own words surprised her. "I'd rather not be any man's property. I'd live for myself and die for myself. I'd be me."

"Then welcome to Troy."

23 ~ The Amazons

That night, with the help of Polymusa, Breeze found her way back through the battlefield. She went through the gate to the washing pool by the Scamander River, and, at dawn, she blended in with the other slave girls doing laundry. From there, she found her way to Achilles' lodge, as she had many times before, and slipped into bed with him. She was relieved to learn that he was sleeping alone.

"Where have you been?" he grumbled at her.

"Incense?" she asked, evading his question. "It smells like sandalwood. You've used it before. Why does a great warrior like you indulge in fragrances?"

"Iphigenia."

"You still think of her?

"I only knew her briefly, and it's been so long since she died that I can hardly remember what she looked like. But I learned then that scent helps calm me, even when you try my patience, as you do so well. So where have you been? Where did you really go, you lover of lies?" he tickled her and wrestled with her in front of the hearth fire.

"Where did you think I had gone?" she asked after squirming free.

"At first I thought Priam had abducted you, to hold you for ransom."

"So, you thought he wasn't really here for his son's body? You thought that eighty-year-old came here to kidnap me and carry me off to Troy? And you say I tell wild tales?" She laughed and tickled him back.

"You have to be more careful," he warned her. "You're at risk in ways you don't realize."

"Yes, oh master, tell me your words of wisdom."

"Let's presume that the old king was tired of the war and wished to end it, but he didn't have the authority to do so. The war has gone on for so long that everyone has lost loved ones and has blood debts they need to pay. The cycle of revenge has become a tornado. a swirling wind that sustains itself until it destroys everything."

"And what does revenge have to do with me?"

Once again, he pinned her to the ground, playfully. "What would you do if you were Priam, and you wanted to end the war?"

"Maybe I'd sneak into the Greek camp at night and pretend that I had come to bargain for my son's body, but I'd be hoping that the Greeks would take me captive. I'd save face because I had so bravely risked myself for my son, but I'd expect the Greeks would hold me for ransom and ask for, as payment, an end to the war, the return of Helen, and treasure as well."

"Exactly."

"And do I get a kiss as a prize for the right answer?"

"But first tell me, what would you do if you were Priam, and Achilles unexpectedly treated you with courtesy, and gave you your son's body, and sent you safely on your way home?"

"I'd celebrate my good fortune."

"No. Remember you want to end the war."

"You don't mean—"

"Of course."

"But what good would it do to abduct me? I'm just a slave girl."

"You're the girl who already nearly ended the war. When Agamemnon took you from me, I pulled out of the fight in anger, and the Greeks, without me and my Myrmidons, wouldn't stand a chance against the Trojans."

"So, the Trojans would hold me hostage?"

"And they'd only return you if I swore an oath that I and my men would never again take up arms against them."

"And you'd do that for me?"

"Yes. But don't breathe a word of that to anyone. It would be dangerous for you if people knew how much you mean to me. You need to slip into the background. We need people to believe I share my bed with Iphis and Diomede, instead of you."

"Iphis and Diomede?"

"When you vanished, I wanted to stir everyone up to search for you. But Phoenix warned me that if I reported you missing and asked for help, that would signal, once again, how important you are to me. The Trojans aren't our only enemies. I've aroused the envy of many a Greek, with my boasting and my success in battle. We already saw what happened when Agamemnon sensed your importance to me. We need to be careful and make people believe that you don't matter to me anymore. If we don't, someone will try to get back at me by hurting you."

"But how can we change what they already know?"

"Trust Phoenix. When I sought his help in finding you, Phoenix explained the risk, reminding me of all the outward signs by which I testified to my passion for you. Then Menelaus chanced upon us, and I'd have told him, too, that you were missing. But Phoenix stopped me with a head shake, and I quickly turned the talk to Patroclus, like I was still mad with grief for my friend. Fortunately, I said nothing about your absence."

"So, I have to stay away from you?"

"When others are around."

"And you have to make a public display of affection for Iphis and Diomede?"

"Yes."

"But sometimes I get you all to myself?"

"Every night."

"I can live with that." She kissed him on both cheeks and on the forehead and the chin.

"So, it doesn't matter to you that I can't acknowledge you in public, that you'll have to fade into the background, as just another slave?"

"I don't care what people think, so long as I have you and bear your child."

"And if and when it becomes clear that you're pregnant, you can't let it be known that I'm the father."

"Of course. For the same reasons. I wouldn't want to put our son or daughter at risk."

"Good. We're in accord. Now tell me where you were."

"At Troy."

Achilles chuckled at her wit. "Then you met the great Penthesilea?"

"She's a blond giant, as much taller than you, as you are taller than me."

"And beautiful, as we heard tell?"

"That, I don't know. Her helmet masks her face. She wears a bright red helmet, as do all her Amazon warriors, and she never takes it off in public."

"So, she's a horrible Medusa, and a glance of her face could turn me to stone?" he laughed.

"So, don't go near her."

"Have no fear of that. If I see a dozen red helmets together, I'll go to the opposite end of the battlefield to avoid them. There's no glory to be won fighting women. And I'll not have their blood on my hands."

"Good. That's what I told Andromache."

"Andromache?"

"Hector's widow. She summoned the Amazons and feels responsible for them. I told her that I'd tell you that they're the ones with the red helmets and, knowing that, you'd steer clear of them."

"You think so little of me?"

"You don't fear them, of course, but I do. Iphis and Diomede are enough competition. The only wild warrior woman I want you to fight is me."

"And you're a wild warrior woman?"

"I could be. You yourself said I had the build for it. "

"And who is going to teach you?" he chuckled.

"You, of course. Who better than you to show me how to use sword, javelin, and bow?"

"You actually wish you were an Amazon?"

"I hear you like strong and forceful women."

"You're strong and forceful enough already."

"And if some beautiful Amazon queen came along and fought as well and as hard as you, you wouldn't fall in love with her?"

"So, there's a motive behind this sudden urge of yours?"

"If you have fantasies about wild warrior women, I want to be such a woman."

"I haven't had such a fantasy, but I'd delight to see you adorned in bronze and leather."

"And so you will. I'll make new dreams for you. But first I must train. Otherwise, you'll just see me as a little girl, role-playing. Let me be a true Amazon in your eyes."

"You trickster. You disappear and make up this wild story about going to Troy, all to get me to train you as a warrior? Yes, if you want to learn, you can learn. I won't deny you anything. But people can't see me training you. That would undermine what we're trying to do. Rather, let Phoenix be your teacher, as he was mine. That could work to our advantage. Be seen with him often. I'll say that I've given you to him, that, in my pride, I don't want you anymore because you've been with Agamemnon, even if Agamemnon didn't touch you."

"Fine. Make me a cast-off. Make me a nobody. Just make love to me, and no one else."

24 ~ Wiggle Room

Ten days later, as was now her habit, Breeze slipped out of Achilles' lodge just before dawn and walked to the mouth of the Scamander River where she stretched out on the ground, took off her sandals, and let her feet play in the current and the sand. The period of truce has been like a honeymoon for her and Achilles. She wanted it to go on forever.

Achilles had no duties. During the day, he lounged outside his lodge, playing the lyre, singing, dancing, sometimes even spinning and weaving. He learned those skills growing up disguised as a girl at the court of the king of Scyros, where his mother had hidden him, trying to protect him from his fate before Odysseus had tricked him into revealing himself and recruited him for the Trojan War. He had such self-confidence that he felt comfortable doing whatever he wanted to do, whenever he wanted to, without concern that anyone would dare to think him effeminate. He enjoyed engaging in women's tasks with beautiful women.

He and Breeze being together in such a group presented no problem. They both felt an erotic buzz in that setting, constantly aware of one another's presence, because they had to make a conscious effort not to look at one another, or touch, or talk to one another in public in a way that would reveal their true relationship. To Breeze, it was like they were performing in a play.

Achilles also used this time to improve his skill at cooking, which had been Patroclus' role. After putting Breeze through her combat drills, Phoenix helped Achilles prepare supper. Sometimes Breeze couldn't resist the temptation to join in. She enjoyed seeing Achilles' surprise at how much she knew about cooking. In those times, cooking meat, like hunting, was considered men's work.

Breeze enjoyed her military exercises with Phoenix. And at night, when she and Achilles were alone, she'd put on leather and bronze and show off what she had learned. Then the two of them tussled erotically as if they were at war with one another. When her muscles ached, which was often, she let him know, and Achilles, solicitous and tender, soothed them with the tender touch of his powerful hands.

This time of truce is *out of the story*. Breeze had no prior knowledge of what would happen. She wanted to forget the story. She wished that they could extend the truce, that they could end the war, that there was nothing inevitable about Achilles dying or Troy falling. When it rained, she joked that the war should be canceled for bad weather.

A few times, she woke up sweating and panting from nightmares about the capture and destruction of Lyrnessus and the death of her family. But she always woke up in Achilles' arms. Sometimes there was a moment of hesitation, seeing him first as a vicious killer, whom she should kill to clear a blood debt. Then, his tender touch on her temple brought her back to herself, and she hugged him passionately, in relief.

Now, with her sandals off and her feet in wet sand, she felt queasy. She scrambled to get up and waded a few feet into the river in case vomit should rise to her throat. She had said nothing about her symptoms to Iphis and Diomede. She didn't want them to suspect that she was pregnant.

As usual, Iphis and Diomede joined her a little later, bringing laundry. They are washing the pieces of cloth that they used during menstruation. Their periods were in sync. It was their time of the month, and they had bloody rags to wash. Every scrap of cloth was hand-woven. No one would consider throwing away such valuable material. And the cloth was not very absorbent, so they needed to change a dozen times a day.

Diomede was short, blond, delicate, pale, and submissive. Iphis was the opposite—tall, black-haired, sturdy, bronze-skinned, and self-assured. Both of them wore gold jewelry, all the time. Word had spread that they were now in favor with Achilles, so leaders like Odysseus, Idomeneus, and Antilochus gave them gifts in hope of help in getting the ear of Achilles. While Breeze always turned down such gifts when she was the publicly acknowledged favorite, Iphis and Diomede wore them proudly, delighting in tangible confirmation of their new status. They needed such reassurance because Achilles, who publicly made it seem like he's pleased with them, hadn't been to bed with either of them since Briseis returned from Agamemnon. Each of them presumed that Achilles was sleeping with the other but didn't want to ask. Only

Phoenix knew the real arrangement and he, following Achilles' orders, made much of Briseis in public, as if she were now his prize.

"What do you think Achilles will be like when the war starts again?" asked Iphis.

"I keep hoping the Trojans will agree to terms, and the war will simply end," replied Diomede

"But they aren't even talking, and the truce ends in two days," Iphis continued.

"Yes, we should be realistic, I suppose. After all, it was a miracle that the truce happened at all."

"I hear that Agamemnon kicked a hole in the wall of his lodge when he heard that Priam had been here and that Achilles let him go for nothing when we could have held him hostage to end the war," said Iphis. "And then he broke the jaw of his personal guard when he learned that Achilles had, without consulting anyone, offered a twelve-day truce and expected the whole army to abide by it."

"I wish I could have seen Agamemnon then," noted Diomede. "Better still, I wish that Achilles could have seen him. If they had confronted each other then, face-to-face, they'd have exploded at one another again and the war would be over."

"Diomede, you're such a dreamer," Iphis added.

"No, Briseis here is the dreamer, saying not a word, just scrubbing away, and those aren't even her rags she's scrubbing."

"Briseis, I appreciate the help, really I do," noted Iphis. "The flow is really heavy this month."

"It's no problem," Breeze answered. "You'd do the same for me if my flow were heavy."

"But this month you're late, and you're never late. Do you think you're pregnant?"

"No. I don't think old Phoenix has it in him."

Iphis and Diomede chuckled.

"He must be quite a contrast to Achilles," said Diomede.

Iphis suggested, "Maybe you're late because you're still tense and distracted from what you had to go through with Agamemnon. You haven't been the same since you came back from him."

"Not since Phoenix asked you to seduce and tame the wild Achilles," added Diomede.

"And Achilles hasn't been the same either," Iphis said.

"I still don't understand what happened that night, what made Achilles change," Breeze commented, to keep up the pretense. "I did everything in my power to arouse his desire, but he rejected me. And he hasn't wanted me since. Thank the gods for Phoenix. If it weren't for him, I'd be a drudge shoveling latrines."

Breeze continued washing. Maybe her trip with Hector's corpse to Troy was a dream. Maybe her supposed knowledge of the future was nonsense. Maybe she was just a pregnant slave girl, a nobody who could never make a difference in the world. Maybe nobody ever made a difference. Fate or no fate, we had just a few moments of pride and bluster, then we settled back into the numbness of habit and routine.

Then she spotted another slave girl, a stranger, walking nimbly along the shore, carrying an urn and fetching water. The girl was performing a task that everyone did, following orders. But as she walked, she wiggled her hips and moved her feet in time to music that only she could hear. She was trapped in this time and place, trapped in a role that she didn't choose, but yet she had wiggle room in which to be herself.

25 ~ Achilles in Action

The two armies advanced at a steady pace, row upon orderly row—first chariots, then foot soldiers, archers to the rear.

Breeze left Achilles' lodge before he did, dressed in her practice armor, bringing shield, javelin, and sword. Her green-crested helmet covered all of her face but her eyes. She joined a dozen other warriors who had assembled before the horns sounded.

She needed to see Achilles in action.

It was as if she were the lover of an Olympic swimmer and had never seen him swim, a great pianist and had never heard him play, a great dancer and never seen him dance.

She also needed to know if there was any way to edit the story she found herself in. If Achilles avoided the red-helmeted Amazons, anything was possible. And she wanted to see that for herself. She wanted to be an eyewitness if and when fate was broken.

No one paid attention to her. She was just another soldier. Her lessons with Phoenix had not been enough to make a fighter of her, but she did know how to hold shield and javelin, and how to march in formation. She took her cues from those around her, like a dancer taking cues from her partner. She focused her attention on putting one foot in front of the other, in step with her fellow soldiers, alert for shouted commands.

She felt the queasiness of morning sickness, but, despite that, managed to stand tall and keep pace.

As Achilles' Myrmidons advanced, the other Greek troops parted and let them march through until the Myrmidons held the position of honor, in the center of the front line, with green-crested helmets and with green banners unfurled.

To the rear of the Myrmidon contingent, archers knelt with arrows notched and ready. To the front, chariots took position ahead of the foot soldiers and Achilles with his charioteer, Automedon, was in the lead. Achilles held high the javelin with which he would signal the charge.

This was before the time of saddles, bridles, and stirrups. Riders could not easily control their mounts in battle conditions. So, chariots instead of cavalry dominated the battlefield.

Achilles waved his javelin, and the Myrmidon archers loosed a volley.

Other leaders to the right and left issued their commands in their own ways.

Soon, a return hail of arrows descended on them from the Trojan side, and the Greek foot soldiers knelt, holding high their shields.

Achilles signaled again, and the foot soldiers stood and advanced at a deliberate pace, stomping the ground loudly in sync with drums and in sync with one another, shields still held high to block arrows that continued to fall in their midst.

Arrows bounced harmlessly off the armor of soldiers near Breeze. One struck and penetrated the thigh of a man ahead of Breeze. He fell, dropped his javelin, and grasped the shaft of the arrow, and stifled a moan of pain. The soldiers behind him stepped around him, not missing a beat.

When they got within a hundred feet of the enemy, Achilles signaled again, and every other man raced forward and hurled his javelin, then dropped back to get another javelin from stacks near the archers. The others, including Breeze, continued to march forward, javelins at the ready.

Soon, a hail of javelins from the Trojan side rained down on them. One pierced the shield of a man to her right, passed through his throat, and stuck in the ground. The man behind him walked around him without a word or a gesture of help.

The chariots raced ahead. Front lines engaged front lines. Soon lines became blurred and what had been a coordinated operation became a series of fights between individuals. Arrows and javelins landed randomly. Some warriors raced back and forth fetching and throwing javelins, but most, like Breeze, simply advanced, until, in the confusion of hand-to-hand combat, it was impossible to tell which way was forward. All semblance of order dissolved. Breeze couldn't tell who was Greek and who was Trojan. But the fighters seemed to have no such difficulty, recognizing subtle differences in armor and weaponry.

Phoenix hadn't taught her how to distinguish one side from the other. He focused on how to march and how to fight, not how to tell your enemy from your friend. He never imagined that she'd go into battle. He thought she was training for the exercise and for the play-acting make-believe. When she set out that morning, on impulse, she had no idea what she was getting into.

As the summer sun rose high in the sky, her bronze and leather armor began to burn against her skin. She was thirsty and hungry. She had to pee. What do soldiers do when they have to pee in battle? she wondered, and she restrained herself from laughing. She nearly tripped, stumbling on a severed head that was oozing brains.

Her bladder was painfully full, but she controlled herself, soldier-like.

Then, with the wind blowing in her face, she smelled shit, wet loose shit. She saw brown liquid dripping to the ground between the legs of the man in front of her who was exchanging sword stroke for sword stroke with the Trojan in front of him. She realized that others were human, too. She let loose her bladder.

That freed her mind to remember that she was there for a purpose, not just to play soldier.

The air was hot, stale, and still. A mist of dust and blood obscured her view. The stench of sweat and gore. The clash of bronze on bronze. The grunts and screams of pain. The shouts of celebration and congratulations.

She couldn't see Achilles or any of the chariots.

She couldn't see anyone with a green-crested helmet.

She wanted to withdraw to safety but had no idea which way was which.

Bodies.

Pieces of legs and arms.

Dogs feasting on the gore.

It was pointless for her to be there.

She couldn't see what was happening on a large scale and couldn't understand what was happening nearby.

Andromache and Polymusa talked as if war were glorious. But this was random butchery.

She found herself face-to-face with another warrior. A Greek, she presumed.

His eyes met her eyes as if he recognized her. She was tempted to risk asking him to lead her to safety in the rear.

His helmet didn't have the green crest of a Myrmidon. But he could've been one of Menelaus' men or Agamemnon's. He could've been from any of a hundred other independent Greek cohorts, a guard who had flirted with her at the washing pool.

She hesitated, reluctant to speak, not wanting to give herself away with her voice if she could help it.

She imagined him smiling behind his helmet.

She took a step forward. If she were close to him, no one else would hear what she said in this noisy chaos.

He lunged at her with his sword, and she, by reflex, well-trained, deflected his blow upward and skewered him in the belly, below his breastplate.

As his head hit the ground, his helmet came off.

He was a boy, no more than fifteen. A handsome lad he would be if his face weren't contorted in pain.

A soldier to her left saluted her with his sword and shouted congratulations.

A sudden breeze cleared the air and through a gap in the fighting, she saw Achilles, out of his chariot, running, slashing again and again with his sword, striking one Trojan after another, in the back, all fleeing him, none facing him. He ran forward faster than anyone else could run away, slowed as they were by the confused mass of their fellow fighters and the random bodies and body parts at their feet.

With each kill, the Greeks around Achilles shouted congratulations, inspiring one another with renewed enthusiasm and confidence.

Breeze barfed uncontrollably and stumbled to the ground, her face inches from the face of the dying boy, his agonized face now covered in her vomit.

This was no art. This was frenzied, brutal slaughter.

Ahead of Achilles to his left, advancing in his direction instead of fleeing with the rest, she saw a dozen Trojans with bright red helmets and shields.

Achilles turned and dashed toward his chariot, which was following in his wake. He leapt abroad, took the reins from Automedon, then turned the horses to the right and lashed them hard with his whip, turning them to race off to another part of the battlefield, far from the red-helmeted soldiers.

Achilles had listened to her. He had believed her. He was doing as she asked him to do. He would fight somewhere else, far from the Amazons, pursuing a new destiny.

Without the threat of Achilles, the Trojans in this sector stopped their retreat and turned and fought.

The wind died down. The mist of dust and blood rose again. The battle raged on, hour after hour.

Slaves brought up wagonloads of water and soupy stew in bronze cauldrons. Then they filled those same wagons with dead and wounded and carried them back to camp. Other slaves dug shallow latrines behind the row of archers.

At twilight, Breeze caught another glimpse of the red-helmeted soldiers holding their ground.

She followed the wagons back to the Greek camp.

She believed that she had fulfilled the mission she had set for herself. She had saved the Amazons. She had broken fate. Everything was possible. Achilles could live and could pursue a new destiny.

26 ~ Penthesilea

Breeze bathed in the river, perfumed her whole body, then sat on the porch outside Achilles' lodge to wait for him.

The Myrmidons returned before nightfall—all but Achilles and his charioteer.

There was no word that he had come to any harm. The Myrmidons presumed that, as usual, he was still fighting in the dark, that he had not yet tired of killing. They weren't concerned about him. He was invulnerable. But if, as Breeze believed, they had broken out of the story, then anything was possible.

Breeze took up a lyre and sang softly. Phoenix sat near her, resting his sore back against one of the struts that supported the porch.

Finally, after midnight, they heard an approaching chariot. With one hand, Automedon guided the horses and with the other, he supported Achilles.

Achilles' eyes were open, but he was unresponsive. Automedon and Phoenix helped him into the lodge and onto the pile of rugs that served as his bed. He had no visible wounds. Automedon had searched for him on foot in the dark and had finally found him wandering aimlessly among corpses near the walls of Troy.

Phoenix insisted that everyone leave except Briseis. To her he whispered, "Work your magic."

Alone with Achilles, she kissed him, first gently on the forehead and cheeks, then passionately on the lips as if he were enchanted and a kiss would wake him.

She kissed him on the ear and whispered. "I was there. I saw. You stayed away from the Amazons. They all survived. You've broken out of the fated story, my love. You're free. We're free. Totally free."

She took up her lyre and sang love songs that he had often performed for her.

Still, he didn't respond.

Then she stripped, and she lay down on top of him, massaging his body with hers.

Still, he didn't respond.

Her joy and passion turned to concern, and her concern mounted. Lying on top of him, she sobbed, then pounded his chest to break him out of this depression. He had done what he had thought was impossible to do. They should celebrate. What was wrong?

On impulse, she took a pin from her hair and shoved it hard into Achilles' left palm. He showed no sign of pain. But he sat up, shook his head. Then, seeing her, he lay back down, rolled away, and covered his eyes as if he didn't want to see her, as if he didn't want to return to this reality.

She didn't let him move away from her. She wrapped her arms around him and rested her head on his shoulder. "You were wonderful," she whispered. "I was there, on the battlefield, disguised as a soldier. I had to see. I had to know what was happening. You must have been sorely tempted to attack, but you held back. You avoided the Amazons. You restrained yourself. You've changed the world, not just for you and me, but for everyone."

"What did you see?" he finally asked in a tense, controlled tone that she had never heard from him before.

"You were advancing toward the red-helmeted soldiers, and they were advancing toward you. Then you took the reins of your chariot and rode off to another part of the battlefield. All thirteen of the Amazons survived today's battle."

"All thirteen of the soldiers in red."

"Yes, of course."

"Are you color blind?" he shouted.

"What?"

"Can you tell the difference between red and blue?" he shouted again.

"Of course."

"Then perhaps the god who informed you was color blind."

"What do you mean?"

"The soldiers in red were decoys. Yes, I rode off to the far-right flank because of what you had told me, but also because the Greeks on that side were hard-pressed. The Trojans were threatening to break through at that point. At the forefront, fighting like demons, were twelve warriors and their giant leader with helmets and shields painted bright blue."

"Oh, god, no," screamed Breeze. She leaned forward to bury her head on his chest, but he pushed her away, roughly.

"I charged them all at once, with my sword swinging with a strength and skill I had never felt before. It was as if Ares, the god of war, had taken possession of my body. I was in a frenzy. My body acted independent of my will, out of my control. Soon, the only blue warrior standing was the giant.

"Our swords and shields clashed, again and again. The frenzy continued. If I was possessed by a god, this giant was as well. Time and again, I felt the blade strike me, but it left no wound. Time and again, I could have sworn that my sword hit true. If this had been an ordinary mortal fight, we'd have both been dead a dozen times over. We fought for hours, until long after dark, and still, my arm was fresh and strong.

"Then, as I was about strike again, the giant removed its helmet. It was a woman, the Amazon queen, Penthesilea. She shook her long blond hair and smiled. I was dazed. I just wanted to stare at her. But my body was still possessed. My sword arm kept moving. I couldn't stop it. I slit her throat. She fell.

.   "Only then did I regain control of my body. I caught her before she hit the ground. She draped her arms around me." He shut his eyes as if reliving that moment, his face muscles quivering, barely under control.

"The cut was not deep, but it had severed a blood vessel. She was alive and conscious but losing blood quickly. There was nothing I could do to save her." He paused to catch his breath, then continued. "She spoke of her blood debt for having accidentally killed her sister. She said that now the debt was paid."

He paused again. "She said that she knew that I was Achilles, that she had come to find me, and that I was indeed the fighter she had heard I was.

"She said that she loved me for my strength and my courage. She said that she could only love a man who was greater than she was, and she had never met such a man until now.

"As she grew weaker, she could no longer talk with her voice, but her eyes, her bright blue eyes were locked on mine. I could hear the

Furies screaming in my brain that I had killed the woman I loved and that I now owed a blood debt that could only be paid by my own death.

"Why did you tell me about her?" he shouted at Breeze. "Why did you create those Amazon fantasies? Why did you arouse me with the thought of her before I met her? And worst of all, why did you trick me with the change of color? You talk of fate, but, without your meddling, this would never have happened. I would not have met her on the field of battle today. Or having met her, I would never have fallen in love with her as I did. You did this to me. Why? I thought you loved me."

Breeze couldn't find words. Achilles' body was cold and distant.

"You should leave now," he ordered. "For your own safety. I have no idea why you did this to me. But I know that I once loved you. And I don't want to do violence to you when the grief and anger well up in me again."

He was shaking, struggling to control himself. She pulled back from him. The wild look in his eyes expressed what might be hatred but could be fear that he didn't know what he might do next. She retreated to the far end of the lodge.

"Yes, go," he commanded. "And don't come near me again. Don't make the mistake of Thersites."

"Thersites?"

"A braggart, a nuisance. No one will miss him."

"What happened to Thersites?"

"He stood by and watched my fight with Penthesilea. When he saw that she was a woman, he mocked me for having found my true equal — a mere woman, as strong as me. When he saw that I cared for her, cradling her in my arms, trying to ease her pain, trying to express my love in those final moments, he mocked me again. He said I liked my women big and preferred them dead. I waited until she turned cold. Then I grabbed hold of Thersites, and, with my bare hands, I tore off his arms, then his legs, then his head."

Breeze didn't sleep with Achilles that night — she didn't sleep at all.

27 ~ The Undead

For seven days, Breeze didn't sleep—she didn't wake, either, dragging about, zombie-like, and speaking to no one.

Each night, Iphis and Diomede waited on the porch of Achilles' lodge in case he might call for one or the other of them, which, given his rage, they now dreaded rather than wished for. Phoenix and Automedon stood guard nearby in case he should emerge in a rage. But Achilles stayed cloistered and spoke to no one.

Breeze spent most of her time sprawled on the beach near the mouth of the Scamander River. Iphis and Diomede brought her food and forced her to eat. They tried to coax her out of her depression. But Breeze didn't share her feelings with them, continuing to act as she did before when she was pretending to have been rejected by her lover. Now that act required no effort because he actually had rejected her.

She no longer had the energy to mask her morning sickness. Iphis and Diomede recognized the symptoms and presumed that Phoenix is the father and that that was why Achilles now refused to see her. They figured she was in deep depression, with the emotional swings of early pregnancy added to her alienation from Achilles. They wanted to stay near her to help and support her, but she avoided them, wanting to be alone, and not wanting to talk to anyone.

On the morning of the seventh day since the end of the truce, Breeze saw a tall regal woman walking along the beach. She had an urn on her shoulder, wiggling her hips in time to unheard music. As the woman came closer, Breeze recognized her but thought she must be hallucinating.

Breeze scrambled to her feet and stumbled toward the apparition, reaching out her arms, expecting them to pass freely through the empty vision. But instead, she fell into the friendly embrace of Andromache.

When Breeze woke up, her head was resting on Andromache's lap, and Andromache was wiping her forehead with a cold wet cloth. Nearby, dozens of slave girls stamped on their wash in the pool by the river.

"Andromache?" she blurted out. "Here? How could you risk this?"

Andromache hushed her and leaned close, whispering, so only Breeze can hear. "Risk? What risk? I could wave my arms and shout, 'Here I am, the widow of Hector. Free for the taking.' No one would believe me. It's too improbable. People see what they expect to see. But I shouldn't boast. It's never wise to mock the gods or the Fates. They'll find ways to knock the pride out of you and put you back in your place. So, I'll do what I wish, but quietly. I'll take my chances, but I won't flaunt my freedom."

"Freedom? What freedom?" Breeze whispered back.

"The freedom you gave me, the freedom of knowledge you gave me with your prophecies. I will be alive when Troy falls. Then I will become the captive of Pyrrhus, son of Achilles, and he will bash the skull of my infant son against the ruined walls of Troy. Knowing that, why should I fear anything now? If the prophecy is true, I am safe for now. And if it's false, what could happen that could be worse than what you foretold? Tell me that it's false. Tell me that you misheard the words of the gods," she insisted.

"I was wrong. I blundered. I'm worthless, useless," Breeze wept and shivered with a sudden chill.

"Would that you could be wrong. But thus far, you have been all too right."

"The Amazons, yes, the Amazons."

"Memnon, as well."

"Memnon?"

"The king of Ethiopia, son of the Goddess of Dawn, came just as you said he would, bringing an army of black men. He killed Antilochus, son of Nestor, as you said he would. Then, just yesterday, Achilles cut him down, and his leaderless army fled."

"Memnon?" Breeze asked in disbelief. "So that prediction, too, came true. And the Amazons as well. They all died, slaughtered by Achilles, and all your hopes and plans were dashed."

"Yes, the Amazons, Penthesilea and her warriors, killed by Achilles, just as you foretold."

"I'm sorry. I'm so sorry. I don't understand how it could have happened as it did. I coached Achilles well. I must have misheard what you said. I expected them to wear red, but they wore blue instead. I don't know how I could have made such a mistake. Perhaps the gods muddled my thoughts. Perhaps that was a trick of theirs to ensure that what was fated came about just as fated. I was a fool to think that I could outwit them."

"No, Briseis. It was my fault. I didn't trust you. You admitted that you were the lover of Achilles. I thought you'd tell him everything."

"I did. Of course, I did. Just as you told me to."

"I thought when you told him that the Amazons were in red, and he would go straight to them and slaughter them. So, I had them change colors. I thought that would ensure their safety."

"I told him that they were in red, and he tried to avoid them, as I asked him to. Then he stumbled on them in blue and slaughtered them. In seeking to undo fate, we helped fulfill it, fools that we are."

"I should have trusted you."

"In your place, I'd have done the same. But it's over. So why then did you come here like this? And how did you get here?"

"Polymusa."

"What? You mean Polymusa's ghost led you here? I'd believe anything at this point."

"No. Polymusa herself. She knew the way in the dark." Andromache stood up, raised her urn high over her head and moved it back and forth. A woman emerged from the bushes a hundred yards away and sauntered toward them. It's Polymusa.

Breeze stared in disbelief. "How did you survive?" she asked the Amazon.

"I was knocked unconscious," Polymusa replied. "My body was covered with the corpses of my friends. Everyone in Troy believed that I had died with the rest of the Amazons. I thought it might prove useful to seem dead. No one knows that I survived but Andromache, and now you."

Breeze paused, then concluded, "That means that the story that will be told about the battle will say that you died."

"Yes, that's what people will say," agreed Polymusa, "if they choose to say anything about someone so unimportant as I."

"But yet you're alive."

"Evidently," Polymusa smiled.

"So, the story and the truth are not the same."

"That's not unusual." Polymusa smiled "Truth is sometimes slippery."

"Then maybe all isn't lost," Breeze noted.

Andromache smiled. "That's why we came to you. We suspect that Polymusa's survival might create an opportunity, a breach of fate. But we're not sure what we can do now. Perhaps together we can find a path forward from here, a path of our own."

28 ~ Achilles Must Die

Another morning, another load of bloody rags to wash in the pool by the river.

Breeze, Andromache, Polymusa, Iphis, and Diomede all set to work. And as they worked, they sang and danced. They didn't just do what needed to be done. They did it with style, grace, and rhythm. They performed the same tasks as everyone else, but in doing so in their unique ways, they expressed their creativity and individuality. Breeze realized that when a woman wiggled her hips, rhythmically while walking up the beach, what mattered was not just what she did, but how she did it. For her, work and play were one.

When the washing was done, first Andromache, then the others, picked wildflowers and wove them into garlands for their hair. Breeze joined in. Her fingers seemed to know what to do without her having to think about it, twisting and tying automatically, like the hands of a pianist that continued to play while she looked around the room or chatted with a friend.

"Before we go further," Breeze said softly enough so no one outside their group could hear, "I have to be completely honest with you."

"But you're always honest," replied Iphis.

"Painfully so," added Diomede.

"Our lives are about to change," Breeze insisted. "In a few days, Achilles will die, and then a few months later, Troy will fall. Soon we will all go our separate ways. Only for a brief while are we here at the center of the most memorable event to take place in centuries. If we wish to make a difference, we need to act soon."

"What's this talk about making a difference?" asked Diomede. "Fate is fate. Nothing that we do matters. Why should we try?"

"And what do you mean about honesty?" asked Iphis.

Breeze explained, "Achilles was afraid that if people knew that he cared for me, I'd be in danger; that his enemies could try to hurt him through me."

"You mean that the two of you continued to be close?" asked Diomede.

"Closer than ever. From the time I returned from Agamemnon to the end of the truce, I joined him in his lodge every night and slipped away before dawn. That's over now, of course. Now he hates me. But for weeks I lied to you."

Iphis laughed. "So, it was all a farce? Achilles made it look like Diomede and I were his new lovers. I thought that Diomede was with him every night. And she probably thought it was me. In fact, the only time I ever slept with Achilles was that night when you were about to be taken away by Agamemnon, and Achilles, in a wretched mood, passed you to Patroclus."

"Yes," Diomede added "I haven't slept with Achilles since Briseis returned. I enjoyed the status of being thought his favorite, but I must admit I was relieved that he didn't call for me. Without warning, he can suddenly turn into a beast."

Andromache stood and challenged Breeze, "What makes you think that we can do anything that would make a difference? Do you have anything more to go on than the fact that Polymusa survived when she was fated to die?"

"That and wiggle room."

"What's wiggle room?"

"Dance, song, story, the images you weave and embroider, the way you do everything you do. The facts are the same for all of us. We're born, we eat and drink and work and make love, and then we die. But how we do what we do makes us who we are. We each walk up the beach carrying our burden, but we can wiggle our hips to whatever rhythm we please. Within the framework of the story, we have a space that's ours, a realm of freedom. That's wiggle room."

"So, we can only control trivial details that matter to no one?" Andromache concluded.

"Perhaps. But maybe small changes that are within the realm of our control could have major consequences."

"Like what?" asked Andromache.

"First, let's consider what we want. Andromache, you first."

"Revenge, of course, for what Achilles has done already and for what you say his son will do. Achilles killed my father and my brothers. He raped my mother. Then he killed my husband. And you tell me that his son Pyrrhus will smash the skull of my son and will become my brutal master."

"Polymusa?" Breeze asked.

"Revenge as well. Achilles killed every one of my Amazon friends."

"Diomede?"

"Revenge. When Achilles attacked my hometown on the island of Lesbos, my family and I narrowly escaped and sailed to Thebe where we sought refuge with our cousins, the family of King Eetion, Andromache's father. Then Achilles attacked there, as well, and killed my family and took me captive."

"Iphis?"

"I've been a slave all my life, and my mother was a slave before me. The only man I truly cared for was Patroclus. His killer is already dead. Fate is fate. There's nothing I can do about that. I have no blood debt and no need for revenge. But I will stand with you all and will help you do what you need to do."

Breeze added, "Like most of you, I have a blood debt owing. But I don't feel as strongly about it as the rest of you. Achilles killed my father and my brothers. But that seems so long ago, so far away, it's as if he's a different person now, and I'm different, too. Like Iphis, I have no need for revenge."

"But I do," Andromache emphasized.

"And I," said Polymusa.

"And I, too," added Diomede, "though I hadn't thought about it for a long time because there was nothing that I could do. What you can't change, you learn to accept. Are you saying we should kill Achilles?"

"No. I want to break fate mainly because I want Achilles to live," Breeze admitted. "According to fate, in just a few days, he will die, struck in the heel by a poisoned arrow. I don't expect that we'll be able to satisfy everyone with what we do, whatever it may be, but we should focus on what matters most to us."

"You're still speaking in riddles," insisted Andromache. "What can we do?"

"Consider what happens next, after Achilles dies. The Greeks will retrieve Philoctetes, the arms bearer of Heracles, from the island where they abandoned him on their way to Troy. He has the poisoned arrows of Heracles, and he'll use them to wound Paris. Paris will die from the poison."

"You've told us this before," Andromache complained. "What's your point?"

"Paris will die of poison. But the poison could come from another source. Do you like Paris?" asked Breeze.

"He's a vain and cowardly rascal," Andromache admitted. "If it weren't for him, there would never have been a war. And yet he will be the one to kill the great Achilles. There's no justice in that."

"Then would you prefer that Paris die at your hand, rather than a Greek's? Would you prefer that it be an agonizingly painful, slow-working poison?" Breeze asked again.

"He deserves no less. But to do that wouldn't leave my soul in peace."

"And what would?"

"To save my son," says Andromache.

"And how would you do that?"

"Substitute someone else."

"And you'd have some other baby die?"

"No. The guilt would be unbearable," Andromache admitted.

"Then do you have another idea?" asked Breeze.

"This Pyrrhus, if I were to drug him and cut off his balls, that wouldn't disrupt our story, would it?" Andromache asks.

"Now you're getting the idea." Breeze encouraged her. "But no. That won't work. Pyrrhus will have a son by you."

"This is foolishness," objected Polymusa. "The focus of our anger is Achilles, not Pyrrhus, who isn't even here yet."

"But we can't do anything about Achilles," Breeze insisted, afraid of losing control of the conversation.

"Why not?" Polymusa persisted. "Early this morning, before coming here, I overheard a conversation by the porch of Achilles' lodge. One speaker was gray-bearded but strong."

"Phoenix, the trainer," concluded Iphis.

"The other was tall and wiry, with a jagged scar on his cheek."

"Automedon, the charioteer," said Iphis.

"Phoenix said, 'Achilles still fights with all his skill. But he has no spirit, no passion, and no compassion. He doesn't care who he kills or why. He speaks to no one. He pays attention to no one else's danger or glory. He's just a shell of himself.'

"The other one answered, 'He's in agony. He knows he's going to die and wishes it would happen soon to end the pain. I've seen him toss his shield aside, deliberately exposing himself to the enemy as if asking them to kill him. But his lack of concern for his own safety terrifies the Trojans as if that were proof that he's invulnerable, protected by the gods.'

"Phoenix said, 'It's our responsibility to put him out of his misery.'

"'Yes,' the other replied, 'better that he fall by our hands than by some random Trojan.'

"'Better still,' suggested Phoenix, 'we should find a way to help him end it all quickly, and yet arrange the scene such that everyone believes that he died nobly in combat against a worthy foe.'

"'If only cows had wings,' answered Automedon. 'We could never do that. And imagine the horror and the shame if we should try and fail and be caught at it.'"

Iphis reacted to this revelation, "If Patroclus were here, he'd do it."

"Patroclus was a sensitive, loving man. I, too, miss him dearly," noted Breeze.

"He was not as special as you may think," said Iphis.

"I realize that Patroclus came to Achilles' father as a runaway murderer, banished from his homeland."

"That's not what I mean," added Iphis.

"Then what do you mean?"

"I shared his bed, as a slave, for nearly twenty years," Iphis explains. "He was as close to a husband as I will ever have. I could never ask for a better master. But he was not just the best friend of Achilles, but also the man who more than any other resented, envied, and hated Achilles. Yes, he was sensitive and intelligent. His voice and his touch were tender. But he always stood in the background. He was always second best. Peleus treated him like a second son and told him repeatedly that if he had had no son, he'd have adopted Patroclus as a son. But one time in his life, Patroclus took first place."

"Of course," Breeze broke in, trying to regain control of the conversation, "when he put on Achilles' armor and led the Myrmidons into battle."

"No, earlier than that, in Scyros, on the wedding night of Achilles and Princess Deidamia," Iphis continued. "Patroclus drugged Achilles and took his place in bed with the bride, without her knowing. He did that three nights running until he felt confident that she was pregnant by him."

"How do you know this?" asked Breeze.

"I was Patroclus' slave even then. He had me pour the drug into Achilles' wine. Until this moment, I was the only one, aside from Patroclus, who knew that Pyrrhus is the son of Patroclus, not of Achilles. Patroclus could be so patient, so understanding, so willing to stand in the shadow of Achilles, because he knew that his seed would one day be king. But the boy, Pyrrhus, is vicious. Achilles himself, who had no doubt that Pyrrhus was his son, wanted to keep the little devil far away, and insisted that Pyrrhus stay in Scyros rather than join him here at Troy."

"What happened to Deidamia?" asked Breeze.

"She died in childbirth."

Breeze was shocked. "In other words, the child I am carrying is Achilles' only child, even though that fact will never be publicly known?"

"Iphis," insisted Andromache, "what's the point of this confession of yours?"

"Patroclus, his best friend, would and could kill Achilles if he were yet alive," explained Iphis. "Phoenix and Automedon, his comrades in arms, wish they could, but don't have the guts to do it."

"We could do it," concluded Polymusa.

"Who could?" asks Andromache.

"All of us together," suggested Polymusa.

"All?" asked Andromache.

"Yes. Every one of us should have a hand in it," Polymusa continued. "We should all feel responsible. That's the only way for all of us to pay our blood debts and be free of him. And, yes, Briseis, that way we'd take our fate in our own hands."

"I'd risk anything to make that happen," swore Andromache.

"Theoretically," Breeze reluctantly admitted, "we could do the deed in private, then set up the situation so it looked like everything happened as in the story. So long as the public story stays consistent with fate, anything can happen."

"That way his reputation remains intact. He keeps his honor," Iphis recognized

"Let's do it tonight," urged Andromache.

"No. We're not thinking this through." Breeze tried to dissuade them. "We're talking about Achilles, the son of a goddess, the greatest fighter who has ever lived."

"Achilles is not himself," answered Diomede.

"Achilles is in agony," admitted Iphis.

"Achilles is suicidal. We'd be doing for him what he can't or won't do for himself," added Polymusa.

"He's a wild animal," Andromache said. "We should kill him with no more sense of guilt than if we destroyed a mad dog."

"This is not what I intended," Breeze objected.

"But it's the obvious answer to the questions you raised," Andromache continued. "It's inevitable. Nothing can stand in our way."

"Thetis," Breeze suggested, in a final effort to turn the tide.

"What?" asked Andromache.

"His mother, the goddess. How could we kill him if a goddess stood in our way?" Breeze asked.

"You, who are so rational about other matters, believe that his mother is a goddess and that she is an obstacle?" Andromache objected in disbelief.

"Yes. I don't know why or how, but life in this world is woven together in ways I never imagined. Yes, there could be gods and goddesses. Yes, there could be a Thetis. We'd be foolish to presume that there isn't."

"Then call to her," ordered Andromache. "Ask your priest friend Calchas to invoke her. Nothing must stand in our way."

29 ~ Thetis

"In olden days," Calchas explained, "man and nature were connected in ways that today we find difficult to imagine. Gods and goddesses were immanent in everything—every stream, every tree, every flower. Today, when man and nature are at odds, and men are in strife with other men, no one sees the gods anymore."

"Don't gods sometimes appear in the form of ordinary people, taking over a human body and speaking with that human's voice?" asked Breeze.

"Yes, so they do. So, it sometimes seems with you when you get your falling sickness. That's what the gods do when they decide to intervene in human affairs; but they do that on their own account, not because someone invoked their presence."

"But people pray to gods all the time."

"Yes, but that's one-way talk. When people pray, they say their piece and hope they're heard. That's not what you're asking for. You want a two-way conversation with Thetis to learn from her how to help Achilles in his anguish. Are there any conversations with gods in the story you know from the future?"

"Achilles himself invokes his mother several times and has lengthy talks with her. He has a special tie with her. She can sense his troubles and his wishes from a great distance, deep under the ocean, at the home of her father, Nereus, the Old Man of the Sea."

"Then Achilles should ask for her himself."

"I wish that he could. But he's in despair. I fear for his sanity. Something must have broken his link with her, or she'd have come to him already. What can we do? What would you do if you were in my position?"

"She's a sea nymph. Water must be important to her."

"What should we do with water?"

"Go to it. Immerse yourself in it. Swim in it. Dare to put yourself at risk. It's important to show that you care enough about what you are asking to risk your life for it."

Richard Seltzer

"Are you suggesting that I swim out to sea, beyond the point where I could safely return to shore and hope that Thetis will save me and talk to me? That's asking a lot."

"You're asking for an audience with a goddess. Would you expect that to be easier than seeking an audience with a king?"

"But there's no assurance of success."

"Of course not. If you knew you'd be safe, there'd be no risk, and your act would not be a gesture of faith and commitment."

"Would you do that?"

"No."

"Well, what would you do?"

"I'd sacrifice a bull and pray."

"Has that ever worked for you?"

"Never to the point of seeing a god or goddess."

"And you have no other suggestions?"

"Just one. Remember that the gods appear in interconnectedness and disappear in separateness. When you try to invoke the goddess, you should act in consort with others, all of whom are willing to risk their lives, trusting one another. All of you should be truly connected, your wills united."

"You ask the impossible," said Breeze.

"No, my dear, it's you who ask the impossible. But if you should succeed, that would be the kind of experience that gives meaning to a life that would otherwise pass unnoticed."

Breeze relayed this information to Andromache, Polymusa, Iphis, and Diomede, expecting that that would be the end of the matter. It would be impossible to invoke Thetis, and hence it would be impossible for them to kill Achilles. Everything would proceed in accordance with the fated story. Her presence, her life, and the lives of these others would make no difference. They should simply enjoy their few days upon this Earth as best they could.

But the others were not willing to give up.

Diomede suggested that instead of swimming out to sea together, they should swim toward one of the many rocks that only surface at low tide. There they could join hands and float near the rock, singing to Thetis in hopes that she might come.

Andromache suggested that they climb to the top of Mount Ida, behind Troy, and pray at the spring where, by legend, Paris met the goddesses Hera, Athena, and Aphrodite, in the beauty contest that led to the Trojan War. "The gods have always favored mountain tops," she added.

Polymusa suggested a place at the base of Mount Ida that she had scouted weeks before as a possible camp for the Amazons. Several streamlets racing down the mountain joined there to form the Scamander River and then went over a waterfall so high, that when the water hit, it bounced, and a mist rose. "There's something visionary about rising mist," she noted. "If I were a goddess, that's where I'd want to appear."

"And what would be the risk there?" asked Breeze, still hoping that this discussion would lead nowhere.

"Just below the waterfall, the river is narrow and deep, with rapids," Polymusa explained. "There's a place where we could stretch across, forming a human chain, linking arm to arm, with those on the ends holding a firm grip on tree trunks. We'd have to trust one another. And especially the one in the middle would be at risk."

"The one in the middle should be the strongest swimmer," suggested Andromache.

"I don't swim at all," admitted Iphis.

"Me neither," added Diomede.

"But you were the one who wanted us to float for hours in the sea," objected Breeze.

"Floating is one thing, swimming in white-water rapids is something else."

"I'll do it," volunteered Polymusa.

"But you come from Hyrcania, beyond the Caucasus, from the plains of Scythia, nowhere near any river or sea. You don't have experience swimming," Breeze pointed out, and Polymusa backed down.

"Then I'll do it," said Andromache.

Breeze objected, "For the last ten years, you've been stuck inside the walls of Troy. When was the last time that you swam?" Andromache backed down as well.

Then Breeze admitted, "If we are going to risk this, then I'll have to be the one in the middle."

***

That very day, they did as Polymusa suggested, linking arm to arm across the rapids, facing the waterfall and its mist, as the droplets of water, struck by the rays of the setting sun, generated a rainbow that lent a hint of divinity to the scene.

At first, Breeze held her ground, wedging her feet between boulders on the river bottom to give her stability. But Polymusa noted, "If you do it that way, you don't need us, do you? You don't need to trust us, so we aren't really connected."

So, Breeze let go—let her legs drift downstream with the current and held tight to Andromache on her right and Polymusa on her left. She shut her eyes with fear. "Thetis," she whispered with her voice and shouted with her mind.

When she opened her eyes, in the mist, just beyond the rainbow, she saw the face of a woman. Moments later, without any of them having moved, they're all sitting on rocks, under the waterfall, sheltered by the overhanging ledge. Thetis once again appeared in the mist, this time viewed from the other side, looking toward the sunset. She was larger than life and luminous.

"What do you want?" the goddess spoke directly to all their minds, without sound.

"Achilles is in agony," Diomede blurted out loud. "It would be a mercy to put him out of his misery."

"He's fated to die just two days from now. Let nature take its course," Thetis said.

"We have blood debts that need to be settled," replied Polymusa. "If nature takes its course, we'll have no hand in his death, and it will bring us no peace."

"Death rarely brings peace to anyone," answered Thetis.

Polymusa objected, "He's fated to be killed by the vain coward who stole Helen and caused the war. Better that he dies by other hands, even if the world thinks that it was Paris who did it."

"And for that you invoke a goddess and try to tamper with fate? What about you, Briseis? You're the one who spoke my name. What do you want of me?"

"Why did you kill your other sons, Achilles' six brothers?" asked Breeze.

"I didn't kill them," Thetis explained. "They were sickly infants. They died despite everything I did to save them. Do you have any idea how often human infants die? And do you have any idea how difficult it is for a cross-species child to survive, the offspring of a human and a god? And can you imagine what it feels like to lose six infant sons, one a year for six years?"

"But don't gods have the power to save human lives?" asked Breeze.

"What a quaint thought, that gods have power greater than fate. Would that it were so. None of this would have happened if Zeus himself had the power to change fate. I'd never have married Peleus. I'd never have given birth to any of my seven sons. And I would not now be on the brink of watching my one surviving son struck down in battle."

"What happened?" asked Breeze.

"I loved him," Thetis answered.

"Who?"

"Zeus, of course, the king of the gods. I loved him. He loved me. All he had to do was set aside Hera, his sister, his wife, and the bane of his existence. He was ready to do that, but then an oracle told him that some god who was yet to be born would overthrow him, just as he had overthrown his father, Cronos. He became obsessed. He wanted to track down whatever female was destined to give birth to the one who would destroy him. Prometheus knew, but wouldn't tell. So, Zeus chained Prometheus to a rock and had a vulture peck away at his liver, dooming him to eternal torment unless and until he revealed the name. While Prometheus was loyal and brave, even gods have their limits. Eventually, he spoke. He said that it was me. I'd be the mother.

"Zeus, like you, wanted to change fate. So, despite his love for me, he refused to couple with me, and he made sure that I wouldn't mate with any other god. He interpreted the prophecy to mean that my son would be far greater than his father. So, if I mated with a god—any god—Zeus would be at risk. But if I mated with a human, Zeus would have no reason to worry.

"He arranged for me to marry a human, Peleus, in a formal ceremony to be attended by all the gods, with all the gods swearing to honor and preserve our union. That was the only time that a god or goddess formally married a human. And once I began to bear children, Zeus was content that they died, one after the other. That was the safest outcome. As for Achilles, his fate was well known. He would die at Troy. And nothing I did, from dipping him in the River Styx, to disguising him as a girl in the palace at Scyros, nothing could change that. I realize that now. The gods themselves are not above fate."

"Might there be a middle way?" asked Breeze.

"What do you mean?"

"When Achilles spoke to me—and he hasn't now for weeks, obsessed as he is with his personal agony—he used the dual number and the middle voice. You, too, I notice, use the middle voice in the thoughts you send to me."

"I've never heard the term *middle voice,* but, yes, gods have their own ways of thinking and speaking," Thetis explained. "For us, everyone and everything is connected. We don't just do things and have them done to us. Our actions continue and have consequences that have consequences in an unending chain. Yes, there was a time when everything was alive, even the rocks, and all beings had thoughts and emotions, and everything was connected."

"So even violence led to connections?" Breeze asked again.

"Yes, even killing. The hunter in killing his prey was bonded to his prey."

"Humor me, please. Tell us more. Teach us. That's why we're here."

"Gods dwell in connections, in the connectedness of all things. Once men spoke and thought in a connected way, the way of caring, and, in those days, the gods dwelt among them. Over time, more men gloried in their separateness and thought and spoke only in terms of what they did as individuals and what was done to them as individuals. They acted as if they were free and independent, forgetting the interdependence of all creatures."

Breeze interpreted, "The entire earth was a single eco-system, a single organism, self-regulating, self-perpetuating."

"You use strange words, girl, but I sense your meaning is similar to mine. Gaia, yes, the Earth was once alive. Everything on Earth had its own in-dwelling spirit. But today, earth is just the passive soil from which meager living things sprout for a few days or a few seasons. Today, the world is in a fallen state. Only a handful of heroes, mainly those reputed to be the children or favorites of gods, continue to speak in what you call the middle voice. And even they only use it rarely, at times of great emotion. The fact that Achilles addresses you that way indicates his special bond with you."

Breeze replied, "If I understand you right, when Achilles killed Hector, that was not an act with a beginning and an end. From the moment Achilles was born, he was fated to kill Hector, just as Hector was fated to be killed by him. The act of killing Hector didn't end Hector, rather it affirmed their connection with one another."

"Your turn of phrase implies that it was an act of love," noted Thetis.

"But isn't that what your words mean? There's emotion in connectedness, even the connectedness of revenge and blood debt. Achilles and Patroclus were a natural pair, as close as twins. Hector killed Patroclus, affirming his connectedness with Patroclus' spirit. So, Achilles in killing Hector in revenge, became reconnected with Patroclus."

"There's some sense to what you say," Thetis affirmed. "Those are relationships we would express with what you call the middle voice."

"So, you'd say that when Achilles killed the Queen of the Amazons, that created a special bond between him and her?" Breeze asked.

"Yes, and that bond is driving him mad, for he can't revenge her death when he's the one he'd have to strike against."

"And, by the same token, whoever kills Achilles will be tied to him for all time," Breeze concluded.

"You must be mad, young lady. By that logic, if you killed him, that would be an act of love."

"You say that he will die two days from now. And you say that whoever kills him will be connected with him for all time. If that's true, I'd rather that it be me than Paris."

"That's nonsense."

"Then why do you stay here and listen to a fool like me?"

"To a human, what can matter more than life?" asked Thetis.

"How you die, when you must die."

"But that's a matter of fate."

"Only if you let it be. It's a question of wiggle room," said Breeze.

"Wiggle what?"

"We have to go from here to there. We have to be born now and die then. But along the way, we have some degree of freedom. We can sing and dance and whistle. We can wiggle our hips. Fate may control the outline of the story of our lives, but spirit, emotion, art, and love can fill it out. And within the limits of the fated story, we have the power to make changes, so long as the story, as publicly told and publicly known, remains the same."

"You mean you could kill Achilles?" Thetis asked.

"A day before he's fated to die."

"And patch things up so it looks like everything went as fated?"

"Yes, I believe that. But do you believe it too?"

"Perhaps. It's intriguing to think that fate could be cheated. I've always wanted to cheat fate."

"Then let's do it."

30 ~ The Death of Achilles

Diomede and Andromache supported Achilles' head and shoulders while Iphis brought the goblet to his lips. The scene reminded Iphis of when she drugged Achilles years before, in Scyros on orders from Patroclus. But this time, the wine was laced with hemlock, not sleeping potion.

Iphis let go. She couldn't do it. The blood-red wine poured down his neck and chest as if someone had slit his throat.

In a deep exhausted sleep, he didn't seem to notice.

Polymusa prepared another goblet and handed it to Breeze, but Breeze refused to take it. She hoped that Achilles was still invulnerable, that poisoned wine couldn't hurt him, that only an arrow in the heel could kill him, and only on the day that that is fated to happen. She didn't want to be the one to test that theory.

Andromache tried next. "This is a special medicine," she urged him, deliberately pouring some on his forehead to arouse him. "It tastes like the finest wine, but it cures the pains of the heart." She put the cup to his lips and held back his head. "Drink deeply and your misery will end."

Without opening his eyes, he opened his mouth and swallowed. Then he smiled with satisfaction.

Polymusa prepared another, and Diomede handed it to Andromache. This time Achilles half-opened his eyes, took hold of the cup and swallowed with gusto. He stood up and handed the cup back for more.

Polymusa handed the next one directly to Achilles, and he gulped that down.

"Excellent," he announced. "Where did you get this?"

"It's an old family recipe," claimed Polymusa.

"It's got quite a kick to it," he proclaimed with joy. "Enough to wake the dead."

This was the day before Achilles was fated to die. The Greeks and Trojans had declared a one-day truce, as they often did, to collect and bury the bodies of the dead. Breeze had convinced Phoenix and

Automedon that they should let her and her friends try to rouse Achilles from his grief-induced lethargy.

The five women had assembled in Achilles' lodge at dawn. To get their revenge and thereby pay their blood debts, they all needed to feel that they're responsible for his death. But only Polymusa had ever killed anyone before, and that was on the battlefield. When it came to murder, they were all amateurs.

Achilles stood with a bright sparkle in his eyes. His gloom seemed gone, along with his beastly temper. "Who's this slave?" he asked Breeze, pointing at Andromache. "I don't remember seeing her before."

"She belongs to Odysseus," Breeze quickly improvised. "He sent her over to help us with you, to try to arouse you from your anguish."

"What's your name?" he asked.

"Andromache," Andromache answered, shocked that she has spoken the truth.

"The same name as the wife of Hector?"

"Yes, it's a common name," noted Diomede. "I have a cousin named Andromache. It means *war with men*."

"So many women are at war with men?" Achilles joked.

"Indeed," said Polymusa. "That would be a good name for an Amazon."

"And who are you?"

"An Amazon."

"Yes. Now I remember. I saw you before. I once doubted the existence of Amazons. Unfortunately, I was wrong," he laughed, then coughed. "It hurts to think of Amazons. It will always hurt. What's your name?"

"Polymusa."

"Many muses? That's a name for an entertainer, not a fighter. Entertain me, please. I'm told I don't have long to live."

Polymusa kicked him in the shins, tripping him. He fell over backward. Then, before he could get his bearings, she jumped on him, pinned his arms with her knees, and grasped his neck with both hands, trying to strangle him. He smiled with delight, rocked back, booted her in the butt with his knees, then rocked forward pinning her on her back. He gave her a quick kiss on the lips. He helped her to her feet.

"Magnificent," he pronounced. "What better entertainment could I ask for than a woman wrestler? And a fine one, too. You women are amazing. This wine is better than any I've ever tasted. And now this. After the way I've been treating everyone, I appreciate your going to all this trouble for me. Especially you, Iphis, and Diomede. I haven't been fair to you. You're both so beautiful and lovable and caring. In another life, I could have married either or both of you and been happy."

"Iphis and Diomede know about us," Breeze told Achilles. "They know about you and me and our child."

"Are you well?" he asked Breeze, relieved to be able to freely express his concern.

"Yes. I feel great." She smiled ironically. "I have this delightful queasiness in my gut every morning."

"Let me be with you tomorrow morning. I only have one morning left. I wanted to spend time with you these last days, but it didn't work out that way."

"I'm sure you've been with me in spirit," Breeze replied.

"And for what little time is left, I hope to be with you in body as well." He reached out and pulled her close and kissed her. She hugged him back, caressing his shoulders. He cringed and groaned. "The more muscles, the more muscle pain." He chuckled, slow to move, like an athlete after a grueling contest.

"You need a massage," suggested Andromache.

"With four hands," added Polymusa.

Achilles obligingly returned to the dark side of the room, away from the blazing hearth, and stretched out on his belly on the stack of rugs he called a bed, shutting his eyes in anticipation.

Polymusa straddled his legs. Andromache straddled his head, facing toward Polymusa. Each of them held a bronze knife in both hands and with a nod to one another, they struck him in the back.

He moaned.

They struck again with their full strength

He moaned again.

With weary arms, they did it yet again.

Then they noticed that his moans were moans of pleasure, and they noticed, too, that no blood flowed from the wounds.

"Incredible," he exclaimed. "I've never had such a massage, such total relaxation. What do you call this technique of yours?"

"Acupuncture," Breeze answered quickly, delighted that nothing could hurt the man she loved. "It's a practice from the Far East. Blows with sharp instruments relax the muscles."

"If only you had a way to stop this throbbing headache that has been plaguing me since the battle with the Amazons."

"Indeed, we do have such a cure," Diomede quickly volunteered. "Your problem comes from too much blood."

"High blood pressure," Breeze improvised.

"What's blood pressure?" asked Achilles.

"When you're in danger," Diomede added, "your body produces extra blood to give you greater strength. And when you are in anguish, with tension and grief, your body can be fooled into acting as if you were in real danger, when you're not. Then your body produces more blood than it needs, which gives you headaches and muscle pain, and is bad for the heart."

"That's why we must bleed you," added Breeze, amazed that so barbaric a procedure could sound logical. Like a nurse, she placed an urn beside his bed, held his wrist over it, and quickly, with a knife she took from Andromache, she made two deep cuts. Achilles cringed with the pain, then leaned back, patient, and trustful, to see what would transpire. His blood flowed freely from his severed veins. The women watched in amazement. This demigod, for whom sharp knife strokes in the back caused no pain and no wound, might simply bleed to death. It might all be over in a minute or two.

Shocked and frightened, Breeze reached out, ready to apply pressure to stop the bleeding, but before she could, and before anyone could stop her, the bleeding stopped on its own, leaving a tiny scar.

"Terrific," he exclaimed, sitting up. "The headache is gone. Diomede, why didn't you tell me you had such skill in medicine?"

Diomede was speechless.

"With all that you women are doing for me, I feel like a new man. I haven't felt this alive in weeks. Thank you."

"Let's play," suggested Andromache.

"Play?" asked Breeze, who hoped that they had come to the end of their murderous attempts.

"Of course," answered Andromache, quickly grabbing a sheep's skin and throwing it over his head. "Quick, Polymusa, throw me that rope," she hollered.

"What's this?" asked Achilles, intrigued and offering no resistance. "What kind of game is this?"

"A guessing game," answered Andromache, tying the rope over the sheepskin and around his neck.

"I love guessing games," he admitted, his voice muffled.

Andromache gestured for the others to help her pull the rope tighter. "Keep your arms to the side," she insisted. "No peeking."

With a nod from Andromache, all but Breeze pulled on the rope with their full weight as if this were a tug of war.

"What are you doing?" asked Achilles.

"We need to make sure that you don't peek," repeated Andromache.

Stumbling and groping to get his bearings, he banged his heel on a log by the hearth. "Ow," he exclaimed and started hopping in pain. He quickly broke the rope and tore the sheepskin off. He sat down on the bed, holding his heel.

"Not your heel again," exclaimed Breeze.

"Yes, indeed, it doesn't take much for that damned heel to act up. It's sensitive to anything and everything. It always has been. A javelin can bounce off my shoulder, and I'll hardly notice it. But the tiniest bump to my heel and I'm in agony."

"Let me rub it for you," Breeze suggested.

"Yes, please do, as you have done so well so many other times. I only wish that you and your friends had a cure for this as you've had a cure for everything else today."

"Perhaps," noted Diomede, as she gestured to Andromache, Polymusa, and Iphis. While Breeze caressed the heel and washed it with a warm cloth, the other women met on the far side of the lodge. When they came back, Diomede had a pin in her hand.

"My brother had a problem like this," Diomede explained. "He was a great warrior, but he had an elbow that was sensitive. I relieved his pain with an ointment I received from a priest of Hermes, an ointment I have with me now."

"That sounds convenient," Achilles said, with a hint of suspicion.

"We came today at the bidding of Phoenix, to do all that we can to ease your pain. We brought with us everything that we thought might help."

"Then let's try your ointment. But let Briseis do it for me, my lovely Briseis, healer of my soul and mother of my child."

Their eyes met. This is the Achilles she loved, the Achilles of the honeymoon truce, the Achilles who played the lyre and danced, and whose passion she could arouse with the touch of a fingertip. As she leaned forward for their lips to meet, Diomede put the needle in her hand and her hand moving independent of her will, Breeze delivered the point of the pin to his sensitive heel.

He sighed with deep satisfaction. She sighed as well; the kiss having brought her close to him.

Then he told her, "You've done it again. Whatever ointment you have on that pin is amazing. The pain I've felt in my heel every day of my life has eased. It's not gone yet, but I'd never have believed that such relief was possible."

"Allow me," suggested Polymusa. She stepped up with another pin and inserted it as well.

"Yes, yes," he exclaimed. "More, give me more."

Then the others stepped up in succession, Iphis, Diomede, and Andromache each inserted an ointment-coated pin.

"My heel feels numb, completely numb," he said with joy. Then he reached out and touched his calf, then his knee, then his thigh, with growing surprise, "My leg, my entire right leg feels numb, blissfully numb."

"It's the poison," Breeze sobbed, falling to the floor beside him.

He reached down and pulled her up to him, putting his nose to her nose. "You'd kill me?" he asked in disbelief

"Part of me would," she stumbled over her words, trying not to look him in the eye.

"So, you did feel the weight of your blood debt?" he concluded, still holding her tightly, but tenderly, forcing her, with his eyes and his will, to look at him and only him.

"You were a different person back then," she objected. "That wasn't you who killed my family."

"I am who I am," he insisted with a voice that was weakening. "I'm responsible for everything I've done, even that which I didn't intend to do. That's what it means to be human, to be responsible, never to run."

"You have every reason to hate me now," Breeze whispered through her tears.

"I love you more than ever before. I never knew you'd have the courage to do this. You've accomplished what the greatest warriors of our day couldn't."

"I didn't mean to kill you. I thought you were invulnerable. I thought that there was no way we could change what was fated to be. I only went along because I thought we couldn't succeed."

"No excuses, my love. You are who you are. You've done what you had to do. I'm proud of you."

"I'll never be able to live with this guilt."

"Don't talk like a child at such a proud moment. You've shortened my life by just a day. Can that be called *murder*? You've given my death, and hence my life, a meaning that otherwise, it couldn't have had. I die at the hands of the woman who loves me, the woman I love. What more could I ask for? You've cheated fate as I never could, as even my mother, a goddess, never could." He tried to hug her tight, but, to his surprise, his muscles didn't respond to his will. His grip weakened. Then he let go of her, with no strength left in his arms.

A frightened look passed through his eyes. This was the moment that Breeze had dreaded most, the moment when his death became real to him, not some romantic theory, but painful and immediate: the end of everything. But it was not for himself that he feared, "What about you?" he asked. "What about our son? How will you escape? I could never rest in peace if I knew you'd be punished for this." He was so frantic that his head, the only part of his body he could now control, began to shake.

"Don't trouble yourself, my love." She tried to comfort him, cradling his head in her arms. "You have no reason to fear. The fated story says nothing about what we did here today. No one will know but us."

"And what will be said?"

"What you always knew would be said. For the public, everything will unfold as expected. In the stories told for thousands of years about the great Achilles, you will die a hero in front of the walls of Troy at the Scaean Gate, shot through the heel with a poisoned arrow."

"I'm not good to the women I love. I leave them or kill them."

Breeze wiped away her tears and smiled. "Are you forgetting your lines? Now is when you're supposed to say that I'm the only one you truly loved."

"What are lines?" he asked faintly.

She kissed him quickly on the forehead.

He whispered, "You've thought of everything, my love, everything but your own safety. When you've done everything you must do, leave here. Phoenix will help you. Head east and go as far as you can. I don't want you here when our son is born. I don't want you here when Pyrrhus arrives."

"I'll do as you tell me."

"Some might say that I'm doing this to myself, that I wished this kind of death, that I willed you to do this for me, that I'm sacrificing myself to pay my blood debt to Penthesilea for killing her. But I can barely remember her now. Briseis, you're the only image in my eye. If I'm a sacrifice, I'm your willing victim. What's your prayer to the gods? What's my life worth in trade?"

"The end of fate. The beginning of freedom."

"Fate is greater than the gods, my love."

"But perhaps there are other gods in other worlds."

"Can worlds collide?"

Before Breeze could think of an answer, Achilles' eyes closed, and his head grew still. She leaned forward to give him a final kiss, but he sat up suddenly, knocking her to the ground.

"Do you think it'll rain tomorrow?" he asked. "Perhaps they'll call the war off for rain. Yes, let's all go home."

31 ~ Achilles Dies Again

Breeze kicked and scratched and punched to keep the others away from Achilles. She was sure that he was still alive, even though he lay limp on his bed of rugs.

He was smiling.

He looked relaxed.

His eyes were open.

But they were glazed.

His pupils were fully dilated.

He didn't move.

Didn't breathe.

Finally, the other women were able to restrain Breeze and tied her up. They left her in a corner of the lodge near the hearth. There, she tried to conjure up and preserve memories of Achilles as he was during the truce, singing and laughing and playing the lyre.

Meanwhile, the others scrambled to get everything ready before the body stiffened. First, they put his armor on him, including his helmet, which served as a mask. Then they arranged all his body parts, so he'd be straight and look natural, and with his feet positioned so he appeared to stand.

Iphis and Diomede fetched Achilles' chariot, harnessing his favorite horses.

Meanwhile, Polymusa and Andromache dressed themselves in Myrmidon armor, with helmets disguising their identity.

In less than an hour, they were ready, but the body wasn't. They had to wait for rigor mortis to set in. Polymusa was the only one who had been intimate with death and dying. She killed repeatedly in battle, but she never handled corpses. That was work for priests and the slaves of priests.

They sat in the lodge and stared at the body. From time to time, one of them reached out and shook a hand or a leg of Achilles and found it still limp.

"What do you know about this?" Andromache asked Breeze, who was still tied up near the hearth.

Richard Seltzer

"Nothing. I know nothing. From this point on, I know nothing," she whimpered in reply.

"He's not like mortal men," Andromache continued. "It took forever to kill him. Will it take forever for him to stiffen? Will he ever stiffen?"

"I know nothing," Breeze spat back. She hoped the plot would fail, that they'd all be caught and punished.

Andromache brought in a skin full of wine, took deep swallows, then untied Breeze's hands, and passed the wine to her. Breeze gulped repeatedly.

"You know so much," Andromache pursued. "You know far more than you've told us. You got us started down this path because of your confidence in the story that's fated. Tell us more. What happens next and next? It's unnerving sitting here helpless, just waiting for nature to take its course. What happens to Pyrrhus? What happens to me? Am I to have a long and miserable life?"

"Pyrrhus kills your son. Yes, he makes you his whore slave. Yes, he takes you home with him to Greece where he reigns as King of Epirus. But later, he's murdered by Orestes, son of Agamemnon. Then your life begins anew. You marry Helenus, son of Priam, twin brother of Cassandra the prophetess, and together you reign over Epirus for many happy years. And Molossus, the son you have with Pyrrhus, will reign after you; and his son after him, and his son's sons, generation after generation for hundreds of years. And seven hundred years from now, a descendant of yours named Alexander will lead a vast army through this very place, where Troy once stood. And at dawn, he and his friends will strip and run naked around the funeral mound of Achilles, doing his memory this great honor, before setting forth to conquer all of the known world."

"You mock me."

"No," Breeze gulped more wine, welcoming the numbing and the confusion that came with intoxication. "The play must go on. Such is the story—that's what happened and what will happen. I didn't see it, but I did hear about it, thousands of years after it happened."

"You scare me." Andromache took the wineskin, swallowed, and passed it on to the others.

"I scare myself."

"Then we will succeed here and now?" Andromache asked.

"Of course."

"What could be *of course* about such a hare-brained scheme?" she asked again. "Yes, you were right time and again when you foretold what would happen here at Troy. Yes, you summoned a goddess. Yes, you helped us kill the great Achilles, despite the well-known edict of the Fates. But how can we trick everyone into believing that this corpse is a living warrior, single-handedly challenging all of Troy? How could the Trojan people be that gullible?"

"And the Trojan Horse?"

"What?"

"Those same rational citizens of Troy will be tricked into bringing a giant wooden horse into their city to please the gods, when in fact the horse is hollow, with a dozen Greek warriors hidden inside, who will open the gates to the entire Greek army."

"Impossible."

"History is full of tales of the impossible, even a tale like this one. Two thousand years from now, a corpse will win a battle, and inspire a nation for many generations."

"What?"

"A warrior named The Cid, who's dying of his wounds, will have himself tied to his horse in full armor. When his corpse has stiffened, his men, following his orders, will prod his horse toward the enemy lines and, he, as a dead man, will ride forth leading his knights into battle, and terrifying the enemy."

"You're drunk," Andromache objected, drinking more herself.

"I'm no more drunk than you are," Breeze shot back, taking the wine from her again. "But if you could know what will happen, you'd be more drunk than wine could ever make you. Imagine a teenage girl, a shepherdess who never held a weapon, suddenly becoming commander of nation's army."

"Would that I could see such a thing," Polymusa interrupted. "A world in which Amazons rule."

"That teenage girl will command an army of men, professional soldiers, perpetual losers, and she will lead them to victory after victory. There will be other moments like that that defy logic but change the course of history. This will be such a moment, but no one but us will ever know that this happened. Official history is rich and varied, full of surprises. But moments like this, what happens in the gaps of the story, that historians know nothing about, that's far more amazing."

"And what else do you see with your prophetess' eyes?" asked Polymusa. "What will happen here tomorrow?"

"I don't know. But I can imagine. Before dawn, the body will be stiff enough. We'll prop him in place in the chariot. Andromache, masquerading as an archer, will stand by his side and hold him. You, Polymusa, will act as charioteer.

"You'll ride up to the main gate of the Greek encampment. Achilles' chariot and armor will be clearly recognizable. He sometimes goes out to the battlefield alone before dawn. The guards will not be surprised. They'll open the gate and cheer him on.

"Polymusa, you'll whip the horses to a frenzy. They'll race across the Trojan plain. "Andromache, you'll hold tight to the rail with one hand and to the armored corpse with the other.

"When you reach the base of the Trojan wall, at the Scaean Gate, you'll prop Achilles up and tie him in place so he looks like he's standing on his own. You'll tie a javelin to his hand, aimed toward the ramparts. You'll hobble the horses so they won't run off. Then, Polymusa, you'll shoot an arrow into Achilles' heel.

"You'll finish all this in the dark of night.

"You'll say a quick prayer of thanks to Thetis, then abandon your armor, and run around to the back of Troy, facing Mount Ida. There, Andromache, you'll lead Polymusa to a cave, which is the opening of a secret passage that will let the two of you slip unnoticed, into the city.

"A thick fog will roll in from the sea and extend the night.

"When the fog burns off, Trojan guards will see the chariot of Achilles at the gate and sound the alarm. The name *Achilles* will be whispered, then spoken aloud, then shouted many times.

"Thousands will crowd on the ramparts to see what's happening.

"Archers will shoot at this legendary warrior who dares to challenge all of Troy alone.

"Then someone will realize that Achilles isn't moving and will shout, *Achilles is dead*. Those words will pass from one to another, over and over, in hope and amazement. The bombardment will stop.

"Then, Andromache and Polymusa, you'll shout congratulations to Paris, hailing him as the hero, saying you saw his arrow hit Achilles in the heel. You'll say to everyone that Paris uses poisoned arrows. You'll praise his wisdom for so doing and for his aim, hitting Achilles in his one vulnerable spot. You'll say the arrow of Paris must have been guided by the gods. You'll say that it must be the poison that made Achilles so stiff that he could stay erect even in the moment of death.

"As guards run out to confirm that Achilles is dead and to bring the chariot and the body inside the gates, the Greek army will charge forward.

"Here our private story ends, and the official story starts again.

"The ensuing battle will last all day, with ownership of the corpse switching from one side to the other, more than a dozen times.

"By the time they are done, and the Greeks win ownership of what used to be Achilles. The body will be damaged beyond recognition. Then the Greek chieftains will fight among themselves for ownership of his armor."

"And you," Andromache asked. "What happens to you, Briseis?"

"I see nothing."

***

Three riders raced across the plains toward the east—Polymusa, Breeze, and Achilles.

Achilles was alive.

Night. A campfire. Breeze spoke, and her words echoed. Achilles heard her as if he were inside her head as well as beside her.

"You died twice, but yet you're alive," she explained. "It will take a while for you to get used to your body again. That's what Thetis your mother told me. She rescued you like the gods rescued Iphigenia from her wedding sacrifice. Your mother replaced your body with that of another warrior of the same build. The world thinks you died at the walls of Troy. Andromache, Iphis, and Diomede think that they, together with me and Polymusa killed you the day before that and made it appear that you died in battle at the walls of Troy. That replacement body was damaged beyond recognition in the battle the Greeks and Trojans fought over it.

"The story of your public, heroic death will be told for thousands of years. And your private death satisfied the blood debts of me, Andromache, and the others.

"We're heading to the east now, to the Caucasus and beyond, to the land of the Amazons, in the plains of Scythia. We're outside of fate. There's no story to tell what will become of us, our children and grandchildren, and all future generations. Perhaps I'll become an Amazon warrior, and you'll stay at home, playing the lyre, weaving, and dancing, my trophy husband. Or perhaps we'll make new stories, unlike any that have ever been heard before, and we'll travel the world telling them over and over until we are old and blind, but always happy, always together."

Part Three ~ Body or Soul

32 ~ Too Many Souls

Breeze tried to open her eyes, but her eyelids wouldn't move, her head, her arms, her legs wouldn't move. What the hell was going on? She thought.

Finally, her eyes opened, but all she could see was darkness.

She had vague memories of college life and of the Trojan War, probably dreams. She may have been asleep for a long time. Maybe she was in a coma in a hospital. Maybe she was still asleep and dreaming that she's waking up.

Then she saw stars above—out-of-focus spots of light.

She was lying on her back. The surface was cold. She wanted to reach out and touch it, but she couldn't touch anything. This wasn't like being in a straitjacket, pushing against restraints. She was disconnected from her muscles. She didn't know how to control them. She looked for the *on* switch.

There was a bitter taste on her tongue. She could move her tongue to her teeth and to her palate.

She succeeded in turning her head a little to the left, then a little to the right. Like fighting a cramp, her muscles painfully and reluctantly began to respond to her commands.

She could see torches burning near her feet and stone columns supporting a roof with a rectangular opening in the middle, directly above her.

Then she realized that someone else's hand was holding her left hand. She tensed, a reflex reaction. But she only felt the tension in her mind. Her body didn't so much as twitch.

She focused all her attention on the hand that someone else's hand was holding. Straining, she managed to wiggle her index finger.

The other person's hand squeezed back.

Breeze felt the touch of that squeeze, then the pressure, then the pain, as nerves woke up in sequence.

Her fingertips tingled, as if they're recovering after circulation was cut off.

Then she felt a wave of pain. That other person was deliberately trying to hurt her. She needed to stop that pain. She needed to break free of that grip. She needed to get the hell out of here, wherever here was.

Focusing her attention on her aching hand, Breeze managed to wiggle three fingers at once, pushing back on the hand that's squeezing hers.

The other person screamed, let go, stood up, and ran.

Breeze heard screams all around her. A crowd was running, stumbling, scrambling to escape.

With her elbows, Breeze tried to push herself up to a sitting position. But her arms still didn't work as they should. She succeeded in raising her head a few inches, then lost control. The back of her head hit the hard surface she was lying on. Stone.

It felt strange to her—not just being in this time and place but being in this body. She stretched her arms, slowly figuring out how to control her muscles. She touched her sides, then pulled back in shock, not recognizing the sensations. Touching herself was like touching a stranger. Tentatively, she brought her hands together. Touching fingertips to fingertips, she felt echoes, as if both right hand and left hand were touching the fingers of someone else.

Her hips were huge. Her waist was huge. She was muscular. She was tall. She was naked.

She knew that her name was Breeze. She felt comfortable with that name.

Where were her clothes? Where was her cellphone? The GPS could tell her where she was. The clock could tell her the time, day, and year. She could text or call for help.

She thought that she must be sick and delusional. There was no way she could be naked on a stone altar in an ancient temple.

But she saw and felt too much detail for this to be a delusion. Moss on the pillars, particles of sand under her shoulder blades, the cold air coming in from the night sky above, the smell of sandalwood incense. This was too real. She didn't want this to be real.

Torches in the distance revealed banks of stone benches surrounding her.

A young man was stepping from bench to bench down toward her, deliberately, cautiously. Something scared the audience so much that they panicked and fled. Maybe that man fled, too, and now he was the only one who dared come back.

Breeze tried to stand but couldn't. She felt woozy. Her vision was blurred.

She stared at the man coming toward her. He was hesitating at each bench. He seemed afraid, but, nonetheless, he kept coming.

She had no idea what she should do if she could do anything. She lay quietly, forcing herself to breathe slowly, trying to make sense of the physical reality of this new body and how to interpret its sensations and how to control its movements.

By reflex, she tried to reach out to cover her privates, but her hands swung back and forth, like jack-in-the-box puppets on springs. She couldn't stop them. She had no control over them. They weren't hers. Then they stopped on their own.

The young man reached her. His green eyes were wide open, pupils dilated. He was breathing heavily. The muscles of his face were quivering. The stone she was lying on was as high as his waist. He gripped the stone and leaned forward to support himself. His face was near hers. She could feel his warm breath. His eyes were locked on hers. She saw a face reflected in his eyes, but that face wasn't her face.

"Chloe?" he asked.

She stared at him blankly.

"Welcome back, Chloe," he said.

"Chloe?" she repeated, shocked that she could control the muscles of her tongue and face, that she could speak.

"Yes, Chloe. That was your name before you blacked out and everyone thought you were dead."

"How do I understand you?" she asked.

"What a strange question."

"What language are you speaking?"

"Greek, of course. The language of the Eastern Empire, the same as you."

"But I speak English."

He laughed. "What gibberish is this? Your mind must be addled from what you've gone through."

"And what have I gone through?"

"You were dead, and now you're alive."

"I don't think I was dead."

"Well, your family, your husband-to-be, and your doctor all thought so. You must have been in a coma. Your breath and your heartbeat must have been so faint that everyone jumped to the conclusion that you had died. Such mistakes happen. Fortunately, you woke up before you were buried. You can thank me for that. If I hadn't bought your body and put it through this ritual, you'd still be unconscious, and the day after tomorrow, at dawn, your burial would have killed you."

"I don't remember being sick."

"As far as anyone knows, you weren't sick. You were in full health and happiness. Tomorrow was to be your wedding day. You collapsed, and everyone thought you had died. Such things happen. They are rare, but they do happen. Life is a mystery. Death is a mystery. Call it fate. Call it luck. Your death was a terrible blow to all who knew and loved you. Imagine how great their joy will be when they learn that you're alive."

"They don't know yet?"

"Not yet. You woke up minutes ago."

"What you're saying doesn't ring true to me. And I don't recognize this place."

"You've never been here before. This is what you'd call a pagan temple. You're a Christian, Chloe."

"None of this makes sense. And that name, that's not my name."

"Well, you were unconscious and close to death, so I'm not surprised you have trouble remembering. Your memory will come back soon. I'm sure."

"I have memories. But I don't remember what I see here or how I got here. And I don't remember that name. That's not my name."

The young man hesitated, puzzled. "Well, maybe something else happened. Maybe you did die, and you've returned from the dead. That could jumble your thinking and remembering. Maybe you were resurrected as in your Christian myths, like Lazarus and Jesus Christ."

"Something is very wrong. I know I'm not named Chloe. I've never heard that name before."

"And who do you think you are?" He laughed, nervously.

"Breeze," she answered.

"Briseis?" he asked and stared, his eyes opening still wider.

"Yes, Briseis. My name is Briseis," she agreed. "Call me Briseis."

"And do you remember Achilles?"

After another long silence, she told him, "Yes. I know Achilles."

\   "And what do you remember about him?"

"I remember bandaging his wounds. I remember the taste when I kissed those wounds to make them heal. I remember the firmness of his muscles as I rested my head on his shoulder. I remember riding with him across the plains, far from Troy."

"What do you know about souls moving from one body to another?"

"Nothing. But I've heard of transplants of body parts, moving heart, lungs, kidney, even face from one body to another."

"Maybe that's the word for what happened to you—*transplant*. Your soul seems to have been transplanted in a new body. I don't know how that could happen, but there's much I don't understand. Life itself is a mystery. And you say that the name of your soul is *Briseis*?"

"I don't know anything about souls. But my name is Breeze or Briseis. That's the name my parents gave me."

"And my name is Achilles."

"You, Achilles?" she laughed. "You look nothing like him."

"You mock my stature?" he retorted defensively.

"It's not just your size that's wrong. Achilles' eyes are blue, not green. And his hair is black, not brown, like yours."

"Your memory seems to be coming back."

"Random details pop into my head."

"You really are a different soul," he concluded, in dismay.

"Different from what?"

"You're not Chloe, the woman who died. Your soul is not the soul that once occupied this body. And it's not the soul we hoped would enter it. Where do you come from? How did you do this?"

"I didn't do a thing. I simply opened my eyes."

"And where were you before you opened your eyes?"

"Some other place. Some other time. I can't explain it. I don't belong here. I don't know how I got here. And I don't know how the hell to get back where I belong."

He stared in wonder, then added, "It wasn't supposed to happen this way. It never happened this way before."

Breeze focused on the wavering light of torches reflected in his green eyes. Those were kind, caring eyes. This man believed in miracles and thought that he might have just witnessed one.

"What was supposed to happen?" she asked.

"Sacred writings say that when the ritual is done right, the soul of a young woman enters the healthy body of another young woman who died of an unknown cause. Such an event serves as proof that the soul is separate from the body, that the soul lives even when the body dies, that we can live again and again and maybe live forever. That's the central mystery of the Eleusinian Mysteries."

"We're in Eleusis, in Greece, in ancient Greece?"

"I don't feel ancient." He chuckled. "But this is Eleusis, near Athens, in the Roman Empire, under the reign of Julian. And, yes, this is the temple of the Eleusinian Mysteries. A priestess of Artemis lay down here beside a dead body, the body you now inhabit. I administered drugs to her and to that body that is now yours. I spoke the holy words. The soul of the priestess was supposed to move to the dead body. That's what happened in the distant past when this ritual was performed. And if it were to happen again now, such an event would reaffirm our faith and revitalize our religion. But instead, a different kind of miracle occurred."

"This body I'm in now was supposed to become the body of that person who was beside me?"

"Yes, your body was supposed to become hers. And her body would then be lifeless."

"But she got up and ran away."

"Yes."

"Let me get this straight. To begin with, there were two bodies and one soul, one living person, and one dead body. And if things had gone the way you planned, her soul would have moved from her body to this one. Then there would still be two bodies and one soul, but the soul would be in a different body, and the body that soul came from would be dead."

"Yes. But instead, there are two living people, both her and you, whoever you are."

"And that makes no sense in your religion?"

"Exactly."

"And the dead woman, the woman whose body is now mine, was named Chloe?"

"Yes."

"And the other woman, the priestess, what's her name?"

"That's Eurydice, my betrothed."

"You wanted to marry a woman who was about to vacate her body?"

"It was to be a gesture of love."

"You were going to turn the woman you love into a corpse?" Breeze sat up and stared at him in disbelief. He was slow to move back, and her forehead bumped against his. Her hand, by reflex, reached up at the same time his did. Their hands touched. An awkward moment passed before their hands disengaged.

He broke the silence, "Your skepticism speaks volumes. You don't believe in the traditional gods, and you don't believe in the Christian God, either. Christians believe in souls. A Christian would understand what I'm talking about. You, a participant in a miracle, don't believe in miracles."

"Are you on drugs? Or am I?"

"The soul is eternal," Achilles continued. "If the ritual had worked as planned, Eurydice would continue to live in the new body."

"In my body."

"Yes, in the body that is now, temporarily, yours, like a hermit crab in its temporary shell."

"And her old body, the body that you kissed, that you held, would become a rotting corpse?"

"She's a priestess of Artemis, subject to vows of celibacy."

"This gets curiouser and curiouser. You planned to marry someone who can't marry?"

"In her new body, in the eyes of the law, she'd be a different person, so her religious vows would no longer hold. But to me, she'd still be my soulmate. And we'd be free to marry."

He looked serious and proud, declaring his faith and his love. But Breeze couldn't hold back a chuckle. "The legalities of soul transfer. I'd have never imagined that."

"We prayed long and hard. This miracle would have been a public affirmation of our religion, and it would also have been our personal salvation."

Shouts erupted outside the temple.

"We have to get out of here," Achilles warned. "When the shock and terror of what just happened dies down, those people who ran away will come back angry. And there could be Christians as well and others who are outraged by what just happened here. We're in danger. Can you stand? Can you walk?"

"Yes, of course," she answered, forgetting that she couldn't.

She rolled toward him and they grabbed hold of one another. He helped her swing around so her feet touched the ground. Then she rose, resting her elbows on his shoulders. Her nose brushed against his nose and then his forehead brushed against her chin. Standing straight, his face was even with her breasts.

She shifted her weight from one foot to the other, getting used to the sensations, learning how to keep her balance, but feeling wobbly. She held tight to him, pressing him close, unintentionally enveloping his head with breasts that weren't her breasts, in a body that she couldn't control, but that now sent her a gust of sensations.

She saw panic in his eyes. He pushed her away but pulled her closer at the same time. She was falling into his arms, and he was falling down, unable to support her weight.

They were entangled on the stone floor, she on top, the weight of her new, much larger body pinning him down.

She felt his erection pressing against her groin. She whispered "Achilles."

Then she blacked out.

33 ~ It's Alive

Breeze was dreaming, but she was awake enough to know that she was dreaming. No words. No sounds. Just darkness and the embrace and touch of a man. She was rolling on the floor with him, then cuddling close, her head nestled on his shoulder. She whispered, "Achilles," and remembered whispering that name in another dream, where she was in a different body, and lying on top of another man, his member erect and pressing against her.

Then she awakened, gasping and gulping, her mouth full of a bitter liquid that a woman was pouring down her throat.

Breeze spat and coughed and pushed, and the woman stumbled back across the room.

The woman looked like she wanted to scream, but restrained herself, opening a door and shouting, "It's alive."

The priest Achilles entered, hesitantly, leaning on the doorframe. The left side of his face was bruised.

The woman bowed to him, apologetically. "I'm sorry, master. I know how much you wanted your miracle to work, the right miracle, the righteous miracle. And then you thought you'd have a second chance, that the demon had left, and this body was empty, and you'd be free to try again."

"Enough. I never called her a demon. I never wished her dead, but I thought she was dead. What I don't know of life and death far outweighs what I do know. Fetch us some wine, Eurydice. We all could use some wine."

"Eurydice?" Breeze asked as the woman left. "Is that the woman you said you love?"

"Yes, her name is Eurydice. But no, she's not my soulmate. She's a slave of mine with the same name."

"What a coincidence."

"No, not a coincidence. I gave her that name on purpose."

Breeze couldn't make sense of that. Nothing here made sense. "Where are we?" she asked.

"A back room in the temple of the Mysteries. We should be safe here for a while. My slaves helped carry you here. Orpheus has gone to get a wagon to take you away from here to my dwelling place."

"Orpheus? You named him, too?"

"Of course."

She was naked and cold, laid out like a corpse on her back on a table. She didn't have the strength or the desire to sit up. What was happening was too implausible for her to take seriously. She'd never have rolled on the floor with this man. She'd never have been attracted to him. Impossible. Their bodies are mismatched. He's short and weak, like a computer nerd. She needed a man she could literally look up to. Even in her right body, this man would be shorter than her. And this wasn't her right body. She was taller now. She shut her eyes in hopes that when she opened them again, she'd be in yet another body in another time and place. She didn't care where or when. Anything would be better than this.

She blacked out again, then opened her eyes, then blacked out again. Like a spinning strobe light, her consciousness flipped on and off.

The priest, Achilles, was standing beside her, checking her pulse.

She didn't care about him and the concerns of his life, but she spoke to him to try to make sense of this strange world that she found herself in.

"Why did you name your slave Eurydice?"

"Because I'm a man. I have needs."

"You mean you and she—"

"Yes, of course. She's my slave. She's my concubine. She does what she's told to do. When I found my soulmate trapped in the body of a celibate priestess, what was I to do? We exchanged looks in public places. Her eyes were expressive. I knew she longed for me, as I for her. But she was always escorted by crones. I couldn't get close to her. It took creativity and bribery to exchange written messages. After months of that, I buried myself in study. I sought the advice and instruction of alchemists and magicians, and I delved through the sacred writings of the Eleusinian Mysteries. I sought a way to free her soul from that body that was forbidden to me, a way to allow us to be together forever, as we were fated to be. And all the while, I craved her physically and pleasured myself as best I could with fantasies of her. But that was not enough to meet my physical needs.

"I looked for a slave who resembled her physically, who was married so she wouldn't become emotionally dependent on me, and who was incapable of bearing children. I found the perfect match a year ago and bought her and her husband. I renamed them Eurydice and Orpheus. It's been a satisfactory arrangement. The real Eurydice, my Eurydice knows and understands. It's a temporary fix until I can get this miracle to work, and it almost worked today."

"Such fidelity," Breeze remarked.

"Yes, I'm proud that I was able to find a solution that keeps my love intact and pure while satisfying the needs of the flesh. But the soul transplant will be a far more fulfilling solution. Please tell me all you know about transplants. Please help me find the flaw in what I did and figure out how to fix it."

She turned toward him, on her side, propping her head with her hand, her elbow resting on the table beneath her, deliberately dangling her pendulous breasts in front of his face as a form of defiance. "You lay me out naked like so much meat. I'm your experiment, your failed experiment. You probably want to experiment again with this same body. You're Dr. Frankenstein, and I'm your monster."

"What are you talking about?"

"It doesn't matter what I'm talking about. None of this matters. I feel like I'm auditioning for a low-budget horror movie."

"Is that *English* you're speaking? It certainly isn't Greek."

"And I'm certainly not going to cooperate. From what you've said, you have every reason to wish me dead. You're like a landlord trying to get rid of a tenant. You want me to vacate this body, so you can let your lady move in. Well, I'm not going to go gently into that dark night."

He backed up all the way to the wall. His green eyes telegraphed fear. "Whatever happened to bring you into this new body, happened because of me," he rushed to explain. "I'm responsible for you. I need to make this right. Later, I'll try again with another corpse. But for now, getting your body and soul to adapt to one another, to accept one another, that's our most urgent need."

"Rejection," she offered.

"What?"

"That's often the problem with transplants. I'm not a doctor, but it's common knowledge that the body's defenses get in the way. There has to be a match between the organ and the recipient. And even when the match is close, doctors need to administer drugs to suppress the immune system until the body gets used to its new part."

"That could be what's at issue. Your body is rejecting your soul. That would explain your blackouts."

"But there's nothing you can do about that. You're not prepared to do heart transplants, much less soul transplants." Despite the seriousness of the situation, she couldn't help but chuckle at the thought. She sat up, with her feet dangling near the floor.

"Admittedly, I'm out of my depth. But in my ignorance, by accident, I seem to have gotten a few things right. There must be a close match between your soul and your new body. And the mushroom-based potion that I administered before the ceremony and that Eurydice just gave you, must have suppressed your body's mechanism for rejecting a new soul."

"And what about this body of mine? Was it fresh? Did you keep it cold until you were ready to act?"

"I got it within an hour of death. That was a miracle of negotiation. By good fortune it's winter. And by simple common sense, I kept it as cold as I could, wanting to delay decomposition."

"And that's why I'm naked?"

"Of course. You have nothing to fear from me. I owe it to you to try to make this transplant work. And by helping you, I might learn how to succeed when I try again for Eurydice, with a new corpse."

Breeze looked into his eyes. She wanted to believe that he was the kind of person who would adopt a stray cat or dog, that he'd do what was right for her, even if he had no personal interest in her fate. But before she could figure that out, she blacked out again.

34 ~ Falling in Lust

Breeze woke up to the scent of olive oil and sandalwood.

Achilles the priest, bundled in several robes was hunched over a desk cluttered with books and papers. He was reading by the flickering light of an oil lamp. As he read, he mouthed the words, whispered to himself, like a child who doesn't yet know how to read silently.

Behind him, Breeze lay on a crude bed, hovering between belief and disbelief. What's real? she wondered. Is anything real?

A dog barked loudly, startling Breeze, jolting her out of her lethargy, reminding her that she was naked and painfully cold.

"Quiet, Julian," ordered Achilles, interrupting his work to pat the head and scratch the back of a huge dog, the size of a Great Dane. Julian stopped barking, sat, and nuzzled his master's leg.

Breeze pulled her knees up to her chest, blew on her hands, and pleaded, "Have some mercy, please. Cold is important to keep a dead body fresh. But it's not good for the living." He wrapped her in blankets and called, "Eurydice, bring hot coals and relight the fire in the hearth." He hugged Breeze tightly, apparently to warm her body. "I should never have had her put the fire out. No one should ever put a hearth fire out. It's a sin against Hestia, goddess of the hearth. Yes, that's superstition, not allegory with secret meaning. But I'm as weak as any other man. I hedge my bets," he mocked himself. "Why do things that could anger the gods when the gods might actually exist?" He gave Breeze another hug, then backed off, apparently surprised at how much he enjoyed hugging her. He returned to his chair and went back to sorting through his papers as if there were something important he needed to find.

"So Julian is the name of your dog?" she asked.

"Yes, Julian. He's a mongrel, mostly Laconian, a Spartan hunting dog."

"You named your dog after the emperor?"

"Julian was a friend of mine at school in Athens. We were together when we found a stray. We tossed a coin. My friend Julian won the dog.

A month later that dog had a litter. How was I to choose among seven? I let the mother choose."

"And how did you do that?"

"The traditional Roman way. You separate the puppies from the mother, surround the puppies with an oil-soaked string, and set the string on fire. The mother jumps over the ring of flames and rescues each puppy, one by one, in order of their merit. My Julian here was the clear winner."

"And what hoops will I have to jump through, to prove I'm worth saving?" she asked.

"I'd say your jumping into a new body was plenty enough." Achilles chuckled. "I don't know anyone else who has ever performed such a feat."

"That Julian you mentioned is just a friend of yours, right? You don't mean Julian the emperor?"

"A few years ago, he was a student like other students, a commoner. His cousin, Constantius II, had executed all other family members to avoid challenges to his authority. Julian was bookish and quiet, a threat to no one. So Constantius, on a whim, let him live and let him study whatever he wanted, wherever he wanted. As for Julian, he dreamed that he was the reincarnation of Alexander the Great, but he had sense enough not to let his cousin know that. And he was in no hurry to follow that life path. Sooner or later, it would happen. That was his fate. For the moment, he wanted to learn all that he could, as quickly as he could. We studied rhetoric and literature. That's the usual training for lawyers. But Julian was more interested in the old stories about the gods than he was in legal matters. He believed the power of the state was being eroded by the growing power of the Christian church. He longed for the good old days, the days of the greatness of Rome, and the greatness of Greece. His enthusiasm was contagious. I caught it. Together we attended the Eleusinian Mysteries and became initiates. Then he was suddenly elevated to be commander of the armies of the West, in Gaul. And soon after that, Constantius died, and Julian became emperor. He hoped to be a philosopher-king, as in Plato's *Republic*, and as the emperor Marcus Aurelius was. Already he has made a law that all religions are equal, and everyone is free to worship as he wishes. And he's backing that principle of equality by giving large subsidies to temples like mine and by spending vast sums to rebuild the Temple of Solomon in Jerusalem for the Jews. Right now, he's assembling an army near Antioch and plans to invade Persia, like Alexander the Great.

"If it weren't for him, I wouldn't be here. When he was elevated to emperor, he saw to it that, despite my youth, I became the high priest of the Eleusinian Mysteries. And if it weren't for him, you wouldn't be in that body you're in. He donated a fortune to our temple, which enabled me to bargain quickly and effectively with Chloe's family for that body of yours."

"How did I get here?"

"*Soul transplant* you called it."

"I don't mean how did I get in this body. I mean this place. Where am I now. How did I get here?"

"This is my home, the high priest's quarters in Eleusis, outside Athens. My slaves helped bring you here in a wagon a few hours ago. You had fainted. Nothing would revive you. I needed to study the sacred writings for clues as to what had happened and what I should do next. Also, I was concerned about what the initiates of the temple might do. Those who witnessed the sudden animation of your body were scared and confused, and their wild talk seems to have inflamed the fear and anger of others. A crowd gathered in the street near the temple. I was afraid it would turn into a nasty mob convinced you were possessed by demons. We should be safe here."

"Safe for tonight. I can believe that," Breeze replied. "But what about tomorrow? If I stay in this body and in this world, how will I live? Where will I live? Will I be sold as a slave?"

"For now, you're with me."

"I have no skills. I have no family. You're the only person I know from this time and place."

"Chloe's family may have some claim on you. And the man she was betrothed to. If they wish to exercise their rights."

"There's no way I could live on my own?"

"A woman can't live independently here. This isn't Sparta, where women can own property. Here, as is true nearly everywhere else, women *are* property. First, you belong to your father, then you belong to your husband. I bought you, or rather the body you're in now, from Chloe's father."

"And will you name me?"

"What? You said your name is Briseis."

"I gather that you name the slaves and the strays you bring in."

"Names matter. A man's true name should be an expression of his essence, his ideal self, the idea of who he should be. Your true name is Briseis. You told me that, and it rings true to me. I suspect that your soul was drawn here by my name, that the soul of Briseis needed to be with the soul of Achilles. I feel responsible for that mistake because Achilles is not my true name. I should have renamed myself long ago. I should have called myself Orpheus, after the poet and musician, the lover of Eurydice."

"So why did your parents name you Achilles?"

"It wasn't decreed by tradition. I had no grandparent named Achilles. Rather, it was the wish of my father. He was an athlete. He competed in the Olympics. He came in second in the discus and would have come in first had he not had a cold on the day of the competition. In his prime, I'm told, he looked like the statue of the discus thrower by Myron. There's a marble copy of it in the town square—a continuing reminder to me of my failure to live up to my father's expectations.

"My father named me Achilles hoping that I, who had been born small and weak, would grow large and strong, of heroic proportions. He wished that my life would be a continuation and extension of his own. Instead, my name highlighted the contrast between me and the legendary Achilles. Because of this body of mine, my father didn't believe that I actually was his son. He presumed my mother had been unfaithful, and he turned on her. My parents continued to live together, but they were estranged. She was no more to him than a slave, a drudge. I was their only child.

"I was no good at sports. I had few friends. I became bookish and obsessed about the randomness of how we come to be born with one body or another. I also obsessed over traditional literature, the story of Troy, in particular. I came to revere the old stories of the gods and came to wish that they were true. I became interested in ideas of soul migration perpetuated by the Mysteries of Orpheus and Dionysus and

Eleusis. I wished that I could change my own body. I wanted access to the deepest secrets of the Mysteries. I was fortunate that I knew Julian as a student and fortunate that he became emperor and sought to restore the old beliefs and temples and gave protection to the Mysteries, which the Christians strove to destroy. When, thanks to him, I became the high priest of the Eleusinian Mysteries, I got access to sacred documents that enabled me to uncover the secrets of the soul and of eternal life, the documents that you see here in this room.

"Birth and death are both mysteries. We have no idea where or how the soul exists before birth or how a new soul comes into existence or what happens to the soul at death.

"Many believe in reincarnation, that the soul of someone who has died passes into a newborn. Plato wrote of it. Pythagoras, the great mathematician, believed that he was the reincarnation of Euphorbus, a Trojan warrior who wounded Patroclus and was killed by Menelaus. Christians believe that the soul lives on after death and receives the reward or punishment that it deserves. And Christians also believe in the possibility of resurrection, like Lazarus and Jesus, when a soul returns to the body it occupied before death and that body comes to life again. So why should such miracles happen only at death and birth? I believe that in special circumstances, the soul of a living person can enter a dead body, bringing it to life again. I believe that I might be able to change this body that I'm ashamed of for another, better body. And if that were to happen, if a soul could move from one body to another, that would mean that there is in fact a soul, separate from the body, and that the soul endures even when the body dies. Such a miracle would be tangible proof of life after death, perhaps eternal life. My theory is consistent with the ancient rituals and legends. Initiation into the Mysteries is a symbolic rebirth, like baptism and holy communion for Christians. But to witness the thing itself, not just the symbol, would give new life not just to an individual, but to the religion of our ancestors as well.

"As I told you, I fell in love with Eurydice, a priestess of Artemis, who served at a temple here in Eleusis. She is bound by a vow of celibacy that was forced on her by her parents. Because of her, my goal changed. No longer was I hoping to change my own body for another. I wanted to free Eurydice from her vows, so we could be together.

"I had studied the secret writings of the mysteries, and together with study of modern medicine, I arrived at what I hoped and believed was the right combination of drugs and words and ritual procedures. As I became confident that I could perform the ritual of soul transference, I made preparations for when an appropriate body would become available. I even looked into the legal aspects of this unusual situation, to legitimize what I was doing and to avoid controversies that could lead to delays and hence ruin the chances for success.

"It's rare that a virgin of marriageable age drops dead for no known reason. When I heard that that had happened, I rushed to meet the family and buy the body. People don't normally sell the remains of their loved ones, much less do so within an hour of death, before they have recovered from the shock. And, as it turned out, Chloe was a Christian. Hence it wasn't easy to convince her family to release her body for what they considered a pagan ritual. But there was no time to waste, as the body would soon begin to rot and become unsuitable.

"Fortunately, Emperor Julian had handsomely endowed the Eleusinian Mysteries. Just a few months ago he gave us more money than we could spend in decades. I offered the family a fortune in exchange for signing a sales contract.

"If the body came to life, the new person would belong to me. Nobody believed that that could happen. And if the body stayed dead, ownership would revert to the family for burial. They could keep the money, and I'd pay for the burial. The family thought they were getting a fortune for a delay of a day or two. They could even have the body back in time for traditional burial before dawn on the third day. I had had the contract drawn up by a lawyer in advance. I just had to fill in the name of the body and get the father's signature.

"Those initiated in the Eleusinian Mysteries knew that I wanted to demonstrate that the soul is independent of the body and that eternal life is a tangible reality. Hope was high that I could perform what legend suggested had happened many years ago. Eurydice, too, knew what I wanted to do, and, unlike the others, she knew that the main reason I was doing this was for her, for love of her eternal soul, so we could be together. In a new body, she'd be freed from her vow of celibacy and our platonic love could become natural love, and we could marry and have children."

"Excuse me," Breeze interrupted. "Something here doesn't ring true."

"I'm telling you things that are outside the realm of common experience. I'm saying the impossible is possible. I'm saying I've found the secret of eternal life. And you have one little question? I must be more persuasive than I thought." He smiled at her. Their eyes locked. Then he remembered that he was alone with her, that he was sharing intimate secrets with her, a total stranger, and that she was naked under a loose covering of blankets. He looked away again.

She posed her question. "It's that word *virgin* that's disturbing. In this ritual of yours, do both participants, both the living and the dead, have to be virgins? I hate to throw cold water on your theory, but I'm sure that I'm not a virgin. Whatever body I was in before, I wasn't a virgin, and if I've lived a hundred times, I'm sure I've never been celibate."

"*Virgin* is just an expression, not to be taken literally, any more than the stories of the gods and goddesses are to be taken literally. Those are allegories for higher hidden truths. Those are mysteries to be contemplated like the *virgin birth* of Jesus. Physical virginity is not a prerequisite."

"I suppose that, to you, virginity is no more important than your being faithful to your Eurydice," she interjected.

"Apparently, in the world you were in before, people make more of matters of the flesh than we do here. This world isn't perfect, and we aren't perfect. So why burden yourself with guilt? We compromise. We make the most of what we have. And we do the best that we can, subject as we are to human weakness and temptations. And we make allowances for others as we make allowances for ourselves."

"Spoken like an expert in self-indulgence." Breeze smiled and made eye contact again, which he again broke.

"You're quick to judge. Imagine you had found your soulmate, and you could never be with him because of religious vows."

"Well, I wouldn't buy a slave who looked like him and pretend the slave was my lover."

"But you'd probably have done as I did a few weeks ago."

"And what was that?"

"I believed that I had uncovered the secret of eternal life and that I could give Eurydice a new body. But we needed the right body. And the odds of finding such a body were slim. We might have to wait for years. We might never have the opportunity. But our physical desire for one another had peaked when we knew that it was truly possible that we could be together. We plotted and bribed, and one night Eurydice slipped away from her temple and joined me here."

"You did it with her? Did your souls orgasm?" Breeze provoked him.

"No, and our bodies didn't either. I expected too much."

"Performance anxiety," Breeze chuckled. "There's justice in the universe."

"I wasn't able to consummate our love. Even fantasizing that the real Eurydice was my slave didn't work. Fortunately, she was inexperienced in sex, so it was easy to convince her that what I did with my hands and my tongue is all that physical love amounts to, that our physical lovemaking was an amazing experience."

"And she believed you?" asked Breeze, incredulous.

"From what she said, she was fully satisfied with my performance. And I'm sure she'll be even more satisfied after the ceremony when there's no such stress, and I can perform at the level of my natural ability."

Breeze noticed a tent-like rise in his robe near his crotch.

He realized what she was looking at and turned away, returned to his papers and books and placed an open codex face-down on his lap.

Breeze stared at his back, silently, until he turned and looked at her again, shamefaced. He tried to explain, "I'm sure it would upset Eurydice to see you in that body, in Chloe's body, here alone with me. What man wouldn't be attracted to you?" he admitted. "And what woman wouldn't be jealous of you? She'd have been delighted if that were her body and if she were here now as you are. That's who she feels she is or who she deserves to be, someone physically attractive, so attractive that her beauty is like an unstoppable force of nature. But she'd be outraged to find someone else in that body and that body naked in my bed."

Breeze replied, "It's hard to know how to take compliments about this body when it isn't my body. I'm a visitor in it. I haven't even seen it except from the awkward perspective of looking down at myself. Do you have a mirror? I'd like to look at myself in a mirror."

"Eurydice," called Achilles, "Please bring a mirror. The big one. Get Orpheus to help."

Breeze remembered looking at herself naked in a full-length mirror on the back of her parent's bedroom door. Back then, she felt sinful doing that, as if there could be something wrong about looking at her own body. She had first taken such a look when she was four. On hopping out of the bathtub, she had raced to her parent's bedroom to look in the mirror, out of curiosity. Then, at the age of thirteen when she looked again, her body looked like someone else's body—not just taller—the breasts, the hips, the curves. It had been very different seeing her entire body displayed like that, very different from just looking down at herself. She expected a shock like that now.

She wondered what this body would look like pregnant.

She wondered what it would look like as she aged here, in this place and time, without ever going to a gym, with primitive cosmetics, with a diet heavy in fat, and with doctors who had little medical knowledge. In this world, she guessed that someone who was forty could look like someone sixty would in the world she came from. If she stayed here, she would lose muscle tone, her breasts would slump, her flesh turn to flab, her hair would turn gray, her neck and facial skin would sag in a maze of wrinkles.

She wondered, how many times, simply through growing and aging, people woke up to find ourselves in a new body.

The mirror was higher than she was tall, made of metal, not glass, probably some alloy of copper, highly polished.

Looking into it and seeing a face that wasn't hers felt weird and disgusting, like discovering she had brushed her teeth with someone else's toothbrush.

She touched her cheeks, her forehead, her chin. Yes, the motions she saw in the mirror matched the motions she was making.

She put her hands in her mouth and stretched her lips and made faces. She stuck out her tongue, which was exceptionally long. She could touch the tip of her nose with the tip of her tongue. Her teeth had never been cared for by a dentist much less an orthodontist. They were yellowish and had random out-of-place twists. But she had all her teeth, and there are no obvious signs of decay.

She thought that a mirror from this time must be distorting, like the mirrors in a funhouse at a carnival. She doubted that the image of herself in the mirror accurately showed what she looked like. But the reflections of objects in the room and of Achilles, standing behind her, were accurate.

She unwrapped the blankets that she was encased in. She flexed her knees and leaned left, leaned right. She did calisthenics in front of the mirror, touching her toes and doing jumping jacks. She was fascinated by the movement of her large breasts which maintained their shape without the support of a bra, and which snapped to attention when she pulled her shoulders back.

Watching Achilles watch her watch herself gave her an erotic tingle. It felt pornographic. She enjoyed seeing herself in her new body, but at the same time she showed herself off to him, inviting him to look, as if she were a stripper or porn star, deliberately turning him on.

But she was more interested in herself than in him.

She had lucked into an extraordinary body. Breeze was now about half a foot taller than she remembered being, well over six feet. She was muscular, with flesh where there should be flesh and curves where there should be curves. Her curly blond hair extended all the way to her crotch, half hiding and half revealing her nakedness. When she ran her fingers through her hair or she shook her head, the long tresses shifted in enticing ways, changing what was hidden and what was revealed.

Even the hair on her legs and in her armpits, light blond hair, looked sexy.

In this body, she was the epitome of blond power.

Any man looking at her would be both attracted and intimidated. He'd be totally at her mercy.

She remembered Penthesilea the Amazon queen who won the lust of Achilles without saying a word. Despite his love for Briseis, Achilles had been caught by the sensual promise of the Amazon's magnificent body.

She wondered, if she were to stay in this world, would this goddess-like body be a blessing or a curse? It might turn out to be like the curse of wealth. How would a woman with wealth ever know if she was loved for that wealth or for herself? And how could a woman with such an exquisite physique ever know if she was loved just for her body?

Achilles stared at her and at the mirror image of her with a far-off look, as if he was hypnotized. She was tempted to seduce him, not because she found him attractive, and she was beginning to find him attractive, but rather to test her powers. This body was a super weapon, and she was itching to try it out.

But maybe that wasn't her, the real her, the soul her, that felt such an attraction. Maybe this body had lusts of its own. How could she distinguish between what she wanted and what this body wanted? How could she feel responsible for what she did in this body?

What she thought and wanted had changed. How could she expect to understand what a man felt and thought in his body? She had never been a man, so how can she know how a man would respond to looking at and touching and holding a body like this one?

This priest Achilles said he was impotent when he was with his soulmate. But Breeze knew he was ready for action when she fell on top of him, just minutes after she had come to life in this body. If she wanted him, she could have him. With no need for preliminaries. His Eurydice would be irrelevant. Was that his moral flaw? Was he incapable of commitment? Or did he deserve forgiveness because this new body of hers was irresistible?

The real Achilles loved Briseis and she him. She's certain of that. Their souls and their bodies fit together like they were made for one another. But he fell for the Amazon Queen. Briseis would have been out of the picture if the Amazon had lived. He was bewitched by her at first sight. But if Briseis had had this body then ,that story would have taken a different turn. Bodymate trumped soulmate. In this body, she could have any man she wanted.

And if, in this body, she was to find the right man, someone she could feel as close to as she had to the real Achilles, and if he were to declare his love for her, how would she know if it was just this body he wanted? And would she care that was what he wanted?

Maybe that's why bodies age, so that everyone, even the most beautiful, can eventually find out if they are loved for themselves. How do the lyrics go? "When I get older, will you still need me, will you still feed me, when I'm sixty-four?"

Achilles was watching her, stupefied, speechless, and lusting for her. He couldn't help but be attracted. She was tempted to let him take this body for a test drive.

She deliberately jostled her hair to see the expression on his face as her breasts and her nether parts were exposed, then covered, then exposed again. She touched herself sensuously, as if she were alone, testing and enjoying the sensations. First his eyes focused on her naked back, then on her front through the mirror. Then their eyes met in the mirror. She blinked, then opened her eyes wide, then blinked again, letting him know, without words, that she wanted him and that she knew he wanted her. She was in no hurry. She knew she could control him, and she was going to savor every moment of this encounter.

Soon they were on autopilot. Their bodies were driverless vehicles. Their souls were along for the ride. They had no inhibitions, no second thoughts, no sense of responsibility, no concern about consequences. It was friction-less freefall into sensory bliss.

When they finished, they were exhausted, too embarrassed to look one another in the eye. They lay on the floor, motionless and silent, except for their heavy breathing. Their naked bodies were entangled. Breeze now realized that she wasn't just in somebody else's body. She was in a body with unexpected lusts and attractions and physical needs, out of sync with her true self, whatever that was. She felt animal instincts and sexual hunger with an intensity that scared her.

Having done this, she didn't know what to expect of herself. Now that it was over, she found Achilles' body ordinary. He wasn't her type. The person she was before would have ignored him, wouldn't have made eye contact with him, much less had wild sex with him.

Achilles broke the silence. "Please don't say anything about this to Eurydice. She'll be jealous seeing you in Chloe's body. What man wouldn't be attracted to you? And what woman wouldn't be jealous? She'd have been pleased if that were her body. But she'd be outraged to find somebody else in that body and that body naked with me on the floor. I need to figure out where you're going to live. You can't stay here."

"I didn't want to do this," Breeze agreed. "I'm not responsible for what this body does. It's not my body."

"And I'm not responsible for how my body responds to yours. I'm human. I had no choice."

"Great story. Tell that to Eurydice. I'm sure she'll understand."

"There's no need to mock me."

"I'm being frank. Go ahead and tell her that. That's her, isn't it, standing in the doorway behind you, watching and listening?"

35 ~ Get Thee to a Nunnery

Eurydice the priestess stood in the doorway.

At the sight of her, Julian the dog whimpered, ducked his head, and retreated to the far end of the room.

Eurydice the slave stood behind the priestess Eurydice, cautiously glancing over her shoulder.

"Let me explain," Achilles blurted out, scrambling to his feet, tripping over Breeze, falling on his face, then pulling himself back up on his chair.

"Oh, yes, you're doing research on the properties of that body that was supposed to be mine. You're thinking of me and only me. You know how much I want and need that body. You're getting ready to exorcise the demon from it. Yes, that's what it looks like. Can I help? I'd be more than happy to strangle this thing."

The two Eurydices could have been sisters. They were both short and chubby, with black hair. But while the slave was submissive and hung her head to avoid eye contact, the priestess stared with fiery eyes and took command of the situation.

"I'm surprised it's alive," the priestess went on. "When I felt it squeeze my hand, I panicked, and the whole audience of believers panicked at my panic. They all raced to get out of there, not knowing why. When I calmed down, I realized that what I felt may have been a reflex muscle movement, a twitch. The body was dead. I overreacted. The stampede was my fault. That twitch may have been a precursor to soul transfer. I rushed back and found the temple empty. I sat in a corner, alone, and prayed and cried, not understanding what had happened, not knowing what I could and should do next. An angry crowd was gathering out front. I didn't know what to expect from them. I slipped out the back and wandered the streets, trying to find my way here. I was here once before, remember, Achilles? A little over a week ago. I was the one on the floor with you then. Are you going to speak now, you cowardly wretch? Are you going to tell me what you intend to do? Are you going to kill this thing and give its body to me like you were supposed to before? Or are you going to give this crazy person to the mob for them to tear apart as a witch and then find a new body for me?"

Achilles struggled to wrap himself in his toga, then wrapped himself in blankets instead, and sat on the chair. He hoped Eurydice would calm down.

Julian the dog ducked his head under the bed.

Breeze stayed on the floor, bringing her knees to her chest, and wrapping her arms around her legs, watching the spectacle in silence.

"Do the priestesses at your temple know where you are?" asked Achilles, trying to change the subject. "We had worked out a cover story and paid bribes so you could get away briefly. If it didn't work, you could slip back, and no one would know or care. And if it did work, there would be no issue. But you've been gone far too long now. How will you explain your absence?"

"How will I explain?" she shot back. "And how do you explain this?"

The dog made squeaky scared noises from under the bed.

Achilles tried to justify himself. "I didn't know what Chloe looked like when I bought her body. She was wrapped in cloth, stretched out on a table, and the family was crowded around. The women were wailing and pulling their hair and cursing their Christian God. I had no chance to examine the body and had no need to. I needed to complete the transaction quickly, so that's what I did. I didn't care what the body looked like. All I knew was that it was an unmarried woman of marriageable age and that she had died suddenly of unknown but natural causes. I wanted that body for you, whatever that body might look like. I'd love you in any body. When we got to the temple, I had slaves prepare the body for the ceremony. At that point, I was sky-high with anticipation and joy, focusing on you and only you, calming your fears, and delighted that we'd soon be together. During the ceremony, I was so focused on you that I hardly noticed the corpse beside you. That was a magical moment. We were true soulmates. You were my other half, straight out of Plato's *Symposium*. I didn't care what body you were in. I wanted to be with you, completely and forever. We'd show that the soul is separate from the body and lives after the body dies. We'd prove that life is eternal. Like Plato said, 'Love is a longing for immortality.'"

"True love, yes, of course," replied Eurydice. "And did your soul enjoy rolling on the floor with this thing, this living dead thing?"

"I'm sorry. I'm human. I'm too human. It was a reflex. It's not my fault that men are built the way we are and that she's built the way she is. How could I be expected to resist a body like that? If I tell my leg to stay still and someone bops me on the knee and the leg pops up, is that the fault of my leg? The penis is subject to reflex reactions. I didn't tell it to get hard."

"Yes, I'm sure it's perfectly natural. You pop up when you see her and wilt when you see me."

"There's so much you don't understand about the male body. You've lived a sheltered life," he tried again.

"Not so sheltered as you might think." She laughed back at him. "What kind of a fool do you think I am? As if you could make me think that your paltry performance last week was great sex? I pity the woman who winds up with you, and that certainly won't be me. You owe me a new body. You promised. I know you can do it. And I expect you to deliver. But you won't be getting me as a prize when you're done with it. You were never going to get me. I needed you to perform your mumbo jumbo, then I'd live my new life without you. And now, you'd better deliver. If I tell the full tale of what you did and what you tried to do, you'll wish you had never lived. Corrupting the Eleusinian Mysteries for your own personal physical gratification."

"I understand." He tried to shake off her words. "You don't need to threaten me. I have an obligation to you. I'll follow through after we sort out what has happened. You don't need to remind me. No matter what the initiates of the Mysteries would think of this, the believers of your temple would want to slit my throat for having defiled their virgin priestess."

She laughed again. "You're such a fool. Take a good look at me."

"Yes. I've never seen you wear anything except your sacred garb before. And I've never seen you except with the makeup with the sacred marking on your face."

She chuckled. "You have it backward. What you thought was makeup was real. And what you now think is real is makeup." She spat on her hands and wiped her face, removing makeup and showing a dark purple mark in the shape of a crescent moon on her right cheek. "That's the birthmark that condemned me to becoming a priestess. Artemis is the goddess of the moon, and I was born with her symbol on me. My parents and the priestesses of Artemis recognized that birthmark as a sign that the goddess had chosen me. Before I was old enough to speak, I was given to the temple and consecrated for a celibate life of service to the goddess. They embroidered that shape dozens of times on my robes. I was revered as a miracle child, holy of holies. I was displayed in pageants. People came hundreds of miles to see the blessed one, the one chosen by the goddess. In a time of growing disbelief, when fewer and fewer people went to the temple and donated to the temple, I was the savior who restored faith in the goddess and filled the temple's coffers.

"I was trapped. The birthmark was a sign of the will of the goddess. I couldn't hide. I couldn't run away. Or so I thought as a child. Eventually, it dawned on me that I could cover the mark on my cheek with makeup. But by then I had bought into the system of belief and superstition. I was sure that even if people couldn't see the mark, the goddess could, and anywhere I might run and hide she'd follow me and take revenge. Many are the tales of the vengeance of Artemis. And I didn't dare to test if the stories were true, or if her powers had declined in these degraded times. When I reached puberty, they started to sell me."

"What?"

"You heard me. They sold me. Yes, this body that so limply inspires you was in high demand. Rich old men afraid of death were willing to pay a high price for intimate contact with the chosen one of Artemis. For my clients, I was their way to get in touch with divinity. That I was young and a virgin, and that making love with me would be a sacrilege for an ordinary man, made the experience all the more titillating. The priestesses who sold me told each customer that he was the only one, that the goddess had chosen him because of his saintliness and his generosity to the temple, and that he must swear to secrecy on pain of angering the goddess, a vengeful goddess. The sales pitch worked well. The customers were primed to believe anything. All it took was some lamb's blood skillfully applied for each to believe that he had deflowered me. And there were some who came back dozens of times and believed that the goddess had restored my virginity so they could take it again.

"The other priestesses are old crones. You can hardly blame them for what they did. There are few believers in our day, and the cult of Artemis is in competition with other cults that advertise the services of temple prostitutes. Sex with me was secret and forbidden, making it all the more desirable. I could spin erotic fantasies that drove men wild. I could make clients feel manly and well satisfied even when they couldn't perform.

"Emperor Julian's largess went to the Eleusinian Mysteries, not to the temple of Artemis. Our temple depends on my services to generate the cash needed to pay the bills, to support the entire community. I could return to the temple at any time, and the priestesses would say and do whatever was necessary to explain my absence. They'd make a miracle of it. Perhaps the goddess invited me to visit her on Olympus. They'd find a way to tell the story such that clients would be willing to pay even higher prices to get their hands on this body of mine, this body I'd so like to get rid of.

"Yes, I had more than one reason to get rid of this body, not just the birthmark, also the tactile memories of what I've done with it. I'm disgusted by this body. Maybe that's why you couldn't respond to it. You sensed my disgust. I wasn't surprised. Some of my clients have reacted that way in the past. The religious sales ladies convinced them that the problem was that they hadn't been saintly enough or generous enough to the temple, and the goddess was punishing them for that. If they wanted the true divine experience, they must be even more generous when they came back again.

"Don't get me wrong. Many of the men succeeded. Many were well satisfied. I'm many times over not a virgin. But I've dealt with men with your problem before and considered their non-performance as a blessing. I had hoped it would be different with you because with you it wasn't a business transaction. With you, I was acting of my own free will. But you were a disappointment.

"I loathe sex with this body, having had to do it so many times with dried up old men who needed fantasy and manipulation to get them going. And you were no better than them. In any case, I need a new body, and you'll get it for me."

A deep loud voice from outside interrupted her, "Chloe? Are you in there, Chloe? What have they done to you? I'm here for you. I'll save you. Achilles, you bastard crazy pagan magician, give me my Chloe. I hear that you brought her back to life. Thank you. But she's mine, not yours. I love her, and I own her. End of story. Do you understand? Give her to me now, or I'll tear you to pieces."

36 ~ I Need Some Body to Love

Achilles shouted, "Orpheus, open the door before he breaks it down."

The visitor ducked to get through the entrance. His muscles had muscles. If Chloe had the body of a goddess, this man had the body of a god. The two bodies looked like they were made for one another. He raced to her and took her in his arms.

But Chloe wasn't Chloe. She was Breeze, and Breeze backed off, pushed him away. She said, "I don't know you. Leave me alone, you brute."

She tried to knee him in the groin, but he twisted out of the way, pinning her arms behind her back.

"You must be Ajax," guessed Achilles, "the man that Chloe was betrothed to before she died."

"Well, obviously, she isn't dead," said Ajax. "Whatever she was and whatever you've done to her, she isn't dead."

"But that's not Chloe," insisted Achilles, pulling blankets around himself and backing away from the furious intruder.

"Stop the nonsense. I know Chloe. We were to be married today. What did you do to her? How did you wipe out her memory? Did you drug her? She'll snap out of it. She'll remember. But even if she never remembers, this is the woman I love. This is the woman I want. This is the woman I own."

"I'm not Chloe," Breeze shouted, spitting in his face.

He wiped the spit off and smiled, "You have spunk, my love. I don't blame you for being confused. It's not your fault that this pagan charlatan abused you with his would-be magic. But you're mine. And the sooner you realize that the better. That's your body, your voice, your smile, the way your curly blond tresses fall to your hips. The way you twitch your shoulders and rumple your nose. You're my love. You'll always be my love."

"This is the body you loved, but not the person," Breeze countered.

"Absurd."

"This is the body of Chloe. But I'm someone else. My name is Breeze, Briseis."

Ajax burst out in laughter. "Enough jokes. Not now. Now is the time for us to hug, to celebrate that you're back from wherever you've been. Call it chance. Or call it a miracle. Say the doctor blundered, and you never died. Or say you were resurrected, and praise God. Who cares how you wound up alive? Come home with me. Let's hold the wedding today, as planned. Let's begin our new life together."

He let go of her to get a better grip, so he could sling her over his shoulder. But she slithered away, stepped back, stumbled, and fell to the stone floor, banging and scraping her left knee.

Ajax and Achilles both ran to her rescue and, together, lift her onto the bed. Achilles fetched a pitcher of water from his desk, then let Ajax gently wash the scratch.

Watching him in action, Achilles laughed.

"And what do you find funny about this?" asked Ajax.

Achilles explained, "I love a woman for her soul, regardless of what body she might have. And you love a woman for her body, regardless of what soul she might have."

Ajax dismissed him, "Enough of your pagan nonsense."

Breeze lay passive, disoriented, surrendering her leg to Ajax, with no idea what might happen to her next. When this body hurt, she felt the pain. Like it or not, this was her body now. She pulled blankets closer around her. If Ajax tried again to force her to leave with him, she'd kick him hard in the groin.

"I'm not Chloe," she insisted. "When Chloe died, her soul left this body, and not long after that, my soul entered this body. If you're a Christian, surely you believe in the soul."

"Yes, of course," he replied flippantly, humoring his beloved, who might be in a playful mood or might be confused at the shock of coming back to life. "We each have an immortal soul. And when we die, that soul leaves the body. If we are true believers in Christ and have lived in accordance with His will, we are saved and go to Heaven, to join the true believers who have gone before and to live in eternal bliss. But there's only one soul per body, love. And the soul only leaves the body when we die. And if through God's grace, miraculously, someone returns from the dead, the soul returns to the same body. Now hug me and kiss me, and let's get on with our new life together."

Breeze pulled back, swung her legs around and stood, bracing herself by keeping a hand on the bed, to take the weight off her sore leg.

"The soul is separate from the body," said Achilles. "Some say that the soul leaves the body not just when you die, but also when you sleep."

"Pagan nonsense." Ajax chuckled.

"Some say that the same soul can be reborn again and again in different bodies," Achilles persisted.

"Chloe, you don't believe that pagan nonsense, do you? You know better than that. When your family heard you had come to life, they ran to the church and rang the bells for joy, and told everyone that you had been singled out by Christ for the miracle of resurrection. When you appear before our congregation, your friends and relatives who wept over your dead body, their screams of joy will rock the city. Thousands of pagans will convert to Christianity when they see and hear the good news that you were dead and now you live. You will be tangible proof of Christ's power and his mercy. Let them rejoice. I don't care about theology. I don't need to explain the unexplainable. All I care about is you, having you back"

"Stay away from me," she shouted, stretching out her hands to keep him back. Then she appealed to Achilles, "Please save me from this madman."

Achilles intervened, "Back off, Ajax. The lady needs time and space to sort out who and what she is. How can we imagine what it's like to die and then come back to life? What would we remember from before? Any promises she made to you before her death were canceled by that death. At death, you did part. Regardless of whether there's a soul, regardless of whether the soul in her body is the same soul as before, this woman is a new person with a new life, born not of woman and man, but rather born of a miracle, unlike any miracle that I've ever heard of."

Ajax raised his hands in frustration and took charge of the conversation. "You don't know anything about her. You don't know how she died, if she really died. Nor does her family. I was there. Her father lost his job last year when Emperor Julian decreed that Christians couldn't teach rhetoric, literature, and philosophy. Lord only knows why Julian did that. Maybe just to show that he could, to give the bishops and archbishops notice that he's going to knock the Christian church down a notch. Her father went from being one of the wealthiest men in Eleusis to being destitute. He had three marriageable daughters, and he could no longer afford dowries for them. He wanted to put them all in a nunnery. Before that, he'd never have considered me as a suitor. I wasn't rich enough or socially elite enough for his daughter. I inherited my family's farm and cattle, but I have no education. I'm not in her class. I fell in love with her just from the look of her, and I admired her from afar. Then when I heard that her father had fallen on hard times, I offered to take her as my wife with no dowry. And I converted to Christianity, to eliminate that barrier. Chloe didn't want to go to a nunnery. She was flattered by my offer, and that I was willing to convert and to do anything else that might help to win her. And she wanted me for my body, too. Our bodies are a perfect match. She could see that as well as I could. The date for our wedding was set for today. She invited me to her bed last night. She was impatient to make love with me and wanted the intensity that would come from doing something forbidden. As we had planned, I climbed in through her bedroom window. We were afraid that her father would find us in the act, and we were both sky-high from the intensity of the moment. She had an immense orgasm and collapsed in my arms.

"She has an amazing body. Aphrodite herself would choose such a body if she wished to take human form and enjoy human pleasures. When Chloe went limp in my arms, that's what I thought had happened. The goddess of love had possessed her and had suggested such a reckless adventure, and having satisfied herself, the goddess left her body. But then I couldn't arouse her. Her heart had stopped. She wasn't breathing. I screamed, and her father came running. He sounded the alarm, and the whole family assembled, and the dogs began their death howl. That's when I realized she hadn't just fainted. She had died. This was a corpse in my arms. I fled in horror.

"Only later did I hear the rumors that her father had sold her corpse for a fortune, that some pagan priest magician claimed he could bring her back to life, but rather than asking her family to pay for her resurrection, he was paying them on condition that once she was restored to life, she'd be his.

"The terms made no sense. You offered a ridiculously large sum. What you claimed you could do was impossible. And if you didn't succeed, you'd return the corpse to them for burial, and pay for the burial, and they could keep all that you had paid for the body as well.

"It was clear to me that this was bogus. You were obsessed with Chloe, just as I was. I can't blame you for that. There was no way her Christian father would let her marry the high priest of the Eleusinian Mysteries. You probably heard that she and I were getting married. You paid off a household slave to lace her food or drink with a drug that would make her fall into a coma, and it would look like she was dead. Then you rushed over and made your fabulous offer before the drug wore off. And by the strange terms of your contract, when she woke up, she'd belong to you. She'd be your property to own as a slave or to marry as a wife.

"As soon as I figured that out, I raced to your temple. When you weren't there, I asked around and found your home. And now I'm here, to put an end to your nonsense. She's mine. And I'll take her now, or I'll take legal action to get what's mine."

Achilles objected, "Nonsense. Total nonsense. Though I do commend your creativity. You should write a play with a plot like that, with mistakes and heartache and confusion when a beautiful young woman seems dead, but really isn't. Bravo for your storytelling. But you have no legal right to this woman. You aren't her husband. Her father might contest the contract, but I don't think he wants to. I'm sure he's delighted that his beloved daughter is alive. But he wants the money, so he'll let me keep her, as agreed. As for you, if you wanted to contest this issue in court, you'd have no standing."

"On the contrary, I'm the father," Ajax insisted.

"The what?" asked Achilles.

"The father of her baby."

"This is too much. What are you talking about?" asked Breeze.

He answered, "At the moment of climax, I felt it, I knew it, and you must have, as well. That moment was unlike any lovemaking I had had before. You had this look of ecstasy on your face, and then you weren't there. Your body went limp. I screamed. Your father came running. The grief, the shame. I was devastated, paralyzed with disbelief, as your father pounded me with his fists and your mother and sisters cried and tore their hair and prayed to Heaven to undo what had been done, prayed the Father, Son, and Holy Ghost to forgive your sins and bring you back to life. When the dogs started howling, I jumped out the window and wandered the streets in grief and despair. Later I heard that this priest arrived in less than an hour and showered your father with gold and took away the body that I loved. Now you're alive again, Chloe. Our sins are forgiven. We have a new chance. And I feel certain that the life we started in your womb lives, too. I'm sure that you are with child, with our child. It's a miracle. We're blessed. And no one can keep us apart."

"You're out of your mind," Breeze persisted. "You do it once with this body, and you're certain you fathered a child? "

He smiled broadly. "Well, to tell the truth, it wasn't just once. We coupled many times over the last month, discreetly, when and where there was no danger of discovery. But none of those times was the climax as earth-shaking as that one yesterday."

Breeze stared in disbelief, but Ajax's words prompted a gut-twisting doubt. She had no idea if the body she was in was pregnant. And she had no idea if she could be pregnant from the life she was in before this one and if pregnancy there could have carried over to here. She thought she was on the pill, but she didn't know if pills taken when she was in her old body would have any effect in this new body here. And she had no idea if her wild, unexpected roll on the floor just minutes ago with Achilles might have impregnated her. So not only did she not know if she was pregnant, she also didn't know who the father might be.

She looked at Achilles, then at Ajax, this godlike hunk of a man. Then she looked at Achilles again. If she had to have one or the other, which would she choose? What if Achilles and Ajax could swap bodies, if she could have Achilles in the body of Ajax, a body that was very much like the body of the real Achilles, the Achilles of the Trojan War? She felt a tingle in her nipples. She never had sensations like that before.

She never had thoughts like that before. This new body was sexually charged, easily aroused.

Then she noticed Eurydice, staring in awe at Ajax, knowing that if the ritual had gone the way it was supposed to, she'd be in Chloe's body now and this godlike Ajax would be hers. It was clear from the look on her face that Eurydice lusted for Ajax.

Seeing Breeze staring so intently at Eurydice, Ajax turned to look at Eurydice himself. "What's that on your face?" he asked her abruptly.

Eurydice was lost in thought or fantasy and didn't respond.

"Is that dirt on your cheek? Or makeup?" Ajax asked. "Why would you have a mark like that? What does that mean to you?"

Eurydice blinked, then touched her cheek with her fingers. She wiped off the makeup. The birthmark was showing. She covered it with her hands. "I've lived with that my whole life." Tears ran down her cheeks. "The priestesses of Artemis said this is a sign from the goddess. It means that I'm blessed, that the goddess chose me to serve her. My birthmark is a holy mark, not a random mistake. I'm ordinary in every other way. My body is nothing in comparison to that marvel of physical beauty that you lust for. But I have a mark of divinity. I'm entitled to some respect for that."

Ajax walked over to Eurydice and gently touched her birthmark. "I meant you no disrespect. I'm shocked, that's all. That's my brand. You were born with my brand, the brand with which I and my father and his father have marked our cattle. If I didn't know better, I'd say that you were fated to belong to me."

He shook his head in disbelief, then rushed back to Chloe, lifted her onto his shoulder, and strode out the door.

Breeze was caught by surprise. She was outraged to be treated that way. But she felt her muscles respond to his muscles, as she settled comfortably with her head cradled on his shoulder, just before she blacked out.

37 ~ Post Traumatic Death Syndrome

When Breeze woke up again, she was lying on a bench in a large hall with marble walls and pillars. Ajax, Achilles, and Eurydice were standing nearby, facing the front of the room, where a man on a platform, flanked by a pair of Roman soldiers, glared down at them with an air of authority.

"Who's the plaintiff in this case?"

Eurydice and Ajax both answered, "I am, your honor."

"One at a time, please. We must keep order. Young lady, what's your name?"

"I am Eurydice, priestess of Artemis."

"I see in the notes that this case involves the Eleusinian Mysteries. Yes, I understand that Emperor Julian, our dear supreme leader, has seen fit to grant special protection and privileges to the Eleusinian Mysteries, so any issue having to do with that comes to me, as a representative of the government. But what does Artemis have to do with that? Those are two different cults. You people have so many gods, how do you keep them all straight? The Christians have the right idea — one God, one bureaucracy. Why are you here? Why are you taking my time? Let's get this over with."

Eurydice pointed at Achilles, "I charge this man, the high priest of the Eleusinian Mysteries, with grand larceny."

"What has he stolen?"

"My body," she replied.

"The theft of a cadaver is a serious matter. That's more than ordinary larceny."

"And he didn't just steal it, your honor. He desecrated it."

"In what way did he desecrate it?"

"By bringing it back to life."

"What nonsense is this? Where's the body in question?"

Eurydice walked over to Breeze, who was now standing and shaking her head, like trying to wake up from a bad dream. The long blond hair waved back and forth hit Eurydice in the face and got in her mouth. Eurydice spit the hair out and backed away.

"Here it stands," she answered

"That's not a dead body," noted the judge.

"Of course not. He brought it back to life."

"You mean the priest of the Mysteries?"

"Yes, Achilles, the one with the bruise on his face."

"And that is your body, you say?"

"Yes, of course, it's mine," she asserted.

"In what sense is that your body? Is she your slave?"

"No. That body was promised to me. That body was supposed to be me. I was supposed to be in that body. She's wearing it now, but I should."

"You claim that this woman here has no right to the body that she is now in? You say that her body should be your body?"

"Yes, my soul should be in that body."

"And what soul should be in the body you now occupy?"

"This body should be empty and dead."

"You're asserting that a crime has been committed because your body isn't dead. And you claim that that woman over there is occupying a body that should be yours, that you should be in the body that she's in?"

"Your honor, this may sound foolish, but it's well-grounded in what we all believe. Christians as well as believers in the traditional gods all agree that everyone has a body and a soul."

"Yes, that sounds right."

"Well, that body over there is my body, but someone else's soul is in it."

"Let me get this straight. A body without a soul is a dead body."

"Yes, of course."

"And a body with a soul is alive."

"Yes."

"You are alive."

"Yes."

"Then you must have a soul."

"Yes."

"Then what has been taken from you?"

"My body, that body, like I told you."

"Then whose body is the one I'm talking to now, the body where your soul is right now?"

"This is my old body, the body I should have left behind."

"You're saying that you wanted to take her body. Aren't you then the would-be thief?"

"Her body was promised to me by him, the high priest of the Eleusinian Mysteries, Achilles."

"And how could he promise you any body at all, much less her body?"

"He's a master of witchcraft, and that body was empty, it was dead."

"It isn't dead now."

"Exactly."

"Then whose body is it?"

"Mine, like I said."

"Then whose soul is in it now?"

"Some demon has possessed it."

"Slow down now, young lady. A soul can only be in one body at a time. Right?"

"Yes."

"And you're in this one, not that one."

"That's the problem."

"And who is the soul who resides there now?"

"A demon who calls herself Briseis."

"Who is Briseis, and where does she come from?"

Breeze pushed Eurydice aside and interrupted, "I am Briseis, your honor. And I plead habeas corpus."

"What?"

"That's Latin, isn't it?"

"Yes, but what do you mean by it?"

"I have this body. And I have the right to what I have. It's mine. I'm me. I'm a woman with the right to make choices about my own body." The phrases came to her naturally, though she wasn't sure what they mean. "I have the right to life, the right to as many lives as I can have."

"What's this nonsense?" shouted the judge.

Ajax stepped forward, head bowed respectfully, and explained, "Please pardon her, your honor. Since her death, Chloe sometimes speaks in tongues. She has trouble remembering, and she says things that don't make sense. The doctor says it's temporary. She'll snap out of it. She's my betrothed, your honor. We were to be married today. I'm here to plead her case because she is in no condition to plead for herself. I'm hoping you'll rule that I can take her home so we can marry."

"You aren't married to her now?"

"That's right."

"Then she belongs to her father. Why isn't he here?"

Ajax answered, "Over my objection, despite our betrothal, her father sold her to this priest of the Eleusinian Mysteries."

"Sold her? As a bride? Or as a slave?"

"As a corpse, your honor. He thought she was dead, and this priest offered him a fortune for the body so he could use it in a pagan ritual to try to bring her back to life. If that didn't work, her father would get the body back for burial and could keep the money. If she came back to life, the priest would get to keep her. Her father is delighted that she's alive and is also delighted to have the money he was paid. He doesn't want to challenge the contract for the body. That's why I'm here to plead her case, to free her from the clutches of this pagan priest, to save her from having to go through further horrors. I love her, your honor. I want to marry her. And she loves me, your honor, as she'd say if she could speak for herself."

Breeze objected. "I can speak for myself. I don't know this man."

Ajax explained, "As you see, your honor, she's not in her right mind."

Eurydice stepped forward and protested, "She's not in her right body, either."

Ajax continued, "She doesn't know who she is or where she is or when she is."

The judge asked, "And how do you account for that?"

Ajax replied, "She's forgotten me, her family, and everything that happened before she died. Her family doctor, the doctor who pronounced her dead, has every hope that she'll recover."

"A fine doctor he is," objected Breeze.

Ajax continued, "The doctor thinks it's amnesia, brought on by death and resurrection."

"Post-traumatic death syndrome." Breeze laughed. She didn't know what that meant, but she found it hilarious.

Ajax explained, "You see, your honor, she speaks nonsense and laughs like she's crazy. Death can do that to a person, or so the doctor told me."

"I'm not dead," Breeze protested.

"Have you ever been dead?" asked the judge.

"Have you?" she replied. "How do you know if you've lived before and died, once, twice, even a million times? I'm no different from you, except I know I've lived before, or I almost know that."

"In the name of Hades, what is she talking about?" roared the judge.

"Yes, your honor," Eurydice insisted "She comes from Hades, and I'd like to send her back. Send the demon, not the body—that's mine."

Achilles pushed Eurydice aside and objected, "Please, your honor, may I have my say? I feel responsible for this young woman in the body that used to be Chloe. She wouldn't be alive now if it weren't for me. She's a different person now than the Chloe this man was betrothed to. The body's the same, but she's someone else. She doesn't come from our world. She has no friends or family or possessions here. She's helpless. I have a contractual right to her, as Ajax here testified. And I have a moral duty to help her get started in her new life."

"Enough. I've heard more than enough. This case is outside the range of my knowledge and authority. Get out of here. All of you."

"But, your honor," objected Eurydice, "where can we go? What can we do?"

"Civil courts, like this one, deal with questions of property. For questions about souls, you should go to a religious court."

"Which court, your honor?" asked Achilles. "Ajax is Christian. Eurydice is a priestess of Artemis. And I'm a priest of the Eleusinian Mysteries. Who has jurisdiction?"

"Clerk, remind me, who is the plaintiff?"

The clerk replied, "Eurydice, a priestess of Artemis, your honor."

"Thank you. Then it's up to her to decide which court to go to next."

"Let it be a Christian court," she answered.

"Why that's preposterous," objected Achilles.

"It's her right to choose, and choose she has," decreed the judge. "Next case."

38 ~ Game of Gods

Standing in front of the crucifix and the altar at the front of a Christian church and waiting for a bishop to hear their case, Ajax sat Breeze down and pulled her close with her head on his shoulder. He patted her back, like patting the back of a crying baby. "Just shut your eyes and rest. I'll take care of this. You'll be all right. This is my church. The bishop visits here often. He knows your father. He won't turn you over to a pagan priest. You can count on that. Just stay calm and quiet, and we'll do fine."

Meanwhile, Achilles whispered to Eurydice, "Why did you choose a Christian court? Did you hear what Ajax said? He knows the man who's going to judge this case. And there's no way a Christian bishop will rule in favor a pagan priest or priestess. So why did you move the case here?"

"I wouldn't stand a chance in any traditional religious court going against the high priest of the Eleusinian Mysteries. I'd rather take my chances here. Besides," she smiled, "I've met this bishop before in a professional capacity."

"You what?"

"I did everything he wanted."

The bishop entered alone and explained, "Since two of the parties in this dispute, Chloe and Ajax, are members of this church, I've decided to hear this case in private. We shouldn't have to do this formally as a matter of canon law. Rather, I will act as an arbitrator, helping to bring you to a resolution that you all can live with.

"I've read a summary from the clerk of the civil court. If I understand correctly, you, Eurydice, want custody of Chloe, a member of this church. And you, Ajax, her betrothed, want her as well. I gather that the dispute arose when Chloe died and then came back to life, and now she doesn't remember who she is and can't competently speak for herself.

"The high priest of the Mysteries is claiming ownership of her by contract. That's a bizarre contract unlike anything I've ever seen. And the civil court has ruled that this is a matter of souls, rather than a matter of tangible property. That means the contract is invalid. As for you,

Eurydice, as a priestess of Artemis, what claim could you have on Chloe, and why do you want her?"

"Your worship, Chloe died and is still dead. What you see here is an animated corpse. The Jews call such an abomination a *golem*. It doesn't have a soul, or it has the soul of a demon. It certainly doesn't have the soul of Chloe. It speaks gibberish."

"Can you speak for yourself, Chloe?"

"I sing the raft of Achilles," she replied drunkenly. "Gricks may rise and Troysirs fall, that's what makes life-work leaving."

The bishop smiled again, "I see what you mean, Eurydice. Ajax, do you agree that this isn't Chloe?"

"No, your worship. She's saying strange things, and she can't remember. But that's temporary. I'm sure of that. And her doctor is sure of that, too. I'm asking for custody of her until she's herself again."

"I don't have experience with resurrection, nor, I am sure, do you. The Gospels tell of the resurrection of Lazarus as well as the resurrection of Christ. In those cases, there was no loss of memory and no madness. But there have been reported instances of possession by demons and animation of objects and even of corpses. As Eurydice says, those are called *golems*. For the sake of argument, let's assume that you are correct, Eurydice, and that is not Chloe in Chloe's body. What do you want?"

"I want the high priest of the Mysteries to transfer my soul to that body."

"Let me get this straight. You believe that it is possible to move your soul into that body which we knew as Chloe before she died. And you believe that after the transfer you will continue to be you, with the same thoughts and memories, that you will be the same person you are now, but you will be in that body?"

"Yes, your worship. Imagine me with that body."

"Well, young lady, there's nothing wrong with your present body, but I do see your point. I can imagine your wanting to make that change if it were possible."

"Yes, your worship, and then I'd no longer be constrained by the religious vows with which my father shackled me when I was an infant."

"I believe I understand your argument, but I don't believe for a moment that what you propose is possible," the bishop objected.

"That's because you didn't see what happened in the ritual, your worship. I lay down on the altar next to a dead body. The priest administered the drug and said the sacred words. Then the body's hand squeezed my hand. The corpse came alive. The essence of what the priest was trying to do worked. The body got a new soul, but it wasn't my soul. Instead, a demon entered that body, a demon that speaks in tongues and makes no sense. It doesn't belong here. Kill it. Put it out of its misery and let us do the ritual again. This time, I'm sure, I'll get the right body, that body."

"Let's speak frankly," the bishop addressed all four of them. "You know and I know that this is nonsense. But you, Achilles, did a remarkable job of convincing people that your miracle worked. To me, that's interesting."

"What do you mean, your worship?" asked Achilles.

"I don't know how you produced that illusion. But your ability to do so has potential. You could do a great service for the Christian church."

The Bishop began to warm to this exotic case. "As you know, the rivalry between Christianity and paganism is at a critical point. In a few short centuries, Christianity went from being a persecuted minority to becoming the dominant religion of the Empire. But now, thanks to Emperor Julian, Christianity is no longer the state religion. All religions are now equal under law. Julian is bolstering Judaism by rebuilding the Temple of Solomon, and he's bolstering paganism by endowing and protecting the Eleusinian Mysteries. The secret of the Mysteries is the most credible element of your traditional religion. Everything else is obvious fakery. By preserving the secret of the Mysteries, you have fueled belief in supernatural powers beyond the ken of man and outside the purview of Christianity. If we could discredit the Mysteries, we could convert hundreds, if not thousands of pagans, saving their eternal souls, and the Christian church could triumph in our lifetime, despite the Emperor. The government has transferred this case to me. By so doing, it has turned you, the high priest of the Mysteries, over to my authority. That means that I can do what I like with you, up to and including torture. The protection of the Emperor does not extend here.

"There's no point in debating theology. I want you to put on a soul-transference show like the one you did yesterday. Do it in front of an audience of your believers. Only this time, after you've fooled everyone, the bodies will stand up and admit that it was all a fraud and testify that the Christian God is the one true God and that the Mysteries are an abomination that must be shut down. Hallelujah. Got it?"

The bishop continued, "Fundamentally, there's not much difference between our religions. Yes, the believers talk like they're bitter enemies. They get emotional. They get angry. They get into fistfights. Sometimes they kill one another. But they're playing the same game.

"The god of this and the god of that. The patron saint of this and the patron saint of that. The one side prays to the statue of a god and the other to the statue of a saint. Life itself and what comes before it and what comes after it, those are mysteries that no one understands.

"The common people need answers. They need to believe that there are answers and that those answers are knowable. If anyone challenges the accepted answers, the public bristles and protests. Never challenge fundamental beliefs. Rather, find ways to say what you need to say in the context that they feel comfortable with. This case gives us an opportunity to do that, to refute pagan teachings, and nudge the public toward Christianity. Do what I say, Achilles, and the Mysteries will be discredited, and Christian beliefs will be affirmed. Do it well, and I'll find a post for you in the church. You could go far. Just prove to me that you can do this."

"What?"

"Your show. Your performance. You talk a good talk, like a carnival magician. But can you do a convincing repeat performance? It seems I have more faith in your showmanship than you have in yourself. In any case, I want you to do the best you can, right now. Give me a demonstration. If your act is as good as I think it might be, I'll bet on you. I'll make arrangements. I'll make sure the audience for the real show has a sprinkling of loud and loyal Christians, to cheer you on when you betray the Mysteries and praise the Lord God."

"You want me to do that here and now?" asked Achilles, incredulous.

"Yes. Put on a show for me, here and now."

"But this isn't a trick. What Eurydice described actually happened."

"Then make it happen again. Now."

"But I don't have the potion or the notes I need for the incantation."

"Fetch whatever you need. I'll give you an hour to get ready. I'm not asking for perfection, just an indication of your sleight-of-hand abilities."

"But there's no corpse. It's important to have the fresh corpse of a woman of marriageable age who didn't die of disease, and whose body hasn't begun to decompose."

"Why not use the same one?"

"But she's alive."

"I'm sure we can solve that problem quickly. If we smother her, that won't hurt the body. We could do that right before your act, so the corpse is fresh."

Ajax interrupted, frantic, "But your worship, you haven't addressed my side of the issue. Of course, the battle between Christianity and paganism is important, and maybe this magician's tricks can help discredit the Mysteries. But what about Chloe, my Chloe? I need to be with her, and she needs to be with me. Don't kill my Chloe."

"There's no reason to kill her," Achilles quickly agreed with Ajax. "I can do this without a dead body," he improvised, not knowing how he could do that, but needing to delay.

"Dead or alive, whatever it takes," the bishop replied. "What matters is whether you want to work with me and benefit from my favor, or to work against me and feel the full wrath of the Christian church. I want you to do a trial performance for me here and now, and then put on a public performance to discredit the Eleusinian Mysteries later. Have no fear. I'll protect you and find an important post for you in the church. Remember, young man, the Emperor Julian is an aberration, a bump on the road to the future. He won't last long, and when he's gone, the church, the one true church of the one true God will triumph, and for the rest of time up until the Second Coming, the church will be the source of temporal as well as spiritual power. And you could be one of the heroes in our struggle against paganism. You could be powerful and wealthy in this world, and a saint in the next."

"And what's the alternative?"

"We could go back to the way things were before this complaint arose. Then Chloe here would become a dead body again, to be buried by her grieving family."

39 ~ Soul Swapping

Achilles dashed back to his quarters to get what he needed for a repeat performance. While he had no expectation that the ritual would succeed this time, he had no choice but to try. When it didn't work, he'd improvise and muddle through.

He was disoriented not just by a dead body coming to life with an unknown soul, but also by the transformation of Eurydice. Yesterday she was a virginal priestess who was in love with him. Now she was a temple prostitute who cared nothing for him.

As for this other woman with an alien soul and a heavenly body, whoever she was and wherever she came from, she wouldn't be here if it weren't for him. He felt responsible for her. She was helpless here. And her lost-puppy helplessness would have drawn him to her, even if the physical attraction hadn't been intense. He needed to help her, or she might end up dead or locked up as a crazy person.

He also had to explain to his congregation the failure of his much-anticipated miracle. And he had to justify his involvement with the Christians. He chose a Christian body for his ceremony, and he paid a fortune from the temple's coffers to obtain the body. Then the ceremony failed, and he didn't get the money back. That looked like fraud for personal gain. Now he was spending time in a Christian church, involved with a Christian court. That could be construed as a breach of the secrecy of the Mysteries, and on such a charge not only his position as high priest, but also his life would be in jeopardy, regardless of the emperor's personal friendship.

To save Briseis and to give himself a way out of this mess, he needed to impress this bishop, performing the ritual for him in a Christian church instead of in the temple and with no dead body, but rather two live women. When he performed the ritual the first time, he had confidence that if he did everything as recorded in the sacred texts, he could transfer a soul from a living woman to a dead body. He had brought about a soul transfer, but he hadn't anticipated the arrival of an alien soul. Now he had to do it all over again, with key elements of the procedure changed beyond his control. He wished he believed in the gods he served so he could pray to them with hope that they'd listen and help.

Meanwhile, Ajax, Breeze, and Eurydice stayed at the church, waiting for Achilles to return.

Breeze, oblivious to what is going on around her, did stretching exercises and ran in place. Her leg injury was just a scratch. She hardly noticed it now. She was getting used to her new body.

Ajax sat and stared at her, confused by what had happened and by the bishop's heartless reaction. He was shocked by the new Chloe. She had the same body as before, but she was very different in manner. Her style, her presence, even the way she stood and walked, the way she moved this amazing body of hers was different. She was unpredictable, uninhibited, full of life. If she could just remember who she was and talk like a normal human being, he could love this Chloe even more than the one he loved before.

On his return, Achilles found Briseis stretching, Ajax staring at her, and Eurydice asleep on the floor. He picked up Eurydice to carry her to a couch. Then a disturbing thought occurred to him. Maybe the popular belief was true. Maybe the soul left the body during sleep, then returned when you awoke. If that was true, he shouldn't move her while she slept or her soul might not find its way back to her body. He had trouble enough as it was with bodies and souls. He'd better not add to his problems through foolishness.

He brushed the hair from her eyes and caressed her cheek. Then he shook her.

She responded with a twitch and a start. Then she jumped to her feet, stood with uncertain balance, and shook her head. "What was in that potion you gave me?" she demanded.

"Zeus," he exclaimed. "I didn't take that into account."

"What?"

"You still have that potion in your system. And Briseis does as well. Her strangeness may be an after-effect of the potion, not just the trauma of coming to life in someone else's body. I need to adjust the dosage for our performance in front of the bishop. And I don't know how much, and that's a life-or-death decision."

"What?" she challenged him. "You haven't a clue what you're doing? It's only by chance that I'm alive now?"

"I followed the sacred texts to the letter," he whispered back. "I had full confidence."

"But you don't have confidence now?"

"It's humbling how little we know about life and death, about the soul and what it's capable of. I did my best, and I'll do my best once again."

"And I'm supposed to be reassured by that? From the look of you, you want to try this for real this second time. You aren't going to just put on a fake show to appease the bishop. You're going to risk my life again."

"You want that body, don't you?" he replied. "And if I don't do anything, Briseis is as good as dead."

Achilles laid out his ingredients on a table and began grinding leaves in a pestle with a mortar, like an apothecary. He wore gloves and covered his mouth and nose with cloth.

When the bishop returned, he was pleased to see the display of paraphernalia. "Well done," he congratulated Achilles. "All the trappings of alchemy. Most impressive. Is that parsley?" he asked.

"No, that's poison hemlock."

"Those aren't hemlock needles."

"Of course not. Poison hemlock has nothing to do with hemlock trees. It's a weed that looks like parsley and is deadly. Just touching it can make you sick. Eating a few leaves will kill you. Paralysis starts at the feet and moves upward until it reaches the lungs and shuts them down. You've read Plato's *Apology*? That's how Socrates died."

"Now I understand. That's how you'll kill the body possessed by a demon. But smothering her would be easier."

"No. I don't want to kill her. As I said before, that isn't necessary. Hemlock is an important ingredient of the potion. It's dangerous alone but mixed in the right proportion with the other ingredients, it helps free the soul from the body."

"What are the other ingredients?"

"A kind of mushroom that severs the connection between the mind and the sense organs, letting the mind float freely because the soul can only leave the body in conjunction with the mind."

"And what are those liquids?" asked the bishop.

"Those aren't part of the potion. Rather, they're for use in case of emergency. There's no antidote for poison hemlock. The best you can do is induce vomiting, clear the air passage, then give a little ammonia and distilled wine."

"And those long sharp needles?"

"In case of severe headaches, I'll stick those needles in their feet."

The bishop was amused "I like your style. Is your sleight of hand as good as your talk?"

"I realize you don't believe what I'm saying, but any of these ingredients in the wrong quantities could lead to seizures and death. I have to measure everything precisely as told in the sacred writings."

"And if you blunder, they both might die?" The bishop laughed. "Great showmanship. And the magic words? I presume you have them memorized."

"There are incantations from the sacred writings. The believers expect them, and I'll speak them. But it's the potion that does the work."

The bishop smiled, "As I expected."

"Everything depends on the potion, the right ingredients in the right proportions, mixed in the right order."

"That's the spirit. Keep in mind that I want you to do this with style. For the real show, I want you to put on an extravaganza. The more glitter and flash, the less likely people will be to look closely and figure out that it's fake. I want the revelation at the end to come as a surprise."

"But this isn't fake."

"Yes, of course. I'm sure that's what you say to your initiates. By the way, what cover story do you have for them?"

"Cover story?"

"Your explanation for what went wrong yesterday and for why you think this will work the second time around."

"The sacred books are copies of copies of copies. The original scroll crumbled to dust generations ago. Only by copying are books preserved. But every time they are copied is an opportunity for mistakes to be introduced by human error or deliberately if the copyist were to try to sabotage our religion. That's my excuse. The text was corrupted, perhaps by a Christian spy."

"Do you believe that?"

"Of course not, but it's plausible. I'll say that, after my first try, I found an uncorrupted copy of a key passage, so we'll have a better chance of success this time. If I fail again, I'll say that was another instance of sabotage."

The bishop patted him on the back, "You're a kindred spirit. And what should I expect to see in today's demonstration?"

"These circumstances are far removed from the first attempt in the temple. I don't know what will happen. Probably nothing."

"Or maybe they'll both die?" The bishop and laughed. "Great showmanship."

On Achilles' prompting, Eurydice and Breeze lay down beside one another and held hands. Achilles poured the potion into their mouths. They both lost consciousness.

Achilles intoned the incantation.

Nothing happened. Both bodies were motionless.

Achilles stared, then went down on his knees between them and turned from one to the other, checking their pulses, checking for breathing. From the look on his face, there was no sign of life in either of them.

He jumped to his feet, fetched the emetic to induce vomiting, and poured it in their mouths.

He jumped to his feet again and raised his hands as high as he could. The tendons of his neck were taut with stress. He screamed a prayer, "Persephone, Queen of the Underworld, bless us with your presence, show your life-giving power." Nothing happened.

He lowered his hands and turned toward the bishop with a shrug of despair.

Then the toes of the body that had been Chloe began to twitch, then the feet, then the legs. Then the legs shot up and opened and closed, her robe fell to the sides, leaving her naked.

Eurydice's body was still motionless, unconscious.

Chloe's body leaned back, opened its mouth wide, and made loud guttural noises.

Achilles stared in shock and said nothing.

The toes of Eurydice's body started to move. Then her entire body spasmed.

Achilles kneeled between the two bodies again and put one hand on the forehead of the one and the other hand on the forehead of the other. He shrugged as if he were both surprised and helpless.

"What's going on?" asked the bishop, deeply concerned.

"The temperature of both is fluctuating wildly—burning hot, then cold, then hot again."

He gave them both more of the emetic. Then he stuck pins in the feet of both.

He pulled his hair and shouted, "Dionysus," over and over again.

No sooner did he turn toward the bishop with a look of despair, than the women both vomited and sat up.

"Bravo," shouted the bishop. "Great acting. Great script. Great show. Go for it. You know what you're doing. But you do need more pizzazz. Add music and dance. Nine dancing girls, one for each of the muses. Tell your initiates that's what was missing the first time—no music, no dance. That should be your cover story, not that lame and boring tale about inaccurate copies. Your believers need a story that will capture their imagination. Music and dance are at the heart of religion. Tell them you need to put on a complete show, a spectacle that's so beautiful, so unforgettable that it could wake the sleeping gods and bring them to your temple to enjoy the show. Tell them that the gods will help you do what you could never do without them. Tell your believers that the main purpose of the potion is the aroma. The combination of aroma, music, and dance attracts the gods. The gods do the work, not the chemistry. Tell them that you failed before because the gods didn't come. This time you'll put on a show that the gods won't want to miss."

As soon as the bishop left, Achilles congratulated the ladies. "That was a great performance. You improvised as if you had practiced that repeatedly. You convinced him in a way that I never imagined possible."

The ladies stared at each other, then at him, then at each other.

"Are you all right, Briseis?" he asked.

"I'm Eurydice," said Chloe's body.

"And I'm Briseis," said Eurydice's body.

"Zeus. You did it. You actually did it. You swapped. You swapped souls."

40 ~ Period of Adjustment

After the bishop left, the litigants tried to get their bearings in the new reality they now faced. Briseis in the body of Eurydice. Eurydice in the body of Chloe.

Here we go again, thought Breeze. She tried to scratch her nose but poked her eye instead. Her arms were short now, and they didn't respond as she intended. She was getting used to that other body and starting to enjoy it. Now she had to learn all over again. She was a foot shorter than she was minutes ago. Instead of blond hair extending all the way to her groin, she had short curly black hair. Move slowly, she reminded herself, not wanting to trip and bang her knee again.

Eurydice stumbled, Breeze tried to catch her, and both fell in a jumble.

Lying on the floor, their limbs entangled, they stared at one another while they tried to sort out the implications of what had just happened. Neither of them had imagined that a body could, like a suit of clothes, be changed at will.

At first, to Eurydice in her new body, looking at her old body seemed like looking at herself in a mirror. But in a mirror, everything is reversed. She was seeing her old body as others saw it, as three-dimensional, not a two-dimensional reflection. And at the same time, she saw her new body, Chloe's old body, reflected in the eyes of this other person who now had her old body. Double confusion.

On the other hand, she now had the new body that she wanted. She was no longer Eurydice priestess of Artemis. She could live as she wished. She could marry if she liked. She had a magnificent body that no man could resist. And this amazing hunk of a man named Ajax was already enamored of this body.

To Achilles, the Eurydice he loved just two days ago, for whom he risked his reputation and life trying to move her soul to a new body, had turned out to be a hateful creature. She was a temple prostitute rather than an almost-virgin. And the heavenly body that once was Chloe now had the consciousness of that hateful creature. He had accomplished his goal of moving Eurydice's soul to Chloe's body. But she felt no gratitude toward him, much less love. She wanted nothing to do with him. She had used him. Period. Romance over.

The other young woman now consisted of the consciousness named Briseis and the body that once was Eurydice. Achilles felt responsible for the problems she now faced, having performed the ritual that brought her to this here and now, without her knowledge or consent. He was strongly attracted to her when she was in Chloe's body. Finding her now in Eurydice's body, he was ambivalent, still feeling protective and responsible, but now repelled by the body he associated with Eurydice's manipulation and betrayal of him.

Ajax was delighted. He now had claim to the perfect woman — the body of Chloe with the feisty, forceful spirit of Eurydice. Eurydice performed brilliantly in the trials. And in so doing, she showed that she not only wanted this body that had been Chloe's, but she also wanted him, Ajax. She was attracted by his body as he was by hers. He would have preferred if the mystical crescent-moon brand had moved to the new body along with the soul. That would have given their future life together an aura of fate and inevitability. But this was fine. He was anxious to enjoy this newly assembled masterpiece of a woman. He reached down to take her in his arms.

"No. Stop," Eurydice told him. "This isn't me."

"What?" exclaimed Ajax, stumbling back as if punched in the groin.

"My memory is not just in my brain," she tried to explain. "It's in my muscles as well, throughout my body. Without my body, my real body, I don't know who I am."

"You expect to know who you are?" Breeze chuckled. To her, this was one in a series of bodies. She hadn't been in Chloe's body long enough to forge memories and become attached to it. Whatever body she was in, she would find some way to cope with it. Such was life as she knew it.

But to Eurydice, this was epic. She had abandoned the body she had been in for her entire life. Admittedly, that body had changed over the years. Today's body was very different from the little one she was born in. But the changes were gradual, so she had the illusion of continuity. And all the memories of her lifetime were associated with those bones and muscles. Unlike Breeze, for Eurydice changing bodies was a choice.

Counter to her expectations, she missed her old body and felt strange in the new one. It didn't fit her. She didn't belong in it. When Ajax whispered to her that she was beautiful and he loved her, she couldn't believe that it was herself, her true self that he admired and loved. And when he wrapped his arms around her, and she let his hands wander under her toga to places that should have aroused her, the sensations were muted, as if felt through layers of cloth. She found Ajax very attractive, but only in her mind, not in her new body. The contrast between what should have been, and reality, was unnerving. Maybe that would change over time as she got used to this new body, but she was impatient and frustrated. This wasn't what she had anticipated, and with all the strength of her consciousness and will, with all that she identified with as being her, she regretted her choice.

Ajax was ready and anxious to explore and enjoy Eurydice in her current state. He would do it right here and now in the Christian church, regardless of whether anyone else was around to see. But this woman in his arms felt like a thing, an object, not a person.

Instead of enjoying the sensations, Eurydice felt like a fraud. She had no business being here, doing this. This wasn't her. She was out of sync with her true self, and she had a true self, she must have one. She wanted this whole sequence of events to stop immediately.

Meanwhile, Achilles, who worshipped and lusted for Eurydice when she was in her old body, showed no interest in her in her current body. Nor did Briseis, the creature now occupying Eurydice's old body, show interest in him. Rather, Briseis was self-absorbed, stretching, running in place, deliberately getting used to, and learning this body, as she might have done before with other bodies. Perhaps she was a nomadic soul and found this change natural, as natural as soul transference can be.

Eurydice, despite herself, longed for her original body, and sensed that she always would. She couldn't be herself in any body but the one she always had. She wanted to go home to it, right away. If she possibly could, she wanted to undo this mistake.

Achilles wasn't even looking at the body that used to be Eurydice. He was fussing with his paraphernalia, mumbling to himself, jotting notes. He was trying to make sense of what happened, wondering how it happened, wondering how he could reenact it when he needed to.

Ajax tried once again to help Eurydice to her feet, but she slipped out of his grip, pushed him away, and called out to Achilles, "Undo it."

The words surprised him, as they did the others, who stared at her, confused.

"I want my body back," she continued. "This is a mistake. I want to be me again."

Achilles hesitated, then asked Briseis, "Do you too want to go back to that other body?"

"One body's the same as another to me," she replied. "I don't mind this one. I don't mind that one. I want to return to the other world I lived in, to either of the two worlds I remember. If Eurydice wants to change back, that's fine with me."

Ajax objected, "But, Chloe or Eurydice, whatever name you want to go by now, don't you want me as much as I want you? We've reshuffled the deck of life, and we've been dealt a winning hand. I want you the way you are. I love you the way you are."

"This simply isn't me, and never will be me," she asserted. "Undo it now, Achilles. Please. As soon as possible."

"It's dangerous for you to take more of the drug so soon," he objected "We don't know the residual effects of what you had already. The results are unpredictable."

"I don't give a damn," Eurydice insisted.

She was forceful and decisive at a time when Achilles was uncertain, not knowing what he could and should do next. By reflex, Achilles carried out her wishes. He put together a new batch of the potion. Eurydice and Breeze gulped it down while standing, then held hands, looking into one another's eyes.

In less than a minute, twitching and spasms began. They hugged one another and managed to hold one another up. Then, far sooner than before, the convulsing and shaking ended.

They stood, silent and still, with blank expressions.

Ajax broke the tension, taking hold of the body that once was Chloe. He turned her toward him, with a look of compassionate concern. "Eurydice, enough of this nonsense. There's no reason to take this risk again. This priest doesn't know what he's doing. Eurydice." He shook her. "Speak to me, Eurydice."

"I'm not Eurydice," she answered.

"What?"

"I'm Briseis."

"But this was Chloe's body, and a moment ago it was Eurydice's." She looked down at herself and laughed.

He turned toward Eurydice's old body, "Is that you, Eurydice?" She nodded.

"He did it again?" Ajax was incredulous. "And so quickly? The two of you are back to the bodies you started with? Are you okay?"

Eurydice nodded again.

Ajax picked her up, cradled her in his arms, kissed her on her birthmark, then on her lips. "You're amazing, Eurydice. That took courage."

She reached out to Achilles, took his hand, and squeezed it. "Thank you, Achilles. I didn't realize your power was so great. The rush was amazing, more powerful than any drug I've ever had. And as a priestess, I've had many."

"It's probably the mushrooms," Achilles guessed, "the mind-altering effect of the mushrooms."

"It's more than that," insisted Eurydice. "I've eaten all kinds of mushrooms. What I felt was much more than a drug. Imagine what it must feel like for the soul to break free of its body—the rush of liberation, the feeling of unlimited power, that anything is possible."

Ajax lifted her high and kissed her again. "Maybe it's me that makes you feel high," he suggested.

"Maybe it's the hemlock," added Achilles. "By restricting your breathing, it slowed the flow of oxygen to your brain, as if you were being choked."

"Whatever it is, give me more of it," Eurydice pleaded.

"We have to be careful," Achilles warned. "There's no guarantee that it will work again or how it will work. We're not going to do it again. It could kill you. You're going to have to stay in this body you have now, the body you started with. You're still a priestess of Artemis, subject to your vows of celibacy, or at least the semblance of celibacy. Can you live with that?"

"Forget the vows. I'll convert to Christianity. You'd like that, wouldn't you, Ajax? I'll ask the bishop for his protection. I'm in my own body, and I'm in the arms of the man I want to be with. I couldn't ask for more."

"Be careful," Achilles cautioned "The emotional high you feel now may be temporary, artificial, a matter of chemistry."

Breeze grabbed him from behind, lifted him, and kissed him on the neck. "I want you," she whispered.

"Are you going crazy, too?" he asked.

"Your potion triggered something in me. I still feel the buzz."

"Neither you nor Eurydice should take any more of it. It's dangerous. Thank the gods that you're still alive."

Breeze laid him down on the ground and got on top of him, pinning him. He struggled to free himself, but the pressure and the friction of their playful struggle excited her and him even more than the first time they had rolled on the floor together.

"I don't think this is over," she told him. "I think I have the power to do it again. Maybe I always had that power. Maybe that's how I got here and got to other places and times before this. I had it in me by nature and your potion made that power stronger. I believe I could do it again, at will, under my control."

"No more potion," he repeated. "Do you understand?"

"There's no need for more."

"Never again. What we do for the bishop's grand event will be a sham. That's all he wants. We won't take chances with your life. I don't want to lose you."

"But I can't abandon this power now that I've found it. If you ever experienced it, you'd know what I mean."

"Impossible. End of story."

41 ~ Transgender Soul Swapping

The following morning, Achilles and Breeze went to a nearby beach on the Aegean Sea. Breeze was giddy, still high from her soul moving from one body to another. She was gaining confidence that she could cope in this strange new world. Instead of obsessing about the dangers she was facing, she was enjoying each day as it unfolded.

"You should try the potion. I brought the last of it with me," Breeze coaxed and tempted Achilles. "Just take a swallow and find out what it feels like for your soul to move to another body,"

"You want me to move to your body?" he asked in disbelief. "Men and women can't swap souls and bodies. The sacred records say that souls can only migrate from one woman to another."

"You told me the transfer can only take place between a dead body and a living one. Now we know that's not true. Unless you try, you won't know if you, too, can have this experience."

"Well, even if it were possible, I wouldn't want to try. It's too risky."

"You had no problem taking risks with me and Eurydice."

"You were dead, or rather Chloe was. Eurydice desperately wanted a new body. And that was the only way she and I could be together."

"Enough with your excuses. You need to try this for the experience and for what you would learn about life and death, about the nature of the soul. Wouldn't you like to know what it would be like to be a woman? To be in my body?"

"You have a bizarre imagination." He gave her a warm hug and a sloppy kiss.

She laughed.

"What's so funny?" he asked

"I'm imagining me in your body, with your hormones and lusts, feeling your sensations, seeing through your eyes."

"Enough."

"No. I have the last of the potion with me. If you won't drink it, I will. Then maybe I can make the switch happen without you."

"Impossible."

She swallowed it before Achilles could stop her, then put her hands on his shoulders and stared into his eyes.

He smiled in disbelief. "There's no way you can, all on your own, move your soul into my body and my soul into yours."

Soon his muscles started to twitch, then to spasm uncontrollably. He fell on the sand and went into convulsions. He vomited, retching repeatedly. Then he sat up and said, "How in Hades did you do that? On the other hand, I'm still in my body. You made me feel sick, but that's all."

"Let's try again."

"Fortunately, that was the last of the potion. I'd have to mix more, and I won't do that."

"No matter. I may have enough of it in my system already." She led him to the water and splashed him to clean him up. Then she put her hands on his shoulders again, stared into his eyes again, and ordered him, "Don't look away. Focus on me."

He smiled and indulged her.

Once again, he started shaking. He dropped to his knees. The water was up to his waist. Then Breeze fell into the water beside him, limp and lifeless. He grabbed and lifted her. As he was dragging her to the beach, his legs went one way and then another, out of control. He struggled to keep his balance, then fell face down on the sand.

He felt a painfully strong urge to urinate. He stood and reached to take hold of his penis, only he didn't have a pens.

Up the beach, maybe ten feet away, he saw himself urinating, the stream arching high and far.

"That's amazing," he said, without him thinking or willing those words. "I always wondered about that,"

His legs started churning. He was running along the water's edge, off-balance, leaning so far forward that he barely managed to stretch his feet out for the next step. Then, panting from exertion, he stopped abruptly, squatted, and stretched out on his back.

He heard himself say, "That was fun." Only his voice came from somewhere else.

He tried to turn his head to the left, but it went to the right instead.

"Check it out," his voice said.

He touched his body. Breasts? Large breasts? Unfamiliar sensations resonated through his body.

"Okay, I believe you," he managed to say in her voice. "Now can you get us out of this?"

Before he saw her, she was on top of him; only she was him and he was her.

In the afterglow, lying in one another's arms, they flipped back to their original bodies, Achilles told her, "That was amazing. Are you a goddess now? Can you do that at will? And how did you know how to reverse it?"

"I haven't a clue," She laughed.

42 ~ Soul Projection and Eye Reading

"Where were you?" asked Eurydice when Breeze and Achilles returned from the beach.

"We went for a walk, waded in the sea, and swapped."

"You what?"

"We moved to one another's bodies and made love," she answered matter-of-factly as if that were an everyday occurrence.

"You-as-him made love with him-as-you?"

"Yes, you could put it that way."

Eurydice didn't hesitate, "Show us how. I want to do that with Ajax."

At Breeze's insistence, Achilles mixed a new batch of the potion. Then, following her instructions, both Eurydice and Ajax drank it, put their hands on one another's shoulders and stare into one another's eyes. Nothing happened.

"I'm sorry," Breeze apologized. "For us, it was instantaneous, and I was the only one who took the potion."

"Let's try again," says Eurydice. "This time, I'll drink the potion and Ajax won't."

Still nothing happened.

"Let's try yet again," she insisted. "This time give me a double dose."

Achilles objected "We don't know the right dosage. It probably differs with the person. Too much might kill you. Briseis and I were lucky. We never should have taken such a risk."

"That's for us to decide, right Ajax? You want this as much as I do?"

He answered her by taking her in his arms. He looked dazed, drunken, and wildly happy.

"Give us more," Eurydice ordered. Achilles did. And nothing happened.

"I'm sorry," Breeze explained. "I may have some special affinity for soul transfer. It may work differently for me than for you. I may be able to do things that you can't."

***

Officially, the bishop found them all guilty of disturbing the peace and instigating religious hatred. They were sentenced to community service for the church, under his direction.

Achilles returned to his temple to repair relations, setting in motion plans for a new soul-transference ceremony and scheduling it to coincide with the annual initiation ceremony. He spread the word that this time he would stage a major spectacle, with music and dancing that would be so good that it would attract the gods, whose help was needed for the miracle to succeed. He explained that he learned from his mistakes and that he was confident that this time the soul-transference would work the way it had in the distant past. Many were skeptical because of his previous failure, but they planned to show up for the entertainment extravaganza. He kept up appearances, carrying out the usual business of the Mysteries. In the evening, he returned to the church for rehearsals. He slept there at night with Briseis.

Eurydice went to her temple to get her belongings and to tell the other priestesses that she was converting to Christianity. She was no longer the property of the goddess. She was under the protection of the bishop.

Ajax went home to his farm and took Eurydice with him, introducing her to his widowed mother as his new bride-to-be. When his mother saw the birthmark that was the same shape as the family brand, without hesitation, she welcomed Eurydice. She read to her from the Gospels and prepared her to be baptized as a Christian. She herself had been baptized just a short while before so that her religion wouldn't be an impediment to Ajax marrying Chloe. She had converted with her whole heart, not as a sham. She was now a true believer and hoped Eurydice would be as well.

Chloe's father insisted that the creature in his daughter's body was not his daughter, but some unholy half-alive thing created by the pagans. He was incensed, but wouldn't sue, because that would jeopardize the money he was paid. Chloe's mother was distraught and confused. The bishop assured her that Chloe's soul was not here, but rather was in a better place, and he set her the task of reciting the Lord's Prayer ten thousand times, which, he assured her, would give her daughter's soul the solace of knowing that she was loved and would bring her happiness in the hereafter.

The bishop deemed that the demon-animated body of Chloe was necessary for the public performance. For now, she stayed at the church. If all went as planned, Achilles could act as her guardian or keeper, if he so chose.

While the others were occupied elsewhere, Breeze stayed in the church, alone, not even daring to walk outside in the sunshine. She napped or stared out windows at passersby. When congregants came to pray or act out their private rituals of worship, she watched from a distance, trying to imagine what they were saying or thinking or seeing. It was on such an occasion that she discovered that she had another power.

Watching an elderly lady at prayer, kneeling in front of a crucifix, Breeze realized that she is seeing the crucifix from the wrong angle, not from her own perspective, but rather from that of the lady. Then she focused on other worshippers, one at a time, and saw through their eyes as well. She had no sense of what these people were thinking, only what they were seeing. This wasn't mind reading. She thought of it as *eye reading.*

Next, with practice, Breeze developed the ability to change the direction of someone else's eyes. If the worshipper twitched, stood, or swung his or her head around in shock and confusion, Breeze broke off contact. She didn't want to raise questions. She just wanted to prove to herself that she could do this at will. And she wanted to refine her skill.

One of her targets was delighted rather than frightened at the sensation. She gushed with enthusiasm describing the experience to the parish priest. She thought she had been touched by an angel.

Breeze didn't want Achilles or the others to know she could do this. With power came responsibility, and she didn't want the responsibility such a power might entail. She didn't want the others to expect her to do such things on demand. She was afraid that she might not be able to deliver when needed.

One day when she was walking through the church, she saw the bishop conducting a service in front of a dozen worshippers. He knelt with a chalice of wine in his hands. He was about to celebrate the sacrament of communion. She couldn't resist the temptation to get back at him.

She focused on him, and he turned suddenly, spilling wine on his white robes. Then he jerked back in the other direction. Then back again, half a dozen times, until he fell on the floor, quivering in spasms, and the parish priest and sexton and deacon came running to his aid.

Breeze couldn't help but laugh, quietly. Then she realized that Achilles was standing beside her, and Eurydice and Ajax were standing behind her. They had all witnessed this demonstration of her new power. Achilles pulled her back to another room, and the others followed.

Achilles told her, "Enough, Briseis. You have to be honest with us. We know you have extraordinary powers. But this I never expected. You projected your soul but maintained control of your own body. You remained standing. You looked like any normal person. But your soul took control of the bishop's body. That's even more outlandish than what you were able to do before. How long have you known you have this power?"

"A few days."

"And you've used it before?"

"I've practiced on random worshippers. Briefly. No one suspected me as the cause. They thought they felt a divine presence. They thought they were blessed. It was different this time with the bishop. I wanted to make a fool of him, to hurt him if I could."

"Enough. Get hold of yourself, please," Achilles pleaded. "We need to talk this out. A power like that could change everything. Don't waste it on pranks. If ordinary people knew what you can do, they'd worship you as a goddess or an angel or a saint."

"That's comical. I haven't a clue what I'm doing or why it works."

"But would you want that?"

"Want what?"

"Would you want to be worshipped? They'd build you a temple and bring you gifts. They'd bow down to you and do your bidding. Emperor Julian himself would abandon his march of conquest and come racing here for the honor of seeing you and witnessing your miracles. Would you like that?"

"No. Never. That's not who I am."

"And now you know who you are?"

"No. I don't. But I do know that that's not me. I don't want power or wealth. I don't want people bowing down to me. I want to be a private person, not a goddess."

"Do you have a choice? Did you have a choice when you appeared in this body? Maybe you have these powers for a reason. Maybe you have a destiny to fulfill."

"Don't do that to me. That's taking away my free will, my freedom. That's like Eurydice's parents deciding she had been chosen by Artemis and giving her to the temple. I don't want that."

"Well, what do you want? The four of us are in this together. The bishop expects us to put on a show that will publicly discredit the Eleusinian Mysteries. Our rehearsals have been a waste of time. We've tried this and that with no vision, no enthusiasm. But the date for the ceremony is coming soon. If we're going to do the bishop's bidding, we need to prepare. And if we're going to try something else and make the bishop's scheme backfire on him, we need to get ready for that."

"What do you have in mind?" asked Eurydice.

"I'd like to sabotage the bishop's plans. But maybe there's something positive we can do instead."

"You're talking like a priest," objected Eurydice.

"Briseis has the powers of a goddess. We don't know how she got them. But we should deal with those powers responsibly. Maybe we can do something that matters not just for us, but for others, maybe even for mankind."

"Don't put all that on me," Breeze pleaded, grabbing her head to relieve the sudden pain that gripped her.

"Okay." He tried to calm her, guiding her to a bench where she could sit, and rest her head on his shoulder. "Tell us what you feel, what you want. You're the goddess-in-the-making. What do you believe? And what do you want your believers to believe?"

"I don't know where to start."

"Start with the soul. That's what this is about, isn't it? The soul's ability to move from body to body, and the implications of that? Plato believed in the soul. He believed that it's eternal and that it moves from one body to another. The soul leaves one body on death and enters another on birth. Christians believe, like Plato, that the soul is separate from the body and is eternal. But I don't know of any religion or philosophy that purports that the soul can move from one living body to another. Maybe they're all wrong. What do you believe, Briseis? From what you've experienced and what you can make happen, do you have answers to the fundamental questions? What comes before birth? Does the soul begin at birth? If not, when and how does it begin? Where was it before birth? Where does it go after death? Or has every soul always existed and will every soul continue to exist forever?"

"I don't know any of this," Breeze protested. "I can see through other people's eyes. And I can change the direction where those eyes look. That's all."

"And you can move your soul into someone else's body and move that person's soul into your body. That's major magic. So, what would you like to do with it? Tell me about the new religion you could create based on that. What do you believe in?"

"I believe that everyone is equal in both body and soul, that any soul can inhabit any body. I believe that magic is in us all, that the secret of eternal life is in us all. I believe that your soul connects you to all people and all times."

"Amen," said Achilles, with reverence and respect.

"But I don't want the tricks I can perform to lead to the creation of a new religion. If I must use this power, I want to use it to wake people up to the miraculous nature of their own souls, of all souls."

Achilles responded, "So instead of exposing the Mysteries as a fake, we should use this spectacle that the bishop has planned to make everyone there feel like they are touched by a god or an angel, to inspire their wonder at the miracle of life and the unknown and the unknowable."

Eurydice objected, "In practical terms, what do you mean by that?"

Briseis answered before Achilles could, "I'll project my soul to people in the audience. I'll go from one to another to another. They'll each feel like they're touched by an angel or a god. I hope that will make them feel a bond of empathy and goodwill toward one another."

"Let's play it that way," Achilles agreed. "I'll recruit musicians and dancers and singers to stage the kind of extravaganza the bishop wants. But instead of the finale being an admission of fakery, you, Briseis, will give the audience a healing, uplifting, life-renewing touch of divinity."

43 ~ Soul Runner

Being in this place and time felt so unreal and fantastical that it was easy to forget about practical matters. In her previous life, Breeze was on the pill. Here, she did what felt was natural, dealing with each day as it came. She and Achilles had taken no precautions. She's been in this body for seven weeks and she had not yet had a period.

She had no idea when Chloe last menstruated or how regular her periods were. And the trauma of multiple soul switches might have thrown this body's schedule off. The potion might affect it as well. Every few days, when her powers noticeably declined, she took a small dose of the potion for rehearsals and to refine her skills, preparing for the performance—the *soul run*, as she liked to think of it.

She suspected she was pregnant but didn't tell Achilles until morning sickness made it obvious.

"No," he said emphatically. "This changes everything. You can't go on like this. You can't take any more of the potion. There's no telling what effect that could have on the child. You have to stop. We can't go through with the plan."

"But we only have one week left to go."

"Enough. This isn't a matter for dispute. We'll scrap the plan for you to do a *soul run*. We'll do the show the bishop's way. We'll start rehearsing for that now. I'll mix some fruit punch that looks like the potion. That's what we'll use from now on. I don't want any argument about that."

Breeze didn't argue. The miracle of new life was growing inside her. Nothing else mattered. Whether they found answers to fundamental questions of life and death, of body and soul, whether they spread their new gospel or just paid lip service to an established religion, none of that mattered next to the wonder of this new child. It didn't matter if the baby had a new soul or an old soul that has existed forever and would continue to body-hop through the ages.

On the day of the performance, after an hour of music and dance, Breeze lay naked on the altar. On cue, she was supposed to stand and gyrate in spasms, as if two souls are struggling with one another, fighting for control of her body.

But before she rose, her eyes made contact with a man in the front row. From habit, she focused her attention and willed her soul at him. She hadn't taken the potion for a week. Today she had only had fruit punch. She was shocked when she saw herself through the eyes of this stranger; and the stranger sat bolt upright with a look of shock.

She shut off the connection with that stranger, then shifted her focus to the woman beside him and entered her; then the next person, and the next, faster and even faster, until everyone in the audience had been soul-touched.

Achilles, Eurydice, and Ajax guessed what was happening and improvised in harmony with Breeze's unscripted action.

As they originally planned, she stood, and the others joined her on the altar. They all held hands. They would announce their discovery and their new faith, with more soul-runner touches here and there in the crowd to confirm the truth of what they said. They would explain that the secret of eternal life is in each and every one of us; that people can be intimately connected to one another in ways they never before imagined. They would empower and encourage everyone in the audience to get in touch with their own souls, and through their souls connect to all people in all times.

They were elated, about to start a new chapter in the history of mankind.

But before they could begin to speak, each of them telling a piece of the story as they had planned, the crowd erupted in mass hysteria and fled.

Epilogue 2 ~ The Miracle of Birth

Achilles had carefully prepared the initiates of the Mysteries for his first attempt at soul transference. The worshippers had known what to expect, and if everything had gone as planned, they would have been awed by the miracle but would have felt safe in the predictability and control that he demonstrated.

When events had unfolded differently, they had panicked and run, and had felt insecure until Achilles explained that the missing ingredient was the involvement of the gods. When they assembled for the second ceremony, they were skeptical that a miracle would occur but glad to enjoy the entertainment. And this time each and every one of them individually felt touched by a supernatural presence.

For many, religion provided protection from the unknown and the unknowable. It gave them explanations for the mysteries of birth, life, and death. It gave them rules and the assurance that if they followed those rules, everything would turn out right, if not in this lifetime, then after death.

It was a simple bargain. Do as instructed. Donate your time, your money, your faith, your love. Then you need not worry about the unknowable. If everyone did his or her job to the best of his or her ability, society would run smoothly. Farmers would farm. Carpenters would build. Priests would deal with the unknown so no one else had to. The church and its teachings provided the wall that kept out demons and doubt, that allowed ordinary people to go about their lives in confidence.

The experience of the *soul run* shattered that social contract.

The Christians, salted into the audience by the bishop, ran to their church and frantically repeated prayers. They were convinced that they had heard the whisper of an angel warning them of imminent death and eternal punishment. They prayed for forgiveness. They promised to rigidly follow the tenets of their religion. They pledged generous donations to the church and promised never to stray again. While the bishop didn't get his wished-for scandal discrediting the Eleusinian

Mysteries, he did get a boost in religious enthusiasm, improved attendance at services, and substantial donations.

The believers in traditional gods who attended the *soul run* sacrificed pigs and chickens and cows and donated to the temple of the Mysteries up to the limits of their resources. Each thought that an angry god had brushed him or her. They feared they might be turned to stone or into trees or beasts, that their soul might be transported to an inanimate object and that they might be stuck there forever, conscious but unable to speak or to act, existing forever in torment.

Both Christians and pagans believed that their religious practices could stave off punishment and personal disaster and protect them from the unknown. Rather than opening themselves to the wonders and joys of life and trying to understand the mysteries of birth and life and death, they shut themselves up in boxes of superstition.

Breeze, Achilles, Eurydice, and Ajax were disgraced, but not punished. A Christian spy working for the bishop replaced Achilles as high priest of the Eleusinian Mysteries. The temple of Artemis closed and was turned into a Christian church of the Virgin Mary. With minor changes, statues of Artemis morphed into Mary, Mother of Christ.

Eurydice married Ajax, and Achilles and Breeze joined them on the family farm, where they lived and worked together. Achilles brought along his dog Julian as well as his slaves Eurydice and Orpheus. Breeze insisted that Achilles free them and let them rename themselves. They picked the names Cupid and Psyche and stayed on as paid laborers.

During Breeze's pregnancy, she and Achilles switched souls periodically so he got to feel the baby move and kick, and so the two of them could share the discomfort. They played cards to determine who would be in the mother's body at the moment of birth. Achilles won, so when Breeze's water broke, Achilles, in Chloe's body, went through childbirth while Breeze, in Achilles' body, served as midwife. Next time would be Breeze's turn.

About the Author

Richard lives in Milford, CT, where he writes fiction full-time. He worked for DEC, the minicomputer company, as writer and Internet Evangelist. He graduated from Yale, with a major in English, went to Yale grad school in Comparative Literature, and earned an MA in Comparative Literature from the U. of Mass. at Amherst. At Yale, he had creative writing courses with Robert Penn Warren and Joseph Heller.

His published works include: *Parallel Lives* and *Beyond the 4th Door,* and *Nevermind* (novels published by All Things That Matter Press), *The Name of Hero* (historical novel), *Ethiopia Through Russian Eyes* (translation from Russian), *The Lizard of Oz* (satiric fantasy), and pioneering books about Internet business. His web site is seltzerbooks.com

ALL THINGS THAT MATTER PRESS

FOR MORE INFORMATION ON TITLES AVAILABLE FROM
ALL THINGS THAT MATTER PRESS, GO TO
http://allthingsthatmatterpress.com
or contact us at
allthingsthatmatterpress@gmail.com

**If you enjoyed this book, please post a review on Amazon.com and
your favorite social media sites.**

www.ingramcontent.com/pod-product-compliance
Lightning Source LLC
Chambersburg PA
CBHW071426260626
47170CB00008B/2609